QUITE ANOTHER CALCUTTA

Edward Ayrton

A Falcon Book

©Copyright 1998
Edward Ayrton

The right of Edward Ayrton to be identified as the author of this work has been asserted in accordance with the Copyright, Designs and Patents Act 1988.

All rights reserved. No reproduction, copy or transmission of this publication may be made without written permission. No paragraph of this publication may be reproduced, copied or transmitted save with the written permission or in accordance with the provisions of the Copyright Act 1956 (as amended).Any person who does any unauthorised act in relation to this publication may be liable to criminal prosecution and civil claims for damage.

First published in 1998 by
M & N Publishing Co.
1 Northumberland Avenue Trafalgar Square LONDON WC1N 5BW

Paperback ISBN 1 899865 71 3

PROLOGUE October 1987

We were sitting in my London club reminiscing about our time in India. Douglas, in his eighties, had retired from the Board many years ago, and recently I had retired from a less exalted position.

"Your marriage has lasted," said Douglas. "Not like so many out there."

I thought of Brenda, our children and the grandchildren. "Yes I've put them first. Yours has lasted too, Douglas, far longer."

"Ah yes, but there's a difference Bob. I knew Edith and her family for some time before we married. In your case, if I remember, you went on leave and married, knowing hardly anything about Brenda."

I ordered some more Scotch. Douglas continued, "I know I have been very fortunate."

We were silent for a time. The drink was beginning to take effect and I leaned towards him, saying with intensity, "Douglas, it seems impossible to be certain that you are fully in love; good, but better may be lurking."

Pause; then Douglas ponders, "When we take our vows in church, if we are devout enough, I suppose that should keep us on the straight and narrow. It isn't easy, is it?"

"You can say that again, Douglas. Don't I know it."

Memories come flooding back. Yes, don't I darned well know it.

1   February 1960

I drive Brenda and the children to Dum Dum Airport. Melanie and Jane are excited. Brenda is glad to be going home, but we are sad to be drifting apart. She has never settled in Calcutta. A tall blonde, who tans easily, enjoys the sun and the Swimming Club, but that's about all. Tries golf. Dislikes the artificial social life. She's bored.

"Just another three m¼"

"Stop jigging Jane, stand still." Brenda turns away to fiddle with Jane's clothing. "I hope they sleep," she says, "Then I'll get some peace."

"Just another three months. I'll be home in May."

"You coming Daddy?" says Jane, four years old.

"Don't be silly," says bossy Melanie, three years older. "Daddy has to work here."

"I'll be home soon Jane." I crouch down, face to face, stroke her hair. "Now be a good girl and look after Mummy."

They bear little resemblance to one another. Melanie is like Brenda: straight hair, straight nose, she'll be good-looking. Jane is more like us, the Bennetts: fair, curly hair, cheeky round face, retroussé nose. They get on wonderfully well together, surprising perhaps, for their natures are quite different. I lift them up one at a time. They kiss me full on the lips.

"Goodbye Brenda, look after yourself." I kiss her on the cheek. I try again. She offers the other cheek. Oh well! It avoids the lipstick.

"Bob, do pack the Dresden ornaments carefully," are her last words as we walk to the barrier.

Jane holds my hand and hugs a Teddy Bear. Melanie carries a little vanity case and a doll. They disappear through the doors. I wait for what seems ages, standing on the balcony among Bengalis, waiting for the passengers to emerge. I wave. Brenda points me out to the kids who wave back.

As the plane takes off and disappears over the palm trees, I have an empty feeling; there's a vacuum. These February mornings are quite cool. Doesn't start to warm up until next month, but it's too humid and you feel sticky most of the time. I walk to the car.

I'll miss the children. Don't think I'll miss Brenda. The kids are the bond that holds us together. Pity she hasn't settled. Family has no tradition of overseas service. I drive away. She'd prefer to run the flat herself, but what about the early morning shopping in the market, I wonder. The servants irritate her, but I don't think she could do without them.

I nearly hit a child as it runs into the road. This wakes me up. I pass a bus on the near side as it hogs the centre. The back step is weighed down by passengers and it makes sparks as it bounces off the bumpy road on complaining springs. The road passes the old Victorian building of Dum Dum Rifle Factory. Blast it! In the rush I've forgotten to contact the Boarding House, Aratoon's. Hope they've a room. I've let the flat to Americans and they'll be moving in this afternoon.

Halfway to Calcutta, the road dips under a railway bridge. When there is a downpour the pool formed here makes the road impassable. You can miss your plane. At such times it is better to use the Airline's bus; then you have recompense. Not many people like these floods; only rickshaw wallahs. They can demand inflated fares when cars are marooned, and when people with good shoes have to cart their shopping home.

I think of Brenda and the kids. Brenda will hope that their early start will tire them, and that she can have some rest. I come to the T-junction where there is a concrete plinth two feet high, on which a policeman can stand to direct the traffic. I burst out laughing, for on the plinth stands a very dark man, clad only in long hair, moustache, shrunken khaki army-issue pullover just covering his navel, and boots, no socks. He is directing the traffic with impeccable hand signals. A mile further and I reach Calcutta proper. Chittaranjan Avenue is in a state of disrepair. A taxi driver had told me that one pothole was so deep that a man could sit in it and read a newspaper without coming to any harm. I had no reason to doubt it.

In central Calcutta I go through Dalhousie Square, the hub of the business area. The name will soon be changed. Reminders of the Raj are being removed. On one side stands the GPO next to the site of the Black Hole of Calcutta. It is ridiculous that this incident should receive such prominence in our history. Probably Suraj ud Dowlah - who locked the men, women and children in this small, stifling room - had no intention of killing them, and did not realise that the rise in body temperature would be fatal. In the same year, expatriates were beheading their servants for stealing.

I park the car outside the office block. Again the lift is not working. This means a plod to the office on the fourth floor. The landlord does as little maintenance as possible. I go into Tony's office.

"I won't be in this afternoon, Tony."

He nods and gets on with his work. He's a small man with a Hitler moustache, very precise, dapper, a capable manager. With Yorkshire candour he says what he thinks, can upset customers. But Tony is fair and helpful.

As I go he looks up. "Would you like to come to us on Sunday, Bob? One of Thora's curry lunches."

"Thanks Tony, yes. Kind of you."

In the next room is Ken Taylor, technical expert, electrical and mechanical. He has black curly hair, wears horn-rimmed glasses. With slight adjustments he would remind me of Groucho Marx.

"Got away all right Bob?"

"Yes, all in order, Ken."

"Where are you going to stay?"

"I forgot to phone Aratoon's. Hope they've a room." I go into my office and I'm about to phone Aratoon's when Ken comes in.

"Wait Bob. I might have a room for you. Donald Morrison. Do you know him? Has a flat in South Calcutta. Want to meet him?"

"Sounds a good idea. Yes."

Ken phones Morrison and it's arranged that we'll meet in his club after work.

"Bob, I don't think you'll want to stay in Aratoon's for just one night. I'll put you up."

"That's good of you Ken. Many thanks."

We go to the Swimming Club for lunch.

"What's Donald like?"

"A Scot. Chief Purchase Officer of Bartley's Agencies. You'll get on well. Well educated."

"Haven't seen him around."

"Bit of a loner. Spends time in his club, where we're meeting him. Full name "The Merchant Navy Officers' Club". He likes a drink."

"Haven't seen him at the CFC or at cricket."

"Don't think he's interested in sport. Goes into the hills, camping."

"Nice flat?"

"Yes, very spacious. Old fashioned. High ceiling you know. View over the Hooghly. Wake up and see the boats in the morning. I think you'd like it."

"How old is he?"

"About your age. What are you now Bob? Thirty-eight? You'll be catching me up soon."

Back to my office, then I go to my flat. It's in a new block, occupied by several British firms; for married employees only. Ours is on the third floor of ten. Tony hasn't moved; doesn't want the bother of moving for he will be retiring soon.

Behind the block is a lawn where children play and talk to each other of their inevitable destiny in prep schools in Britain. Their ayahs sit together gossiping. In front of the block is a large yard, flanked by garages, and a durwan guarding the gate to the *cul de sac*.

Our bearer is at the flat, an elderly man, dark and short, say five feet two inches, powerfully built. I am the opposite, fair and tall, six feet. Probably we weigh about the same. His name is Imdalal Huq, but we call him Bilbo. I complete the inventory then Bilbo helps me to move some things to the car. Then I wait for my tenants.

There's a ring at the door; Mrs Wright with two suitcases.

"Lester's following," she says. She is tall, auburnhaired, tanned, rather scrawny; too much sun-bathing. "Call me Betty," she says.

Lester arrives with more cases and a servant, a Nepali, very smart in white uniform, silver buttons and pugree. Lester is huge, not fat, grey-headed, glasses. A very cheerful man, he beams.

I explain a few things about fans, fridge and so on, introduce the cook. We agree to meet again after a day or two.

I drive to our factory with Bilbo, open the tin trunks stored there, put some things in, take some out. The contents of the trunks remind me of Brenda; she'll be over half way home by now. I've been busy and forgotten her; it worries me that I can do this so easily. I'll phone her tomorrow; she should be over the jet lag by then.

I take Bilbo back to his home. It is a shed-like structure, near a row of dilapidated shops, known as the Thieves' Market. If, for instance, you lose the car headlamps you will probably find them here and buy them back.

After dumping my things at Ken's flat, I drive to Donald's club.

2

The Merchant Navy Officers' Club is situated in a narrow lane just off a main shopping street. You wouldn't notice it. There are two rooms, one with bar, tables, chairs, sofa and bookcase: half-size billiard table in the other. The bar is well stocked, visitors from the ships see to that.
With Calcutta port dwindling in importance, the numbers of ships' officers and shore-based personnel has fallen and so membership has been extended to others considered to be acceptable, like Donald and Ken.

I get on well with Donald who is an excellent conversationalist, slight, pleasant Scottish accent. Comes from the Western Isles. He doesn't have my enthusiasm for sport; isn't a member of the Saturday Club, doesn't dance.

Donald draws me out. I tell him I had worked in a bank just before the War. Was going to their Singapore branch, but joined the TA. Called up in September '39. I was eighteen.

"How did you come to be in this job?" Donald asks.

"A friend in my regiment said his father wanted to help ex-servicemen. Father was chairman of a large firm. "Would you like to go abroad for us?" he asked me."

I want to ask Donald about himself but there isn't time; it will have to wait. All I know is that he'd been in Norway during the War. He is about my age, looks younger, but not too healthy. He has a pale, pasty complexion. He is of medium height and gently rounded. He and Ken are bachelors; can't imagine them being anything else. I sense close rapport between them. I gather that Donald is forbidden to drive as he has blackouts. Liver trouble? I'll be moving into his flat tomorrow.

Donald is about to call a taxi, so Ken offers him a lift. I don't want to go with them. I'm feeling a bit depressed as I drive to the Saturday Club. I think about my family.

Brenda's a good sort, but we are ill suited, have different interests, on music, religion, many things. She won't discuss anything serious. Can't get her to consider the children's education in England. It will involve long separations. I think it's because she doesn't know what to do, so keeps silent. She is furious if I press her for comments. "Will you stop getting at me?" she thunders. I think perhaps it's a clever ploy, albeit subconscious, for getting her own way, whatever that is. Oh Lord God! Perhaps it would have been better not just for me, but also for her, if we had never married.

I wonder what Ken will tell Donald about me. I feel a little uneasy. Ken drives away with a thoughtful Donald.

"Pleasant man, Bob."

"You'll get on?"

"I think so. What's his wife like?"

"Nice girl. Prefers England though. That's why she hasn't waited to go home with him in May."

"What's she do with herself here?"

"Works a few hours in a charity shop. Bores her. In the hot weather spends as much time as she can in the Swimming Club."

"The children?"

"Charming. Seven or eight years old, and the other four, I think. No Donald, they haven't much in common. He would like them all to go the church, but she's not interested. Told me so. Sneers a bit!"

Ken stops the car near the racecourse. Donald's arm finds its way round Ken's shoulders. "Tell me more."

"I don't think Bob's interested in her: but you never know. Donald," Ken chuckles, "he might like you!"

"Pity you didn't move in with me, Ken."

"Bit late now Donald. I don't want to give up my flat; it's very comfortable. Move out, and I'd never get another as good at the price."

Donald's thoughts are elsewhere. "Ken, I've a hell of a hard-on."

I turn into Wood Street and through the Saturday Club gates. It's a place for socialising, dancing, swimming, tennis, squash and bridge. It's called "The Slap", the "tickle" having been dropped.

They've run out of Scotch, so I take a local Black Knight and sit in the shadows; try to unwind. Three months until I go on leave. It's called "freedom", but what will I do with it?

Brenda and I haven't slept together for months. I met her on leave; wanted to marry. Only chance when on leave, bloody hopeless in India. Mixed marriages, Christian to Hindu or Muslim, almost unheard of. Beautiful, well brought up Anglo-Indians including the firm's secretaries. They are taboo. "Don't forget when you marry her, you marry her family," they say. That was the Raj that was, a fucking hypocritical set-up! Yet without segregation the Raj could not have run as it did. Now the Raj has gone; but it couldn't have been so oppressive really, otherwise how could we keep 350 million people in an undivided India in comparative peace with only a tiny occupation force of foreign troops? A Swiss friend was taught at school that at times there were only 25,000 British troops here.

My mind's been wandering. Back to the present. I'll be home soon, to make my marriage work. But how the hell can I? It bloody well doesn't work. I must try anyway.

Next day I move to Donald's place. There are four solidly built, square, flat-roofed blocks standing in well-groomed lawns. Donald leads me upstairs and into the lounge. It opens on to a verandah that has a view of the river. Ships glide past to the nearby docks.

"Here you are, my boy," he says, as he takes me into a bedroom. A plain room, the bare necessities; wide bed, dressing table with mirror, wardrobe or almirah, bedside table, two chairs. There is a huge bathroom with a polished ruby-coloured floor, square space under the shower surrounded by a four-inch wall, sloping towards a drain-hole. Bath and hand basin have large brass taps. There's a magnificent Royal Doulton WC raised on a step, throne-like, white tiled. The room is a temple of cleanliness.

I freshen under the shower, then join Donald on the verandah. We eat and talk. He drinks gin, I Scotch. He is not short of imported brands;

he gets them from his ship friends. He stands up, moves to my side, puts his hand on my arm.

"My dear chap, I hope you'll be happy here with me."

I mutter, "I'm sure I will."

"Where were you in the War, Bob?"

"North Africa, Normandy." He waits for more.

"Weren't you mentioned in despatches?" Ken must have told him. How the hell did he know?

"It was damn all. Tell you later."

"Ken says perhaps things aren't running too smoothly for you."

"Well Donald, I suppose that's true, otherwise Brenda wouldn't have gone home before me."

I could see him thinking.

"Where do you come from Bob?"

"England, of course, Hertfordshire. Born there, parents still live there. And you're a Scot. Where from Donald?"

"The Isles you know. Stornoway, but we moved to Oban, and I was sent to school in Edinburgh. And you?"

"I was at boarding school too, in Essex. Achieved nothing except in sport. And what did you do in the War? Ken told me you had some adventures."

Donald rests his arms on the table, looks down at his hands. "Yes Bob. I was in Norway in 1940."

"In Intelligence?"

"No, studying forestry."

"Then you were there when the Germans arrived?"

There's a bit of a pause, then he gets going.

"Yes their arrival shocked us. I was contacted by Intelligence. Trapped in a house watched by the Gestapo. Me and an Englishman and some Norwegians." He refills our glasses. "There were some children playing outside. One of their hoops fell by the open door. Do you think I look young now, Bob?"

"Yes I do, Donald. Yes, I think I do."

"Well, when I was eighteen I looked very young. I was wearing shorts. I picked up the hoop and bowled it away. They didn't recognise me, so I escaped. If I'd been caught in civilian clothes like that, I'd have finished up in a concentration camp."

Ken had mentioned that Donald helped King Haakon to escape to England. Donald went to a drawer and brought out a medal.

"The Norwegians gave me this. I don't deserve it. Still I suppose someone has to have them. I think the ones I left behind were killed or captured. I feel guilty getting away and leaving them."

"What else could you have done, Donald, other than be captured with them?"

Donald has a good capacity for drink. We are level pegging, but he must have had some before I joined him, for it is beginning to show. He draws his chair close, puts both hands on my thighs, looks me straight in the face with his grey-blue eyes.

"I'm so glad, Bob, that Ken brought us together." A bit of a pause. "I haven't shown you the whole flat. Do come with me."

He shows me the lounge with paintings of Scotland on the walls. Hanging up is a magnificent stag's head complete with antlers. It's eyes seem to follow you. It looks at you as though you are guilty of something.

"Where did you get this, Donald?"

"From one of the army clubs in the Frontier Province."

"Magnificent but sad."

We walk through the dining room into a spotless kitchen. "Arif is an excellent servant," says Donald. Then he takes me into his bedroom: a plain room, no pictures on the walls. There are two single beds.

"Sit down," he says. I sit on one bed; he sits on his, close by. "Ken has stayed here. Why don't you move in, Bob?"

Then I realise I am naive. He leans towards me. "We could see what happens."

Perhaps that's why he had no one staying with him until I turned up. Ken is a bit of a turd not telling me.

"Oh Donald. I'm sorry Donald but you've got it wrong. I don't know if Ken has misled you, but you've got it wrong."

"All right, all right Bob. Steady! Don't misunderstand me!"

"I'm never sure about Ken. Never understood him. Anyway, Donald, I hope we continue to get on well. You still want me to stay?"

Damn it, I don't want to move again.

"Most certainly yes, Bob." He sounds upset. "I wouldn't dream of your going."

I get up, walk to the door. "May I use your phone Donald? Call home. I'll pay of course."

"That doesn't matter at all. Do go ahead."

After a quarter of an hour Brenda comes on, "Hello Bob. How is everything?" I tell her that the handover of the flat went smoothly.

"How are you all?"

"I'm still exhausted. Couldn't sleep on the plane. But Melanie and Jane are very chirpy. Tearing around. "When will it snow Mummy?" they say."

We continue with trivialities.

"How are my parents?"
"I've been on the phone and they are well."
"Tell them I'll phone them. Where are the kids?"
"They're in the bath; Grannie's with them. I won't call them down. Speak to them next time."
"I'll write tomorrow Brenda."
We hang up.

Next day Donald rings from his office. "Please give me a lift home. My car's being serviced." I give him a lift and drive along Strand Road, between the river and the Maidan, that open space some two miles long, north to south, and one mile wide. It is the lung of Calcutta; pray it may never be built upon. Then we turn into Kidderpore, the dock area.

Donald has been silent. Suddenly he springs to life.

"Slow down," he says, "take that turning." I'd never noticed it before, yet I have often passed this way. I slow to a stop, then swing left under a crude wooden and canvas archway, painted green and bearing the odd name "Joshua's Bar". The red gravel driveway is about forty yards long with a gradual curve to the left, enclosed by high bushes. It leads to a shed-like structure, out of view of the road.

"Bet you've never been here before," Donald chuckles. He's right; I would never have dreamt of coming here. This may be an interesting departure from dull formality.

The building, with corrugated iron roof, wooden beams and brick walls, plastered on the inside, consists of a large room with two small ones leading off to the left. One of these is the office and the other, the bar. The main room is open to the front with a lean-to shed attached. Bamboo screens are unrolled and dropped when it rains heavily.

There is an old upright piano on the right of a small stage, and centrally, a set of drums. In front of the stage is a dance space, flanked by metal tables and cane chairs. From these chairs, tiny bugs are known to emerge; it is not advisable to wear shorts. The place is run down and shabby, but its proximity to the docks ensures its continued existence.
Four seamen sit boozing. It is a relief to get away from the ship. Lolling about are three girls, Anglo-Indians, so-called. They all wear dresses, not saris. They do not want to be absorbed into India. They ought to emigrate while the doors are still open. The radiogram plays while the pianist has a rest, feet propped on a chair. He is talking to the manager, a fat, bald Bengali. Later the pianist takes over from the radiogram. He is small and scraggy, grey hair and glasses, his sad face matching the dismal sound he knocks out of the keyboard. Still, it is rhythm enough,

when accompanied by the drummer, to keep the girls' engines motoring their tangos, rock 'n' roll, or mere smoochy shuffling.

The place is filling. The lights are switched on. The atmosphere starts to hot up, the music livens. Two girls are dancing together, twisting and turning. I hardly glance at them as I talk to Donald. Then I turn my chair and look at the dance space. They are good movers, these two. I watch one of them all the time. She looks at me then quickly turns away. I don't know what it is about her, but I want her.

She is of strong but spare build, a dark girl, say five feet tall. She wears a white cotton dress with red cross-cross pattern and black peep-toe shoes. Her long black hair is slightly wavy and hangs down, secured by a clasp. When the music stops, Donald beckons the short girl over. She sits opposite me, lights a cigarette, accepts a bottle of Golden Eagle beer. She is not pure Indian, perhaps part Indonesian or Filipino. On one wrist are four gold bangles, a watch on the other. She wears a gold chain round her neck with a cross attached. She has a retroussé nose, bright brown eyes, an alert expression, on the defensive, defiant. I forget all about Donald. There is only her. She is not beautiful. There is rarely a smile; but she did smile this once and it bowled me over. She revealed a gold tooth behind a small scar at the left corner of her top lip. She told me later that she quarrelled with a man she didn't want, and he punched her.

"Jenny has had a good education," says Donald. "I've told her she's daft to be here."

Donald goes for a pee and I speak quickly to her before he returns. I wonder why I have a sure feeling, as if I had known her for some time.

"Will you be here tomorrow?"

"Yes."

"What time?"

"Seven o'clock."

"Good, seven."

Donald is coming back, so quickly I add, "Free Saturday too?"

"Can be. Just a bit of shopping."

She speaks with a deep voice, surprises me in one so small. It attracts me; so does her smile and the way she moves. Never have I felt such a thrill.

As we get up to go, leaving Jenny sitting, I whisper, "See you tomorrow." Donald notices our contact.

On the way home (it's not late; I feel tired after the eventful day) Donald is silent for a few minutes. Then he says, "I think this is the first time you have really fallen in love, Bob."

"Oh?" I smile and he sees I'm amused. Donald is right about the obvious attraction, but love?

"Yes, I am serious, Bob, I can tell. And she has fallen for you too." I laugh. "No Bob, I'm serious."

Ridiculous, he hardly knows me. Well, he's a bit feminine; feminine intuition?

"How on earth can you say that, Donald?"

"By the way she looks at you when you are not aware. Bob, you are stupid if you get mixed up with her, and," he pauses, "...and she must think you are a little gold mine."

"Gold mine? She'll soon find out that I'm not."

Back in the flat we are quiet for a while. Clearly he is worried, for he feels that I am moving from his influence. "Look Bob. On Saturday week I'm going on a camping holiday in the hills. I'll meet two boys and they will act as guides. Come with me?"

I could imagine the party.

"Donald, it doesn't appeal to me. Anyway, I haven't time."

"Well Bob", Donald went on, "it would be better if you could get away. If you can't come with me, then you should go on tour."

"I've too much to do locally, Donald." He goes and makes coffee.

For a moment I think it would be a good idea if I did get away from Calcutta. But the excitement of meeting Jenny kills the idea. I've hardly met her, yet the attraction is tremendous. It amazes me.
Donald comes back with the coffee.

"Bob, if you go out with Jenny, word will get round. Brenda will find out. Someone is sure to tell her."

Yes, perhaps Donald would hint at it in the club, possibly to Ken, the memsahibs would hear it second hand. What I now know about Donald makes me glad that I'm not going to be with him; better be seen with Jenny than with him.

"And who would do the gossiping?"

Donald takes no notice. "They will say, "Brenda ought to know."

Keep away from these dirty women, Bob." He pronounces the word with a rolled r, which makes it sound even dirtier.

"I don't believe it of her," I say indignantly. "She's better than the others, and you know it."

"I'm only pointing this out for your own good."

I find it annoying to be told by him of all people that it's for my own good. And it's not as if I'm a youngster. We are about the same age, around forty.

I'm angry and I spring up, go towards the door. "I know you mean well Donald." I hope this annoys him too. Then the moment of anger passes and I sit down again. But I notice that his hand trembles as he holds his cup.

He said she shouldn't be in that dive. He called her to our table, no one else. He knows she's better than the rest. I want to help her.

"Donald I'm coming back for a meal after work tomorrow, but I'm going out again."

"I guess you are, Bob, better if you stayed here though. Goodnight, Bob." He's a lonely man.

As I lie in bed I realise that he is jealous of Jenny. Perhaps that's why he senses we're in love.

I can't understand what's happening. I'm on my own. I've never wanted to sleep around. I could have done when Brenda was here, or when I went on tour; but I didn't. Now I feel a tremendous attraction, a most unlikely meeting. People do fall in love at first sight. Heard of it, read about it, where the love lasts a life-time. Physical attraction developing into something far deeper.

I can't know Jenny after meeting for a few minutes. Something strange is happening. She's special. Perhaps it's because I haven't slept with Brenda or anyone for months. I'm meeting Jenny tomorrow. It's like a strange dream; a vacuum doesn't last for long.

3

Next morning Donald is affable; no mention of last evening's altercation. He has started breakfast and is reading the paper.

"Morning Bob."

Just then the door slams below. "That must be Micky going out. He's late this morning."

"Micky?"

"You must have seen him around, Micky Holland. Been in Calcutta for years. Electrical man, runs the department for us. Goes around in khaki shirt and shorts in all weathers."

"Yes, I remember. Fat with a red face."

"That's him."

"A bit of an eccentric Donald?"

Donald gets up. "Bit of a hurry this morning, Bob. I'll tell you about him later. Yes, certainly he's a "one off"."

The driver takes Donald officewards and I follow.

The day can't pass quickly enough for me. At 5.30 I hurry out of the office, down the stairs. I don't take the lift in case it sticks between floors. I drive away, cursing the traffic; a cart has caught its wheel in a tramline. I dash upstairs to the flat.

"Arif, can you give me a quick meal?"

Arif is used to this sort of flap. "Yes, Sahib, fish."

I shower and change, then wait impatiently. The food comes and I bolt it down. I hope to God the phone won't ring with an urgent request to do some job or other, a breakdown somewhere.

I go to Joshua's at 6.45 and buy a beer. The place is half full, mostly men, with a few women. I hardly notice them. I look at the entrance, then at my watch, then the entrance again. I'm in a state: 7.15 and no sign of Jenny.

I'm becoming anxious. A few minutes later, I see a youth come in and walk down the other side of the room, looking around him. He peers at each man, goes into the bar, comes out again and looks at the dancers. He is slim, probably in his late teens. He has a little moustache, out of place on his young face. He wears a white shirt and faded blue cotton trousers, sandals, and a torn green sleeveless pullover. He stands motionless looking around. Then he sees me across the room and makes his way round the dancers.

"Are you Bob?"

"Yes, who are you?" Like Jenny, he has an Indonesian look.

"Here is a note from Jenny."

Oh God! Can't she come? My spirits sink. He makes as if to go.

"Wait! Sit down. What's your name?"

"Arthur."

I read the note: "Dear Bob. Delayed because Auntie Lulu is ill. Coming soon. Jenny."

"Like a drink Arthur?"

He half smiles at this unexpected invitation. "I'd like rum and coke."

"Will you get it? And get me a bottle of Lion." I give him a ten rupee note. He looks at it as if it is a hundred.

I read the note again. I wonder when she'll come. Some people have no idea of time. Arthur returns, puts the drinks down, fishes in his narrow pocket, brings out the change and I tell him to keep it. He sits awkwardly on the edge of the chair, knees together, playing with his fingers.

"Who are you Arthur?"

"Jenny's brother." He is shy, not used to talking to the likes of me. To him I'm an important Sahib.

"Who is Auntie Lulu?"

"Lulu very old lady. Grandma's sister."

I wonder if I should ask him to take me to Auntie's place. No, Jenny and I might pass on the way.

"Are you working Arthur?"

"No, no work."

He wants to go, he's fidgeting. "Thank you Arthur Ask her to hurry." I smile, but he doesn't look at me, remains dead pan.

He drinks up. All he says is, "OK."

It is 7.30. Maybe she will come at eight o'clock, maybe later. Perhaps I've an hour to kill. I watch the dancers shuffling around. One man is smoking, hands his cigarette to his partner and she has a puff. Two are rockin' and rollin'. I recognise the woman who was partnering Jenny yesterday. She sees me on one of her rotations. Next time round she makes a pout and frowns, then smiles naughtily. I think these girls are here, most of them, not because they want to be, but because they must eat. Usually they make friends with their visitors, not just a hop on hop off "quicky". If he likes her, he'll meet her again on his next voyage, may write to her. Whimsically, a'song I'd just heard, comes back to me.

> *I've kissed the girls in Naples and also in Paree,*
> *But the ladies of Calcutta do something to me.*

"Are you using these chairs?" a man asks. Brings me back to earth.

"No, take two."

I keep one for Jenny, hang my coat on it. I go to the bar, chat to the barman, George.

George is an Anglo-Indian. He's getting on in years. He hopes to join his son in England soon.

"I used to have a better job. Barman in the Grand Hotel. Came here last year."

"A bit scruffy."

"Yes sir, it's gone down since the War."

"Who used to come here?"

"Merchant navy, same as now, Army men, a few air ground staff. There used to be a good band and a crooner."

I offer George a drink which he declines.

"Do you know Jenny?"

"Oh yes."

"I'm waiting for her. She's late."

"She'll turn up, won't let you down. Pity she's drifted here. Too good for this."

"Better go back to my seat, mustn't miss her. See you again."

"I hope so, sir."

"Cut out the "sir", George, call me Bob." I give him five rupees. "Have a drink later."

"Thank you Bob, sir."

It's eight thirty. When will she come?

Barely a minute later, "Are you waiting for someone?" a husky voice whispers in my ear. I'm taken by surprise and knock the full glass into my lap. This makes her grin, gold tooth peeping. I stand up and there is a large, damp patch on my trousers. It sort of spoils the moment but it does nothing to dampen my ardour. She collects a cloth from the bar, mops up the mess. She sits down. I'm tongue-tied and my guts turn over. What is it about her that does this to me?

"Jenny," I say. "Jenny. Didn't see you come in."

"Thought I'd surprise you."

I hold her hand, there is warmth. She's quiet. I want her like mad. There is so much still to know about her. She wants me to dance. Her favourite, *Jealousy* is on the radiogram, while the pianist rests.

"My favourite, the tango," she says.

"I can't dance with beer-stained trousers." There's a feeling of what next?

"How is Auntie?"

"Asthma attack, but she is better. Dennis is with her."

"Dennis?"

"Brother."

"Arthur too?"

"My parents adopted him."

"Your parents?"

"Both dead." Silence.

"Let's get out of here," she says.

I hide the damp patch with my coat, walk to the car. I drive to Strand Road and park by the Hooghly. It is peaceful and cool here. I put my arm round her, try to draw her nearer, but these bucket seats, with hand brake and gear lever between, are not designed for lovers.

"Where can we go?"

"Drive to Corporation Street."

I drive along by the river, turn right past Eden Gardens, cross Chowringhee into Corporation Street, into a maze of roads unknown to me.

She directs me, "Turn left." I drive under a building into a yard. The durwan comes forward with his long metal tipped lathi. On his rounds he bangs this staff on the ground to warn intruders. He doesn't want to meet them.

"Give him something," she says and I tip him two rupees.

She tells him to look after the car. We go through a back door to a reception desk. She books in, no details wanted, only money in advance. She takes the key and we go upstairs, into a room with a single bed. All is clean but old and worn.

There is one chair, a table with a mirror standing on it, clothes horse with torn towel next to a cracked wash basin. There is one light bulb with no shade, a bedside table, and a fan - not necessary in this cool weather. At the back of the door are two nails serving as hooks, and hanging there, a 1959 calendar bearing the garish picture of Ganesh the Elephant god with his one tusk.

We use the bathroom opposite, then we undress. Her breasts are small as is common in the East. She is well proportioned, strong, but thin. As I get into bed and touch her, I tremble and swallow, as I did that first time when I was eighteen.

Wham! Something's happening to me, a new awakening. I don't care how many men she's been with; if this isn't love I don't know what is. She takes the clasp off her hair, lets it flow free. I run my hand through it, with its slight natural wave, as that of a South Sea Islander, so deliciously soft, oh how soft, on my cheek.

She lies motionless, undemonstrative, but yielding. We make wonderful love, but something is missing. She is hiding from me, seems to be elsewhere. She puts her arms around me tenderly, but doesn't look at me. I marvel that among millions I have met her. We lie glowing. But I must leave before it gets light.

"We'll meet tomorrow."

"Yes darling."

"Where?"

"At the Green Giraffe."

"At midday?"

She turns towards me, "Yes, I'll be there." I kneel by the bed, stroking her hair. I kiss her face, her eyes, her hair.

"See you tomorrow," she says and buries her head in the pillow.

I leave money in her handbag. It will be a generous surprise. She never asked for, nor hinted at any payment, unusual in these circles where the terms of payment are Cash with Order. If she had thought me a "little goldmine", as Donald had said, then it didn't show. She must like me. It gives me a sure feeling. I look down at her lying there and long to stay, but I must go. Wonderful, tomorrow I'll be with her again. There's no great hurry, it's Saturday.

"Please tell Morrison Sahib I'll be out all day."

"Very good, bahut achha Sahib."

I wonder how long it will be before Arif is informed by bush telegraph that I have a woman, a biwi. I won't be bringing Jenny here; it would upset both host and servant.

At ten o'clock I drive to the office.

"What time do you expect me tomorrow?" I ask, poking my head round Tony's door.

"Oh, twelve-ish."

"Bush shirt order, nothing formal?"

"Yep. And oh, I'm expecting Tim."

"What's he doing over here?"

"Some Bombay work, nothing to do with us."

I go into my office. I'll be glad to see Tim; he was in the Engineers in the War: Western Desert, tank recovery, nerve-wracking business. A major, one rank above me. I write some letters and before midday I drive to the big market. I tell a boy to guard the car. It is a protection racket on a minor scale, cheap at the price. I am pestered by two market porters, official permits sewn on their shirts, and carrying their shallow, round wickerwork basket. It's only a few yards to the Green Giraffe, the small licensed restaurant, not top grade, resident British don't go there. But it's clean and the curries are excellent.

I see Jenny across the street. She holds herself well, very straight back. She's wearing flat shoes and she moves with a slight wiggle like a model on parade. Her light-blue trousers, white blouse, with a hand-knitted dark-blue cardigan are nothing special, but the movement and the get-up are to me delightful. She carries a handbag with its strap over her shoulder, walks into the room and sees me at the far end. She doesn't smile, doesn't turn her head, but glances left and right, taking in the other few occupants. She sits and I seek her hand.

"Tea?"

"Yes please."

I order a pot of tea and some chicken samosas. Sheer happiness. There was fear that she would not come, a thrill when I saw her, the peace as she sits next to me. The joy of it all! What is happening? I gaze at her. She has the high cheekbones of an Indonesian, but her eyes are not hooded, more Caucasian, only slightly slanted and her nostrils are just a little flared. Firm mouth shows determination and character.

"Where would you like to go, Jenny?"

"It's up to you."

"Then let's go the Chandernagar."

"OK, I like a car ride."

She pours out the tea using a little metal strainer. She does things neatly and eats nicely.

"Do you go in a car often?"

"Now and again," she says, and smiles to herself.

"Do you work?"

"I was a Trunk exchange operator."

"But not now?"

"No, I'm a "B" girl.."

My look questions her. She says quietly, "We sell our bodies."

I drive across the Maidan. To our right is the Ochterlony monument, rather like the Monument in the City of London. It's name will be changed to Shahid Minar. There is a gathering of dhotied men at its foot with an orator talking excitedly, waving his arms about.

"Trouble with the trams again," says Jenny.

A bit early in the year for this. Usually shortfuse tempers don't blow until torrid premonsoon May. The Tramway Company is a vital part of the transport system, but it is still British owned.

"The Tramfare Enhancement Resistance Society on the go again. The answer to a fare increase is to burn a few trams, Jenny."

I drive to Strand Road. "How is Auntie?"

"Much better."

We pass the Swimming Club on the right, the river to the left.

"What's your full name, Jenny?"

"Geraldine Margaret. Don't like the names. So I'm Jenny. Family name Sandakan. What's yours?"

"Bennett. Bernard Bennett, and a family name in the middle; Oldfield. B-O-B you see. "Bob"."

"Why not Bernard?"

"They called me Bernie at home and I hated it. Given the nickname "Bob" at school."

I can't drive down busy Strand Road with one hand on the steering wheel and the other seeking Jenny, so I concentrate on driving. We reach Howrah bridge. Howrah, sometimes spelled Hoara, is famous for the main railway terminus and the bridge. From here go trains to Delhi, Bombay and Madras. The Hooghly separates Howrah from Calcutta.

"You know this area Jenny?"

"I go to the station sometimes. I've relatives in Bombay and Orissa."

The bridge is teeming with pedestrians and assorted traffic. In the middle run the single decker trams. They are sturdy, have to be, always overloaded. It is a huge cantilever affair that dominates the skyline, not graceful at all. Before, all traffic went across on a pontoon bridge, or over a bridge a few miles to the north. We cross at a crawl.

"How old are you?"

"Twenty five."

"A big gap; I'm thirty eight."

We pass Howrah station, come to a T-junction, turn right into a road undistinguished in appearance, but distinguished in name: the Grand Trunk Road. This part of it is paved with sett blocks, very uneven. To the left it leads to railway sidings, the Bengal Engineering College and the Botanical Gardens, before petering out.

So we proceed along this historic highway northwards. It stretches all the way to Pakistan and to the Khyber Pass, about 1500 miles.

"A few years ago I drove all the way to Peshawar, Jenny."

We are held up at a level crossing for only a few minutes; lucky, for sometimes it's half an hour.

"Your family isn't Indian?"

"Mother Indian Christian; her mother half Filipino. She married a man from Surabaya."

"And your father?"

"Born in India. His father Filipino, partly Spanish I think. Cousin had tight curls, very dark, some negro blood I think."

"Why did they come to India?"

"Mother's father exported Indian goats."

"Oh yes, I know. Huge, aren't they? Helped turn India into a desert after men cut the trees down. And your father?"

"Stevedore, and his father too, here in the docks. Came from the Philippines."

Jenny is tired of being questioned. So, it seems she is about a quarter Indian and three quarters Indonesian or Filipino. There's something in the chemistry of this bait that has me hooked. She hasn't held out the hook deliberately. I've taken it willingly, or am I the hook?

4

A bumpy, narrow road, running through a string of villages; Grand Trunk it's called. The shops and dwellings are so close that in parts there is no pavement. On the right are many jute mills, next to the river, the gates in their long boundary walls, guarded by men wearing khaki shorts and shirts, pugrees on their heads, lathis in their hands.

It is little more than a congested lane. A bypass road is

planned, inland to miss these villages. This road was adequate fifty years ago, when there were no lorries and buses, only bullock carts and a few horsedrawn carriages and coaches. I point out an inconspicuous lane leading to the left. There is a small sign on a wall with an arrow indicating "Hindustan Motors", owned by the huge Birla combine.

"That's where the Ambassador cars are made. It's a temporary approach road, been here for years. God knows when the bypass will be opened."

"When were these mills built?"

"Between sixty and ninety years ago. That's what brought all the people here. A hundred years ago this part must have been beautiful. Pretty little villages by the river. You don't know this road, Jenny?"

"No. If I come this way to church at Bandel, it's by train."

"We are up and down the roads on both banks, often visiting jute mills, about sixty of them; and chemical works, a tyre factory, cotton mills, all sorts. Last year I just escaped a huge traffic jam, missed it by an hour. Lorry drivers' strike. Traffic solid from Serampur to Howrah, six miles of it."

Today the traffic isn't too bad, but we are held up for twenty minutes at a level crossing in Serampur.

"Tell me about your family, Bob," she says suddenly.

"My wife and kids went home a few days ago. I've let our flat. That's why I'm staying with Donald, and that's how I met you. He brought me to Joshua's. Brenda went home with the kids because she doesn't like it out here."

"How old are your kids?"

"Seven and four. Two girls. I'm very fond of them, course I am, otherwise I'd rather be single again."

"When do you go on leave?"

"In May. I was looking forward to it..."

"Surely you're looking forward to it?"

"Not as much as I was five days ago."

The level crossing barrier lifts and we move on. We reach Chandernagar. To mark its boundary, on either side of the road is a pillar, made of soft stone which is eroded by the weather, but still legible on each is carved LIBERTE, EGALITE, FRATERNITE.

Whose liberty and equality? Fraternity? Plenty of fraternising. As "Blood and Guts" General Patton of the US Army is reputed to have said, in the early months of the occupation of Germany, when mixing with the former enemy was frowned upon, "Copulation ain't fraternisation, s'long as you don't shake hands after it." Plenty of copulation between the races, castes and classes in Chandernagar.

Chandernagar, called by us Chandnagore, with our usual propensity for corrupting foreign names, was a French enclave until 1951, when the French asked the Indian Government, newly independent, to be allowed to stay in this tiny territory. They pleaded, not lacking a sense of humour, but knowing with whom they were dealing, that it would be a good place in which to learn French, but to no avail. Before Independence, Chandernagar was a delightful oasis, free and easy, unlike Calcutta. It was the place to take a girl friend, a night in a hotel, an escape from gossip.

The place is now run down and is of no importance. It's rather sad. But there is still a school, the notice over the entrance proclaiming "ECOLE POUR LES FILLES JEUNES". There is also a pleasant promenade by the river.

"Where can we get a drink, Jenny?"

"Slow down. See that gap in the wall? Drive in there." There is a notice on the wall: Astoria Hotel.

"Used to be a nice place."

I wonder how she knows, as she's only twenty five, but I dismiss this from my mind. I park the car in a small yard, weeds pushing through cracks in the concrete. Up three steps, on the wooden verandah, sits a dhotied man, a little goat beside him, tethered to a table. The green paint of the verandah railings is flaking off. There is no sign of other visitors. We have the peace we want, away from the turmoil.

"You want room?"

"Not staying," says Jenny. "Just resting. And two beers."

The man shows us into the room behind him. There are two cane bottomed chairs, almirah (wardrobe), table, double bed, the minimum. The bed has a plain, sturdy, wooden frame, stained brown. The thin mattress is placed on interwoven cord netting. There are two pillows without covers. I place a towel over them. There is a wooden framework high above, supported at each corner by poles, to hold a mosquito net, if needed. There's a ceiling fan, turned off as the weather is cool.
A servant brings the beer and glasses.

I draw the curtains on the window and Jenny says, "Oh Bob, I'm sorry that I'm not very bright, but I feel tired."

"Are you all right?"

"Yes, just tired. After you left I couldn't sleep, The couple next door were arguing and fighting, very noisy."

I pour the beer. She lights a cigarette. She has a fifty tin of Capstan. The tobacco factory is in South Calcutta on the road to Donald's place. The girls there pack the tins by hand. They take a piece of corrugated white paper, grab a handful of cigarettes, put them on the paper, then plonk them into the tin, fifty exactly, hardly ever need to take one off, or add one.

"Where do you live?"

"Benatala Street, near Park Street."

"On your own?"

"I'll show you Bob."

"When did your parents die?"

"Pa went to sea in the War. Merchant Navy. Never came back."

"And mother?"

"When he didn't come back she was very ill, unhappy, gave up. Died soon after."

"How old were you?"

"All these questions." She changes the subject. "I went to school in Patna, convent school."

"Things were difficult?"

"You can say that again." She is silent. I wait. She stubs out her cigarette. "That's enough for now. I'm tired."

She lies down and I lie beside her. She goes to sleep. It makes me feel horny being next to her, too much to bear, so I get up and sit on the edge of the bed. The frame cuts into my thighs, so I move to a chair, finish off the beer.

I don't want to hurt anyone. I want two incompatible situations to exist side by side. Something is missing in my life and Jenny comes along. The vacuum is being filled. Donald had said Jenny is my first real love. He wished he were in her place. I shudder at the thought. How can any normal man exist in India without a partner? The hypocrisy of the artificial life we have created here, when will it end?

Prejudices, European and Indian, are all too evident; class, caste, colour. But all draw imperceptibly nearer - modern communications, tourism, immigration, emigration, all help.

Coming to India as a young man and finding no female companionship acceptable, to the Establishment, is most unnatural. It is known that one will mix with local girls, but Thou Shalt Not Be Found Out. It's a no-win situation; a bittersweet cocktail of sadness and joy for us to share, if she feels as I do.

She said, "I'm a B-girl", but I'm sure she is very choosy. These girls here are independent, no pimps. I must get her away from all this, but how?

Half an hour later Jenny sits up. "Feel better?"

"Yes Bob." She stretches, yawns. I kiss her.

"Let's get some fresh air."

We go out and the manager is feeding a cigarette to his pet goat.

"Very much he liking cigarette, but he very particular. No cheap Char Minar, only best."

"He likes Capstans?"

"Oh yes please liking."

Jenny gives the animal a cigarette which it accepts with pleasure.

We drive to the promenade, park the car. We stroll under the trees. Sit on a bench facing the river, in front of the lawn of the French school, but there are no little schoolgirls around as it is Saturday. The country boats pass by on the current. Considering the flatness of Bengal, the Hooghly flows with surprising swiftness. It is quiet, very few people. Usually, wherever strangers go, people flock round, inquisitive.

Jenny shows me a photo. She's sitting with a child on her lap.

"Yours?"

"Hmm." She nods. "She lives with my brother Harry and his wife Sadie."

"What's her name?"

"Diana."

"Pretty little kid and a nice name. How old is she?"

"Four. And they have Lucy, two years old. Difficult, but I have Diana with me when I can."

Maybe that's why she's a B-girl, helps keep the child. The telephone exchange didn't pay enough.

"They used to live in a bustee, Moti Jheel, nasty place. I paid for a better place. I'Ll send Diana to boarding School. I let the men see Diana and then they give me more." She is silent. "Bob, I want to go home."

I'm very disappointed. Why couldn't she have told me she didn't really want to come out?

"All right," I say, and I don't hide my annoyance. "I thought you wanted a day out, and a night, too?"

"I've a lot on my mind."

I drive back quickly, annoyed for the moment. She seems to have sunk into her own thoughts, drifting away from me.

Then, "Give me a day or two to get sorted out."

I forgive her. I stop the car, put my arm round her anu kiss her. "I love you," the words just come out; she doesn't answer.

I take a left fork. "I'm going back over Bally bridge." It was built in the early thirties. "I don't know why this was built so far from Calcutta; perhaps for military purposes." The railway runs down the centre, with east and west roads on either side. Just here the Hooghly is straight. Round a distant bend, we can see tall buildings in Calcutta.

I drive on. "Up to the end of 1948 flying boats landed here."

"Why did they stop coming?"

"The journey took too long, three or four days. Landed in Egypt, Bahrain and Karachi. And it was too expensive having customs staff both here and at Dum Dum."

We reach the east bank. "They've renamed the bridge Vivekananda instead of Bally. See, to the left the Hindu Dhakineshwar Temple. "We join the Barrackpore road, turn right, then pass the junction to Dum Dum. Set back from the road on either side are old, square houses, where indigo planters lived many years ago."

We come to a building. "Are you hungry Jenny? D'you know this place? It's quite good."

"Let's stop here then."

The car park is surrounded by palm trees outside a restaurant called Bamboo Khoti. It looks like a jungle dwelling, but the bamboo walls and thatched roof are for show, and hide the concrete blocks and steel underneath. Inside the ceiling is underdrawn with wood and bamboo. The walls are covered by colourful mats and paintings of Indian country scenes. The bamboo chairs have green cushions. The tables are irregular in shape, made from slices sawn from huge tree trunks, polished and finished off.

The waiter comes. He is dressed in a short green coat and trousers, "Bamboo Khoti" written in orange on his breast pocket. We order tandoori chicken, half a bird each, and naan bread. On the table is an assortment of chutneys, lime and mango.

"What you like drink?" says the man.

"I've a bit of a headache. Fruit juice."

"We have mixed fruit cocktail, not alcohol, long drink. Very good."

"Sorry I haven't been lively today."

"That's all right Jenny. Lovely to be with you."

"I'll be better tomorrow. May have a chill. And I've a lot on my mind."

We leave. A cheerful little boy in an off-white vest, full of holes, grey cotton shorts, no shoes, is cleaning the windscreen. I give him a few annas. A car draws up and out gets the driver, Ellis. His passengers are a husband and wife. I've seen them around but can't place them. Ellis nods to me in recognition and his companions look towards us, then to Ellis, who says something.

I have "been seen". That will give them something to talk about.

"Do you know them?"

"I know the younger man. I've seen the couple around." I drive away.

"She'll gossip about us. Well, they all will in their different ways."

"You mean because you are married?."

"Partly, but mainly because we are mixing. This darned social set up."

"I know."

"They think the Raj is still here. Calcutta, stuffier than anywhere else in the whole country. No one brown allowed in the Swimming Club."

"I know Bob."

"Oh well, it'll change slowly. But if they opened up all the clubs, they'd be swamped."

Why can't they open their own bloody clubs? There will be fewer and fewer expatriates. Then either Indians will take the clubs over or they will be closed.

As we approach Calcutta, Jenny tells me to fork left into Circular Road.

"Go to the Killarny Apartment Block."

"I thought you said near Park Street?"

"I'm going to move there tomorrow."

We reach the five storey block.

"Shall I come and help you pack?"

Rather hurriedly she says, "No. No, thank you Bob."

"Then when will I see you?"

"I've a lot to do."

"I must see you." I can't bear the thought of losing her.

"Can I phone you?" I give her Donald's phone number. "I'll phone you on Monday."

What if she doesn't? I feel panicky. What if she doesn't, I can't bear the thought.

"Don't phone me. Please meet me Jenny, you must. Damn the phone. See me at Joshua's."

"All right," she deliberates. "All right. Make it Wednesday."

"Oh why not Monday?"

"Give me time, Bob."

"Right my dear. Wednesday at Joshua's."

We kiss. She walks to the block. The way she walks really gets me. Then the whirr of the old fashioned lift and she's gone.

Her life seems complicated. I was sure she said she lived in Benatala Street. She said she'd sort herself out. So what if her life is complicated, so is mine.

I'll go to the Walshaws' for lunch tomorrow. That can't be too bad. I'll see dear old Tim. Pass the time away. Work on Monday, take my mind off Jenny. I know that I've fallen.

I drive back to Donald's.

Arif says, "Sahib say you go to Holland Sahib house."

5

I rap on the door and a huge man opens it.

"Micky Holland," he says, offering a ham-like hand. I wince at the grip which shakes my whole body.

"Hello Bob," he puts his arm round my shoulders, leads me to the verandah. He is built like a rugby forward but is grossly overweight, glowing red-apple cheeks on a round face. He is almost completely bald, neck and head the same width. His name seems to indicate a Dutch connection. One can imagine him in native costume, baggy shirt, trousers, clogs.

Walking through Micky says, "Strange man, Donald. Could retire. A man from Stornoway said he'd been left forty thousand pounds by an uncle."

On the verandah sit Donald and a light-brown younger man, an Anglo-Indian. He's good looking, medium height, blue eyes.

"Johnny, this is Bob - living with Donald."

Johnny is amused by this.

"Living with Donald?"

"Yes," I say. "My family has flown home."

"Donald told me you were a beer man." Micky hands me a bottle and glass. He and Donald stick to gin. I wonder what else Donald has told him.

"So you are on your own," says Micky. "Don't let Donald lead you astray."

"Don't take any notice of him," says Donald.

"Do you go to church?" asks Micky.

"Not often. Brenda isn't interested."

"I saw you in Messiah last year."

"Ah yes. That went well."

"I was reserve organist."

"He's a good organist," says Donald.

Johnny laughs, "Except the time you had too many."

"Least said about that the better," says Donald.

Micky goes into the kitchen. The fridge door slams.

"He used to be an old devil", says Donald, "until one of his friends was killed. I'll tell you later."

Micky returns.

"What's your job Johnny?"

"I work for Micky. Cabling, so I'm outdoors most of the time. I get browner and Micky gets redder."

Micky sees me giving him the once over. He is dressed in khaki shirt and shorts, and stockings.

"Always wear shorts. Hot or cold, the weather doesn't trouble me." Johnny says, "You go to church like that, eh?" Micky roars with laughter.

"What are you doing tomorrow, Bob?"

"Lunch with my manager. D'you know him? Tony Walshaw and his wife Thora."

"Oh yes, a miserable bugger."

"That's not quite fair Micky. He's never well. Tummy trouble. He's a nice man but a bit blunt."

Micky has drunk too much. "Tony Walshaw! Do him good to let his hair down; get away from the old cow. Bosses him. "The General" we call her. Bring him down on his own. Do him good to have a bit of how's yer father."

I change the subject." I hear you're retiring soon?" Micky doesn't hear. He goes to the verandah railings, arms outspread, gin bottle in one hand. He inhales deeply.

"Oh to be in Calcutta now that England's here."

"April," says Johnny.

"It's February," says Micky.

"He's had too much," says Donald, frowning.

Micky starts to waltz, bottle clasped to his chest, right arm outstretched.

He sings, "Sweet Rosalinda, your Michael is waiting, watching and waiting, heart palpitating."

"And masturbating," sniggers Johnny.

Like many large people, Micky is light on his feet. He is a mixture of clumsiness and daintiness, reminds me of Oliver Hardy. He stops suddenly, sways, walks straight up to me.

"Mr Bennett, may I have the honour of this dance?" this with the utmost gravity.

"I've a bad knee." I get up, pour myself a drink to escape, Micky plonks down in a chair, beaming. He calms down. I wonder how the hell I've got myself mixed up with this odd lot.

"What are you going to do in England?"

Micky is a bit slurred, "Bob, I'll miss India, but I'm not needed. Over age limit."

"What are your plans?"

"I'll buy a pub. One not too busy. Don't need to be greedy; got my pension."

"Where?"

"Devon. I'll take a woman with me. Barmaid."

Donald says, aside to me, "He's a kind man. He's helped several. Brings them here."

"Like Gladstone?"

"I suppose you could say that.

"Some good ones, some bad ones. Sad stories." says Micky. He pours himself another gin. "Bringing two here tomorrow. Lunch. What you doing for lunch, Bob? Donald, Johnny, bring him along."

"Sorry I can't. I told you."

"Must meet Dora and Sheila. Now Dora and Sheila - I'll tell you about them. Bob you must meet..."

"Sorry Micky," says Donald. "We have a meal waiting. See you tomorrow." We go upstairs. "When he starts like that he goes on and on. It bores me. Heard it all before. Then he starts talking about the man who performed in a pew one Sunday; all sorts of embarrassing rubbish."

"What was the shock you said changed him?"

"He was raging drunk. Drove his car into the back of a bullock cart. A bamboo pole went through the windscreen and into his girlfriend's eye. Killed her instantly. Micky was rammed against the steering wheel. Chest badly injured. Lucky to live, but he said he wished he'd died. Funny mixture, Micky. Good in parts."

Arif has left cold chicken, spuds and salad for us.

"You should tell Brenda to stay at home. The children will keep her occupied. Then we can have a really good time here."

He wants me to stay with him. He won't give up trying, but he's wasting his time. I'm glad I won't be here for long; he might wear me down.

It frightens me that I feel some attraction, and I'm worried about it. Donald goes on, "If you worked here and lived with Jenny, you would be social outcasts. She'd never be allowed in clubs. Eventually your firm would send you home, or at any rate, they wouldn't renew your contract. What would you do then, Bob?"

Head in hands, I say, "God knows Donald. Do let it rest. I'll sail home in May. I want a rest. Outside Bombay the pilot drops off into his launch. Wonderful, for two or three weeks no one gets at you. If you fly, just a few hours and you're in London. Message: "Come to HO immediately." Better by sea. At least you can escape for a while."

I go into my room, wash and change.

When I come out he says, "What are you going to do about Jenny?"

"Oh let it rest for Christ's sake. I apologise for being unsociable, but I want to be on my own."

"Won't do you any good.

"You're probably right, but I still want to be on my own. Sorry!"

I decide to go to Princes. I'll be drinking so I leave the car, take a taxi. At Princes I sit at the bar, facing the band across the large dance space. On either side are tables, set for diners. It is spacious, with high ceiling supported by pillars. Races mix here, unlike most of the clubs. Jenny knows the place. I'll bring her here, despite raised eyebrows in my stuffy, obsolescent community.

The South American style band is playing. The leader is wearing a white sharkskin jacket and black trousers. He charms all with his smile. Dolores comes on to the stage, dancing up to the mike, starts singing amusing rubbish, Carmen Miranda style:

> *Mamma gave me a nickel*
> *To buy a pickle*
> *I didn't buy a pickle*
> *I bought some chewing gum...*

She helps fill the place. She's slim, sinewy, sexy, and glistens in the humidity that is Calcutta. She is as hot as the climate; sure has personality.

> *R, I say, R-A, R-A-G, R-A-GEEGEE,*
> *R-A-GEEGEE, M-O-PEEPEE, RAGMOPP...*

I wonder how long she'll last at this rate. Carmen Miranda didn't last long. Short life and a merry one! Perhaps that's the best way.

I've always been here with friends, absorbed in conversation, dancing, eating and the cabaret, hadn't really looked round. Fans hang down on long stems, working like mad, combating the sweat that clings to the dancers in the near 100 per cent humidity. In the centre, above the dancers, suspended high in the dome, is a huge bunch of balloons. They will be released at midnight. It is all very happy, but things are not as good as they used to be. My friend Hamish, nearing retirement, said, "You should have seen us in the days pre-war, laddie. Every night was a Saturday night and every Saturday night was a Hogmanay."

Tim from Bombay walks in.

"Hello, thought you were coming tomorrow."

"Came this morning."

"Did you know you're coming to Tony's curry lunch tomorrow?"

"No I didn't. He thinks I'm arriving tomorrow morning."

"Where are you staying?"

"Here in the Grand."

Tim Cogger went home on leave like I did. Married, like I did. She came out with him. Didn't like it in Bombay, quarrelled and three months later,. she went home. Now they've divorced.

"How's life Tim?"

"Fine, just fine. Glad to be on my own."

"When you going on leave?"

"May."

"Must go. See you tomorrow."

I float out, cool air goes to my head; taxi home. I flop on the bed and pass out.

6

Next morning I get up with a headache, but improve after a shower and coffee on the verandah. Donald is doing a crossword. "Didn't hear you come in."

"Came in just after midnight."

"Where did you go?"

"Princes. Met one of our people over from Bombay."

I go for a stroll to the river wall, helps clear my head. A ship, Brocklebank Line, is going up river to the docks on the high tide; it's wake rocks the flimsy country boats.

Micky has seen me from his flat and joins me.

"You're going out to lunch?. Pity you can't meet Sheila."

"Another time,"

Micky laughs. "You're going to see that twit Walshaw. Bring him down here. Do him a lot of good." Wicked old bugger, Micky is.

Later I drive to the Walshaws. Their fourth floor flat is at the top of an old block in south central Calcutta. Anything south of Park Street is considered respectable. They only just make the grade. Most of the more important expatriates reside in the south, but not as far as Donald, who lives on the edge of what might be termed a jungle area!

I ring the bell and I'm answered by the bark of their smooth-haired terrier.

Tony ushers me in and gestures, "I think you know everyone except Mrs Mukherjee." Mrs Mukherjee, I learn, helps in the Charitable Trust.

Chatting with Thora Walshaw are Mr and Mrs Slater. He works for the insurance company that covers many of our risks. Tony will use this connection to put down some of his party outgoings at the firm's expense. Mrs Slater is holding forth about their children.

"Yes, they have settled well at school in Folkestone. Joan is eleven. Jemima is nine. This is her second term. The games mistress has her eye on her. She runs very fast. Joan is going to be an artist, I think; she doesn't like games."

It goes on and on, with the occasional interjection from Thora; "Oh really?", "Is that so?" when Emily Slater pauses for breath. I retreat and Mrs Mukherjee draws me toward her like a magnet. She's a plump, grey-haired Bengali Christian and wears a sari.

"I was telling Mrs Tomaides about my new flat." Mrs Tomaides is a widow like Mrs Mukherjee. "I'm very happy there in my new flat in Ballygunj, Mr Bennett," she says.

"Call me Bob."

"Yes, I'm happy there. Very quiet away from the traffic. But oh my dear! The girl upstairs! One o'clock in the morning. Walks about on the hard floor. High heels; tuk, tuk, tuk. What on earth is she doing at one o'clock in the morning?" She giggles, "I must ask her to take her shoes off."

"These girls! Oh Mrs M! Don't talk about these young people to me," says Mrs Tomaides, raising her hands in mock horror. Mrs Tomaides is a small woman, white hair, glasses. She wears a dark-blue dress and her fingers are covered in rings. One of her incisors protrudes over her bottom lip like Bugs Bunny.

"What are these young people up to nowadays? I had a nice American boy staying with me. One of my best lodgers. Then, the other day, my eyes are not so good, but I distinctly saw the young lady in the second floor flat in the block at the end of my garden signalling. I thought she wanted to attract my attention. Then I realised she was waving to Daniel. I heard him shout. Dear, dear, Mrs M, I have had to ask him to leave. He went to his office in the morning. Half an hour later I heard the bath water running out his room is over mine. It was the girl from the flat opposite who had stayed overnight. I cannot tolerate such behaviour. What would people say? How are Brenda and the children?" We had stayed in her boarding house for a few weeks. "You must miss them."

"I'll survive, Mrs T, I'll be joining them at home in May."

There is a ring at the door. The bearer and the barking dog answer, and in sails Canon Wheatley, all smiles and good fellowship. He has presence; all turn towards him. I know Reginald Wheatley. He baptised Melanie and Jane. He greets us one by one, speaks to Tony and Thora'

"How kind. A joy to see you at the Service."

Another ring at the door. The bearer beats the dog to the door. Enter Mrs Marjorie Barton, accompanied by Tim Cogger.

"Dear Boy," she says as she sweeps in. "He helped me with the lift, Tony. Someone had left the gate open. Ran up to the first floor and brought it down. We know each other so well now, don't we Tim? Introductions made on the long slow journey to the fourth floor," she pronounces theatrically.

"How are you Tony? Thora? Katisha, I should say. Thora dear, you make a wonderful Katisha. You will dominate the *Mikado*."

Canon Wheatley speaks to me, "How are you Bob?" I tell him Brenda and the children have gone home, that I'll join them soon.

"Oh Reginald, meet Tim Cogger. He's visiting us from our Bombay mob."

Reginald Wheatley also greets Marjorie Barton. He tries hard to mix.

"I went to a party last week. Invited by the Browns of Indian Chemicals. I was told, or I thought I was, that it was a Pimps party. When I got there I asked George Brown to introduce me to the Pimps. But it turned out that I had misheard. It was a Pimms party. Haw haw haw!"

"Lucky to get any Pimms over here," says Tim.

While Canon Reginald and Tim are talking, Marjorie Barton collars me. I'm not sure if she is myopic or what but she peers at me, comes very close and the nipple of her left breast presses against my chest through my thin cotton bush-shirt. She knows I sing and will probably be in the chorus of the *Mikado*.

In her best come-hither voice she says, maintaining the close contact, "Will you come over to my place for singing lessons, Bob?"

I smile at her.

"That might be a good idea," but I've thoughts for Jenny only. Marjorie's husband is constantly on tour, selling mining equipment. She's a good sort and I feel a bit sorry for her; pale face, blonde hair pulled tight off her forehead into a bun at the back. She's lonely and thinks I am too.

Not a bad party of it's kind. There is chicken curry, rice, chapatis and sundries, and for those who prefer less stomach-stirring fare, an assortment of cold meats, quiche and salad; trifle to follow.

I chat with Tim. "We can have lunch tomorrow?"

"Good idea".

"See you." I go home.

In the evening Donald is reading *The World of Susie Wong*.

"This should interest you, Bob, Jenny in Hong Kong. Think you'd enjoy it."

I had read it and don't much like his comparison.

"Donald, if you don't mind, I'll make my calls now." It will be about teatime in England.

Brenda answers and I can hear Melanie and Jane making a noise.

"Hello Bob. Quiet! You can speak to Daddy in a moment. Is everything all right? No problem with the tenants?"

"Everything is fine. I like them."

"Anything exciting happening? Are you going on tour again?"

"I don't think so. I had curry lunch at the Walshaws' today. You remember the boarding house, Mrs Tomaides? She asked after you and the kids. Canon Wheatley, too. Tim was over from Bombay. Seems settled after the divorce. How are you?"

"We are all well, but I haven't got used to the cold yet. Melanie and Jane don't seem to mind it. Here's Melanie."

"Hello Daddy. Grandpa says when it snows he'll make me a snowman."

Chatter in the background, then a nervous "Hello Daddy," from Jane, not yet used to the phone. "Auntie gave me Teddy Bear. Will you bring me present?"

"Yes Jane, I'll bring you both presents."

A mixture of voices, then both of them, "When are you coming, Daddy?"

"Very soon."

Brenda comes on.

"They don't know what to say."

"Well, I'd better sign off now. Love to all."

"Say goodbye to Daddy."

"Goodbye," they both shout.

I find the call has affected me deeply. Then I get through to my parents, a clear line, no interference to add to my father's slight deafness. I feel a tug in my heart. I've been away from home most of my life; boarding school while they were abroad, then the War, now India. Mother comes on first. There isn't much to say. Strange, but most news is exchanged by post. We ask about health. I tell her about the lunch party and the people there, and about our tenants.

"When are Brenda and the children coming?"

"We expect them on Wednesday, very excited."

Dad says, "It's a long time since I entertained young ladies. I shall take them to the woods with the dogs, give them a nature study lesson."

"Well, the bill's mounting."

We say our goodbyes. Brenda and I are lucky; fit parents, no walking frames. Their marriages seem to have run smoothly. I wonder what they would think if they knew of my tangle. If it hadn't been for my introduction to Donald, probably I wouldn't have met Jenny; but if not her then probably someone else. Kay Freestone is absolutely sick of her husband, twenty years older, and she's darned attractive; but I've fallen for Jenny. I can't say why I love her; she's not beautiful, but partly it's because she seems to want me too; and I hadn't been with a woman for a long time. I know I should cut free, but I can't. Perhaps love is an addiction, a drug, the more you have, the more you want. The cure is agonising. Is there a cure?

At last it is Wednesday. In the afternoon I visit a paper mill, then with no intention of returning to the office, go home. If the phone rings, I won't answer. I'm determined nothing will delay me. I go to Joshua's just before seven. Jenny arrives five minutes later.

"No problem. Moved all right?"

She nods. I buy beer. She says nothing, gets up when I ask her to dance. There's a tango on the radiogram. Her face lights up. She guides me; she's small but she takes charge and she's good.

"My brother Harry won a tango competition with me. He used to let me fall backwards and catch me just clear of the floor!"

Jenny's English has little of the Anglo-Indian intonation, the Welsh-like lilt. Nor does she use the quaint phraseology of many English-speaking Indians. She has mixed with so many foreigners. I can detect a very slight American accent.

I'm so happy when I'm with her that I forget any discrepancy in her story, whether she was in Killarny block or Benatala Street doesn't matter. Nothing matters.

After the dance she says, "We'd better move. My friends will be coming. They'll want to sit with us."

I drive to Strand Road, the second time that we've parked by the river.

"Oh Jenny. Do stop visiting these dives. Can't you get a job?"

"I can't go back to Telephone House."

"Can you type?"

"Not well."

"You can learn. I'll buy you a typewriter."

"I can't do shorthand. I don't think I could learn. Copy typing and receptionist's pay is poor." She needs money for Diana.

"Let's add up your expenses. If you work for a low salary, perhaps I can add to it so you've enough." She's not listening. "What's worrying you, Jenny? What's the trouble?"

"You're going away in May. Six months."

"I'm coming back. I want to see the children, but I wish I could stay with you."

"I wish you could."

She leans forward, rests her head in her hands. I draw her towards me." I'll be back."

We shall have the whole of March and April together. It's not funny, but I think of the Mikado. Nankipoo and Yum Yum have one month to live before he is beheaded and she is buried alive. Thank heaven it's not as bad as that. I can understand lovers who have suicide pacts.

"I'll take you to my room." She directs me along the road towards the small hotel as she did last week. Then we go further into a part I don't know; Benatala Street.

"You'll be all right parking here. "She tells a boy to bring Arthur.

"Can you leave it unlocked, so he can sit in it?" I hesitate.

"It's all right, Bob, don't worry."

So I give Arthur my spare key.

We go through an unlit doorway and up a dingy staircase. I'm trembling, partly with being with her, expectant, and partly because I am in territory foreign and taboo. This is an adventure and I am bored; I suppose that's the truth.

We walk along a passage with doors on either side. At the end is a room with no door, furnished with a table, chairs and a sofa. To the left is a padlocked door that Jenny unlocks, and we go in.

"This is it," she says, bolting the door top and bottom.

The place is tiny but neat, all she has, her little world. The head of the bed faces the door. Between bed and door, against the wall, is a chest-of drawers with a wardrobe on top, which touches the ceiling. The wardrobe, chest-of-drawers and two tin trunks under the bed contain all she has. The top drawer is padlocked; perhaps it is her money box.

On the right is a wide window, curtains drawn and beneath is a brown rexine-covered three-seat sofa. There is a wooden chair and a small table with an electric fan on it. At the back is a curtain, drawn open to reveal a wash basin, shower and toilet. Round to the left I can see a small fridge. To the left of the sofa is a radiogram.

I sit on the sofa. She brings a bottle of Scotch. I wonder which ship it came from. She is neat in her movements, so attractive, petite. I pull her on to the sofa, kiss her madly, her face, neck, hair.

She doesn't yield completely, but kisses me lightly, waits for me to calm down.

"I've a confession to make."

"Oh?"

"I wasn't truthful about Auntie Lulu."

"Why? What happened?"

"I met you so suddenly."

She takes a swig of her drink, edges closer, puts her head against my chest. I long for her. If she has a confession, her timing is perfect. It's exquisite torture and I throb. If she had murdered Auntie, I'd have forgiven her.

"I was getting ready to meet you, when my friend Tina came. I was in the shower. "There's a message from Pedro," she says through the door. So I let her in. "He's in the Sailor's Club", she says, "sails tomorrow, must see you." Pedro is a very good friend, an old man. "Why didn't he get in touch sooner?", I ask Tina. He always sees me first day he docks."

"Has he gone?"

"Yes. So I went to the Sailor's Club with Tina. Joseph was ill. He came off the ship against doctor's orders. He is a very nice old man, Bob. Every time he asks me to marry him. "You have good life with me." he says. He has property in California. He gave me two hundred dollars to change on the black."

"He's a nice man?"

"Yes. But he's too old for me, Bob."

If she married him she would have security, but I don't want her to leave me.

She takes off her blouse and skirt, her panties and bra and puts on a cotton house coat. A bra seems unnecessary and I wonder why she wears one. She sits beside me, takes off her wrist watch, bangles, necklace. Unclips her hair. It falls delightfully over her shoulders.

"I told Joseph the same story about Auntie Lulu as I told you. Then I came to meet you in Joshua's."

"Auntie Lulu isn't ill?"

"No."

I don't care if she lied. I tremble as I slip my hands inside her house coat and hug her to me. Then I undress. I try to hurry, so take longer, fumbling with buttons. It amuses her. I turn off the light. No fan on, the night is cool, windows shut, no mosquitoes. She gets up, puts the light on again, goes under the shower. So I go under with her. I tickle her and she shrieks. I dry her and she dries me, and laughs as she looks downwards: I'm standing to attention for her.

"So little Bob wants me," she says.

We get into bed and cuddle close to warm up. I'm nearly bursting. I don't think I could be nearer heaven. We make love. I've never known anything so wonderful. In the night, half asleep, again. Sound, peaceful sleep in heaven, then still half asleep, five o'clock, love again. But hell, I must go.

As I dress she slips from the bed and goes into the bathroom. Then she comes towards me. She gazes up at me in the dim light that comes from a lamp in the yard below. It is a moment I'll never forget. Her face glows with joy; it seems to have a light of its own.

Softly she says, "Go away now." Then she bows her head, puts her hands on my arms, "Go away, darling, before I cry".

Yes, go I must; away from the heavenly dream. Back to voluntary incarceration; back to the open prison of conscience and duty.

"I'll be in Joshua"s this evening." I don't wait for her answer; I know she'll be there.

Reality strikes me as I reach the car. It is Thursday and just another work day; grim reality. My mood lightens with break of day. I remember the show in London:

A hundred and one pounds of fun
That's my little honeybun
Take a load on honeybun tonight.
I'm speaking of my sweetie pie
Only sixty inches high.

Can't get the tune out of my head. In bed I lie completely played out. Marvellous, I'll see her again this evening.

7

That evening we dance at Joshua's. As I'd never been to the Sailors' Club, I ask Jenny to take me there. I drive to the club by the docks. We enter a very large room with a shed roof. There is a bar, full-sized billiard table at the far end, many tables and chairs. A player is in the middle of a snooker break. He has a red nose and receding brown hair. A short man with springy steps, he moves purposely round the table. He is slim, wears grey trousers supported by red braces over a white open-neck shirt. His opponent looks like Anthony Quinn; swarthy, tall. He wears a black and green cowboy shirt, sleeves rolled up to reveal tattoos, blue trousers with thick leather belt.

Two men, they may be Filipinos, talk with another whose face is set in a happy smile, a Chigro. A man sits at a table on his own. He wears a dark blue suit, flashy kipper tie, rings on his fingers. Unblinking and expressionless, he leans on the table over his beer, eyeing the nearby women. Across the room two good-looking lads in pullovers and slacks are playing darts. The women, about ten of them, sit at two tables, not smiling and apparently unconcerned, but waiting to be picked up. They are all in European dress, Anglo Indians so-called, whether they have "Anglo" blood in them or not. One of the women waves to Jenny.

"That's Bella. She lives in the room next to me."

Bella is a large girl, not fat. She wears a red dress, has long black hair, her brown cheeks whitened too much with powder, her lips are very red and full.

As we walk past, a big black man comes to her table. He wears a navy-blue polo sweater and grey slacks, very smart, a good looker. He likes the look of Bella and they move to a separate table. Maybe they will come to an arrangement. She needs money; that's the only reason Bella is here; no National Assistance in these parts. She longs to be taken from all this.

These women are independent, supportive of each other and they don't have pimps.

"Jenny, is there anywhere quieter?"

She leads me into an adjoining room. There is a bookcase and a table on which are spread newspapers. Two men sit reading; they take no notice of us.

"Tell me about yourself, Jenny."

"Let's get a drink first. I'll get them."

She gets up quickly; I think she wants to speak to someone. I can see her through the open door. She says something to a woman, then returns with beer.

"Big Boy has just come in."

"Who's Big Boy?"

"Look around the corner."
I get up and look.
"It's Micky. He lives below Donald."
"I know, but I've never been there," she says.
Micky comes into the reading room.
"Hiding away? Come and join us."
"Micky, you sound like the Sally Army. No, we want to talk."
"I'm taking Sheila home. Bring Jenny."
"Perhaps."
He goes away.
"He helps Sheila," says Jenny.
"Where did you say you went to school?"
"Patna. Run by nuns. I had to leave, we couldn't pay."
"What happened?"
"My father was a stevedore. In the War he joined the Merchant Navy. Mother was told he skipped ship. Went with a woman in L A. Couldn't afford to keep me at Patna. She went on the bottle. Doctor said she'd no will to live. Died of pneumonia. Then I worked in the Trunk Exchange - I speak English, Hindi and Bengali - in the International Section. I remember, by the grave in the monsoon wet and muddy..."

She sips her beer, puts the glass down, gazes at nothing, lost in memories. I study her in repose, tilted nose slightly flared, neat determined mouth, brown eyes, a strong little face. She comes out of her daydream, smiles as she sees me looking at her.

"Why are you looking at me like that?"

"Because I like what I see; very much I like what I see." I take her hands and keep looking.

She laughs and says, "Stop looking at me like that, Bob."

She turns away, her eyes closed, brows knit, she shakes her head, smiling.

"What happened then?"

"We sold the family rooms."

"What?"

"My two brothers, Dennis and Harry, they wanted to go their own ways. I got my own rooms, two, one big, one tiny. I told you Arthur had been adopted. He stayed with me. I taught him to write."

"A difficult time."

"You're telling me. Wish I could start again. Harry took me dancing. I love Harry but he was bad for me. He introduced me to men. I was young and wild. I loved dancing. Was tired, couldn't work properly. Left the Exchange after an argument with the boss. That's enough."

"Hell you must get away from all this."

"Come and dance," she says. The radiogram is blaring. She hooks her handbag over a chair. She dances madly and I can't keep up with her. Then she turns and pulls one of the young men who had been playing darts on to the dance floor. I am very jealous and I cut in.

"Come on Jenny!" I grab her. "Sorry, she's with me." Glad he doesn't cause any trouble. We sit down with the girls. A few, including Bella, have left.

"I want a drink. Get me a whisky."

I hadn't ever seen her in this frame of mind. She's trying to forget perhaps, I don't know. She pulls me towards her, looks me full in the face with a naughty, brazen expression.

"You don't know me Bob." She screws up her eyes. "'I'm really a bad girl, very bad."

She seems to get a kick out of saying it. I take no notice. I go to the bar. All the girls are laughing. I look round and see that they are not laughing at me. I wait at the bar. She worries me, I've not seen her like this before. I've lost a bit of confidence.

When I come back with her drink, I'm alarmed that she's not there. A pixie-like woman, even smaller than Jenny, says, "She's gone to the ladies. I'm Doreen. She's in a funny mood. You're Bob, I know."

"What were you laughing at, Doreen?"

She giggles, "I won't tell you. Ask Micky."

"You know Jenny?"

"For years. You've changed her. Real tearaway."

Micky puts his hand on my shoulder, takes my full attention from Doreen. I think Doreen says that she was called Jenny Wild'un. I think grimly, Wild'un, huh, that's a good name for her. I turn towards Micky.

"You lost her?" he says. "Meet Sheila. I want to take her home to work in my pub."

Sheila has a very short haircut, must be in her midthirties, slim, nice-looking woman, I'd trust her. She wears jeans, shirt and hand-knitted pink cardigan.

I turn to Doreen. "D'you have any trouble here?"

"Any trouble and you're barred. De Mattos, she has a British passport, she was suspended for six weeks."

"Why?"

"Taking them behind this building. Saved time going to her room in central Cal. She's a smoker."

"They pay her in cigarettes?"

This really tickles Doreen. "You bet," she laughs.

But I'm worried.

"Doreen, please go and see what she's doing."

Doreen walks to the ladies' room. Coming past her is a hard-faced, thin, fair-skinned woman, blonde hair hanging lank, but combed. Her eyes lack lustre, pale face expressionless and lined. She wears a pink open-neck shirt, white coatee and green trousers.

"Who the hell is that?"

"The sailors' friend," says Micky. "She sails the seven seas, tending each man's long-felt want. Scandinavian ship".

"They must be desperate." There's more soul and warmth among these Calcutta ladies.

"I call her the Shag Bag. Bob, most of them here are decent and I'm sorry for them."

"Why were they laughing just now?"

"Oh, a bigwig in Burdwan district keeps several girls. He's too old and they're bored. Catch fish in the garden lake. Insert them. Gives them a thrill I suppose, when they wriggle." Heads or tails first, I wonder.

Doreen comes back on her own, says, "What have you done to her?" Then Jenny walks down the passage. Looks miserable; she's been crying.

"Here, drink up Jenny. Do you good."

"Come on home," says Micky.

"Micky wants us to go to his flat, come on Jenny."

She stirs, "OK," then drinks up.

Micky drives away with his friend Sheila, and I follow. How did I get mixed up with these people? Must be mixed up myself! I must get her away from here.

On the verandah it's nippy and Micky lowers the chicks. He goes into the kitchen, brings coffee. He pours brandy into our mugs. "Keep the cold out."

He says he will buy a country pub.

"Lovely county, Devon. You'll like it, Sheila. What d'you think, Bob?"

"Sounds all right. But it's hard work."

"Don't put her off. It isn't hard work, Sheila, not in a country pub, just the hours are long. We'll make friends, they'll take over now and again."

"I agree with Micky, it's a hundred times better than this place."

"A quiet pub. Don't need money, I have my pension."

Sheila says, "It's a big step."

"I'll look after you." And to Jenny he says, "You should get out while the going's good. The government is tightening up on immigration."

"I'll think about it," Jenny says.

"Well don't wait too long. People in the UK say too many are coming in."

"I'll think about it."

"Persuade her to go, Bob."

It would be good for Jenny, but if she goes, then I must go. Leave this job. Can't bear to lose her.

It's getting late. Micky decides to take Sheila home. I don't know why she doesn't sleep here.

"Why don't we use one car?"

"Thanks, but I want to talk to Jenny; don't want to keep you waiting."

Outside her place, we sit in the car and talk about moving to England. I'm surprised she doesn't jump at the idea.

It is after midnight." I must go, Jenny, I have an early start."

Very early; I have to visit three jute mills. The mill people get annoyed if you are late. They think: those office-bound sods don't know what work is.

8

The weather is changing. The cool months have passed. The street hubbub, the shouts, the music, all these noises - bell-clear in the winter - are becoming muffled by the humidity. The heat is coming. Only sheets across stomachs to prevent chills. Mosquitoes don't come to central Calcutta in the hot weather; I wonder why? Fans turn all day and all night. They cool you well in Bengal by evaporating the heavy humidity. We early morning visitors to the mills, come back hot and sweaty. It is easy to catch cold in the air-conditioned office.

April; another month and I go on leave. Tony calls me into his office.

"Bad news, Bob. A letter from the Resident Engineer at Shanagar." We are doing a job at the hydro-electric power station there.

"What's the trouble?"

"Bhagbat's died. Heart attack."

Bhagbat was our supervisor. I smile grimly at Tony.

"I know what you're going to say."

"Sorry Bob."

I know I'll have to go there, up into the hills. There's no one else. "I would have sent Gupta, but he's in hospital."

For a moment I think it's good news. Now I can stay in India longer. Then it sinks in; I shall be separated from Jenny by a thousand miles, and from England, too.

Tony is still talking. "Sorry, Tony, what did you say?"

"I said I must tell Bhagbat's family. I hate this."

"Damn it, Tony. Brenda won't like it; and my parents. But I must get cracking. I'll write you a progress report on all the jobs I leave here."

"Well, Bob, on the bright side, in the hills you'll miss the hot weather."

He hands me the R E's letter. It says that Bhagbat had started to write a report; he was clearly worried. More pipes and valves etc., are needed.

"It's better if you go by train, then you can have the materials with you. If you fly, God knows how long they'll take by train and a bus at the other end."

It is the second of April. I must get to Shanagar as soon as possible. Tony comes into my office.

"I think it would be better if you flew, the sooner you get there, the better. Someone else can bring the stuff by train."

Tony tries the phone but it's hopeless, so he sends a telegram and writes to the R E to say I'm coming.

"We'll send Mewalal with the materials. He's been there before. He can take charge of the gang."

"You were there years ago, weren't you Bob?"

"Yes. The RE was a Sikh, Ajit Singh. This one, Mr James, must be a Christian. I hope the rest house hasn't deteriorated. I was comfortable there."

I ask Molly, the secretary, to book me on the Delhi plane.
After work, I go straight to Benatala Street.

"Just my luck", she says, "losing you in April instead of May."

"You're not losing me. I've an idea. I was thinking about it as I drove here. It's a lovely place, Shanagar. Healthy, clear air, quiet, a rest cure. One thing missing, or one person, I mean. That's you, my darling."

"If you were going on leave, it would be easier for me. But you'll be in India and I can't touch you, only write."

"That's what I've been thinking about. Jenny, how would you like a holiday?"

"What d'you mean?"

"Come with me."

That takes her by surprise. Takes time to sink in.

"Oh Bob. Give me time to think."

"If you're worried about expenses here, then there's no need. I'll take care of all that."

In Shanagar I'll be living on the firm's expenses. Little more than food to spend on, no clubs, no cinemas, no restaurants. No Donald to pay for his room. Cash coming in from the people in my flat. No Bilbo the bearer to pay and no Tulsi, the car seis.

I show Jenny where I'm going on the map, a remote power station, nestling against the Himalayan foothills.

"At the moment it's a suggestion. I'll have to talk to the man in charge there: Mr James. He runs the power station, that's where our men are working. It's urgent that I go quickly, our supervisor has died."

"I'd like to come," she says a bit doubtfully. "I expect the worst and hope for the best; that's my way. But don't be disappointed."

"But you will come, won't you?"

"Oh yes. I mean if you can take me. If the man says I can come. Why, would he refuse?"

"I'm being cautious. He might say his superiors don't want married visitors. I don't know. Wait until I get there, then we'll know."

"Yes, I see."

"Meantime, here's some cash to be going on with. We'll assume you are going."

I tell her what to buy, including a new bedding roll (hers is a bit tatty), pair of strong walking shoes and so on.

"You told me you had been in Delhi. When?"

"A long time ago."

"So you know the north?"

"No. Just Delhi. I went to see my third brother. He ran away. Became a Muslim. I'll tell you, but not now. It's a long story."

"To get to Shanagar I fly to Delhi. Then get another plane to Amritsar. Then a train. Then a hundred miles by bus."

"I hope I can find the way."

"I'll give you very full instructions. I'm used to it. You'll find it easy. Be exciting for you."

I have to leave. I have to represent the firm at one of these absurd cocktail parties. A V I P has called here.

"I'm bloody busy, Jenny. Such a lot to do. I'll be here as early as possible tomorrow. Any time after five o'clock, say. Please wait in."

The first person I meet at the party is my bank manager. He must be bored by these gatherings; same faces, time and again. There are wives present. A few of them are unused to this kind of life and have to learn to relax. Accents change. One Lancashire woman calls her handbag her "harndbarg". The men wear dinner jackets. Custom has it that in Bengal we wear black jackets and white trousers; in Bombay, they wear white jackets and black trousers. Calcutta is the most formal and stuffy of all the centres in India where remnants of the Raj congregate.

I have never been at ease at these cocktail parties. One endeavours to make small talk with someone. Suddenly he appears not to be listening, looks over your shoulder, "Oh, I must have a word with so and so," he says, and drifts away. I stay for half an hour, then go home, glad to find Donald there. Now I can tell him my news.

"Do you remember advising me to get away from Jenny?"

"Oh? Oh yes."

"You thought Jenny would think me a little gold mine. I know you were thinking of my welfare."

"Well?"

"I'm going on tour again."

"Where are you going?"

I explain, but not about Jenny.

"I expect to go on Saturday."

"That's the day I go on short leave. It's a place near Nainital. How long do you expect to be away?"

"It's unlikely to be less than a month. North of Simla. I was there ten years ago. Delightful spot."

At ten o'clock I phone England. Brenda is out, so I speak to her mother.

"Oh they will be disappointed," she says. "What a nuisance, Bob!"

Then I phone my parents and they don't like the news at all. Mother in particular is very upset. I've never known her to express bitterness.

"Does it ever end? We lost William in the War. Now you are away all the time: boarding school, the War, now India. Why did you have to leave us?"

"Oh mother!" Well I didn't send myself to boarding school, they went abroad too.

"Sorry, Bob dear, to grumble. I'm so sorry. Come as soon as you can."

I feel awful about this.

"Anyway, mother, the children will be with you tomorrow."

"Oh yes. It is exciting. No longer babies. Please hurry home darling."

"Donald, I'll pack up everything, but do you mind if I leave a case, and a few things in the almirah?"

"Perfectly all right Bob."

The next three days fly by as I'm busy organising materials and special tools. Also, I have work for the draughtsman. Then ! have to delegate the work, so things don't grind to a halt among the non self-generating staff. I see Jenny every evening. I give her instructions about planes, train and bus. And pray she can come.

Friday evening, and I stay two hours with Jenny.

"I'll write the moment I get to Shanagar. The mail may take two or three days."

I give her money for Diana's care, rent, for fare on the journey and for things she must buy, like a vacuum flask.

"Goodbye darling. Don't come down to the car. Say goodbye here; too public down there."

Back at Donald's it's time to phone Brenda. She will have moved south to my parents by now.

"Hello Bob. So you're delayed. What a darned nuisance."

"Yes it is. I'm just as sorry as you are."

"Why do you always let yourself be put on like this? Not the first time the bloody firm has done this to you. Don't they ever think of us?"

"I've talked to Tony and I agree with him. I must stay here."

"Well, I think it's the limit. It always seems to be you."

"It's just bad luck. It will average out. At least I know I'm needed."

"Can't you refuse?"

"No. I can't afford to refuse."

"Oh Bob. The Jamiesons expect us in Scotland in June. I'm just speechless."

Yes, I've noticed, I think to myself.

"If I'm delayed, can't you go with Melanie and Jane?"

"Oh, I don't know. I suppose so."

"Brenda, Gupta is in hospital, so I must stay here. Just think of Tony. He has the main worry."

"Then when will you be coming?"

"Honestly, I don't know. Nobody knows. It depends on the work's progress. Hopefully I'll be home in time for Scotland."

"Hell, why did you join a firm like this?"

I ignore that remark.

"Sorry Brenda. I'll let you know as soon as I know myself. How is everyone? How long will you be staying in Wheatham?"

"About another week. Everyone is happy here; at least we were until this happened. Come home as soon as you can."

She tells me the children are in the woods with Granddad.

"They're very happy, Bob. I really get fed up with this, living in England and India. I wonder sometimes if you want to come home."

Good God! What a silly thing to say.

"I was lucky to get this job, Brenda. Many better qualified would jump at it."

We say goodbye.

Now I've said goodbye to England and also to Calcutta.

"Donald, the office driver is taking me to the airport. Goodnight. Many thanks. I'll write."

"Goodbye old chap. Excuse me if I don't wake up in time to see you off. I'm catching the evening plane to Lucknow. Then by road."

I set the alarm for five o'clock, a ghastly hour.

9

I'm given a window seat in the Caravelle. To my right is a bespectacled, well-dressed Indian businessman in a smart grey suit. I wear a light-green shirt and white cotton trousers as it's hot outside. Probably put on a pullover later. I'm glad the man doesn't seek conversation.

I try to sleep. I think of Jenny. Was it fated that I met her? When I'm with her it feels so perfect that I can't help wondering if it's predestined. I love my family in a different way. Can you love two people at the same time? I love Jenny. I love Brenda because she and the children are my family. I fear I can never be happy one way or the other. When I'm with Jenny all other thoughts are driven from my mind. My family background and upbringing tell me that I must be an ass: good job; nice family; lovely children. Take things as they come.

I'll be home soon so I'll just see if things sort themselves out.
Jenny. What's she got for me? Wonderful to sleep with? Yes. But it's more. I talk to her as a friend; she's no stranger. She is so used to talking with men. Sense of humour. Listens to what I have to say. It's easy to fool men, our telephonist Katie tells me, but I don't think Jenny is like that. With her it's living with a dear pal with perfect sex thrown in. Nothing jars.

The two-hour flight passes quickly. I'm brought back from muzzy near-sleep, a day-dream - or was it a day-mare? - by the stewardess's,

"Fasten your seat belts". We land at 9.40. Palam, New Delhi, is not an impressive airport and a larger one is planned a few miles away.

At eleven I board the Dakota DC3 bound for Amritsar. It stops twice on the way at small airports with shed-like terminal buildings and tiny control towers.

The three-hundred mile flight is wearisome, taking three hours, an hour longer than from Calcutta to Delhi, and yet only a third of the distance.

From Amritsar I take a stopping train eighty miles northwards to Dharikot, a town important only as a bus terminus. My bus leaves at eight tomorrow morning. I go to the waiting room, no passengers there, take a shower and change clothing; the train journey from Amritsar was very hot and dusty. After a meal of tandoori chicken in the refreshment room, I walk across the railway lines to stretch my legs; visit the ice factory. I make friends with the supervisor, a Sikh.

"Sir, provide much ice for restaurant cars." His name's Gurbux Singh.

"Is this your home town?"

"Oh no sir."

"Don't call me sir. I call you Gurbux, you call me Bob, OK?"

"OK Bob," he grins. "I come from Pakistan side, big trouble time." He is very interested to hear that I've been to Lyallpur. He lived in a village nearby.

"I'm going to Shanagar, I'll come back this way."

"Come see me again."

"Yes I will. When I come can I buy ice for train? Keep compartment cool?"

"Will have special ice. No pay."

I re-cross the lines, go to the hut that serves as a booking office.

"I want first class seat to Shanagar tomorrow morning."

I pay enough for super first class and I'm assured, "seat very best". I sleep well on my bedding roll which I lay out on the charpoy provided, wake early, have boiled eggs and toast in the refreshment room. The waiter fills my vacuum flask with iced water, lime and sugar. At seven-thirty I go the few yards to the bus, which is being loaded. The rack covers most of the roof. It is a noisy business, everyone shouting at once. There are cases of goods, bedding rolls, home belongings wrapped in coloured blankets and tied with cord, a wickerwork basket with red hens in it and my case and bedding roll. There is a rope netting arrangement fitted to the back of the bus, like a huge hairnet, into which packages are shoved. I take into the bus a small bag, vacuum flask and brief case. I have been allotted the front bench seat, meant for two people.

The bus moves off at 8.10. It is not quite full but all spare seats are occupied by bags, tiffin carriers and odds and ends. There are people of all ages. Old men with turbans, white beards, young men wearing Gandhi caps, women with whining children, some with kohl round their eyes.

The construction of the bus does not inspire confidence. The bodywork is locally made and the tinny sides do not enhance the reputation of the panel beater. The appearance hides the efficiency of the engine and robustness of the chassis, which have come from either Mercedes in Bengal or Leyland in Madras.

The driver says it is about 100 miles to Shanager.

"Take long time. Stop town on way. Wait, eh, one half hours. Arrive maybe two clock."

The first two-thirds of the journey are quite quick over flat ground, but with delays at villages. We stop just short of Karampur, a small town at a road junction. Everyone gets out. To the north is a valley at the end of which is a round mountain with snow on top. Fields stretch away from us, rising in terraces. I sit on a grass bank. There are stalls nearby where brightly coloured soft drinks and sweetmeats are sold, and a tin shack restaurant, serving tandoori chicken and naan bread; also corn on the cob. I like grilled corn on the cob, so I buy one, good it is cooked over charcoal.

A holy man walks down the road and sits on the bank near me. He is clad in saffron robes, head shaven, body smeared with ash. He carries a trident-like staff, sits crosslegged and motionless. No one takes any notice of him; Nehru says that ninety per cent of holy men are shams. He ought to know.

At last another bus arrives from the south. There is much shouting and scrambling as baggage is transferred. We are on the move again.

Midday, and air from the Himalayan foothills to our left is cooling us, the skies are clear and the crisp air smells clean. The road twists and turns as we climb. This is the slow part of the journey. At last, just after two o'clock, we arrive at the village of Shanagar. After Calcutta it is like another world.

Shanagar smells dusty, grass worn away with people milling about - a piece of the plains brought to the hills. Many have rosy cheeks from the icy mountain air. They have come from the hills to trade at the busy shops and stalls. I ask the driver where I can phone. "Post office", he says, pointing.

I ring the power station office and am promised transport. Half an hour later a jeep arrives and I am driven to the Public Works Department Rest House, known as the PWD bungalow.

The driver says, "R E come soon. In bangla." He points to the Resident Engineer's bungalow, further up the hill.

The bungalows are on a steep slope with a view towards the west over power station and village. Down to our right, and north, is a stony gully and dry river bed. Further off a scree-covered hill, rising steeply to fir trees far above. To the left, the road winds upwards past the bungalows and continues to a valley of apple orchards. Maybe I will have time to go there, but this place is heaven enough; 4,500 feet up, clean, clear, peaceful.

A man shows me a bedroom. He wears grey flannel shirt, cotton trousers and waistcoat. There are two bedrooms with connecting door. The place is spotless. Each bedroom has two beds and a bathroom with hand basin, shower and hot water, and a gleaming white WC. When I was here ten years ago there were only thunder boxes, emptied each day by the sweeper.

Next to the bedrooms is a sitting room with a table, four wooden chairs, an armchair, a sofa and a large open fireplace with logs piled at the side. The kitchen is a shed-like structure next to this room.

I shall have to get used to the silence. There is occasional birdsong; the sound of a rare truck driving past in low gear; the distant roar of water dashing from the turbines through the tailrace to the stream. Without this water, the stream would be almost dry; when the rains come it will be a torrent. The turbine water comes at great pressure through monster pipes from a lake behind the hill to our north. The hill is covered by boulders, with patches of scree, bare of trees except where the slope flattens at the top. This place smells fresh, clean, uncorrupted by man.

I hear the RE's tread on the gravel as he comes to the door, which leads through a porch into the sitting room.

"Mr James? Bob Bennett."

"Mr Bennett, good afternoon. I hope you had pleasant journey, yes?"

He sits down. He is of medium height, greying hair, glasses, a pleasant, ordinary man. He wears a dark-green pullover, light-grey tie, grey flannels, strong brown shoes. He has a gold ring on his left middle finger. We discuss the difficulties which I shall have to sort out, excessive pressure in some ancillary equipment.

"A sad business, your Bhagbat. A good worker. He was cremated by river. I have his belongings, Mr Bennett. Will hand them over to you."

The man comes in. "Ah, Kailash," says Mr James. "You like tea?" he asks me. Kailash is plump, shirt lap hangs out, he has black hair, large moustache. "Kailash can cook. He will look after you."

"What do I pay him?"

"We pay him. He will shop for you, give you bills. He will be happy, Mr Bennett, never make loss." He smiles.

"I'll give him a bit extra, Mr James."

Kailash brings tea and biscuits.

"We meet in the office tomorrow, Mr Bennett?" Mr. James leaves, walks up the hill to his bungalow.

In the evening it's not cold enough for a fire, but I don a pullover. Kailash grills me roast chicken, potatoes and peas, followed by rice pudding.

After the meal he says, "Money for market sahib." I give him an advance. He produces a "cook's book" like the cook had in Calcutta; the cook's book is "cooked" no doubt. No cook is out of pocket. Lists of purchases are entered here.

I write to the office and to Brenda. I wonder what the children are doing. It will be afternoon in England now. I go to bed early. The silence is strange to me; not a sound.

Next morning I take the short cut to the power station, picking my way between the rocks at the side of the dry river bed. There's a mere trickle of water. On the way to the office I go to the switchyard, where the transformers link to the cables. The pylons take the cables westward and over the horizon.

One of the fitters, Kartick, sees me and runs, calling his three mates. I tell them that Mewalal is coming to take charge. The money order for their pay is late, so I advance them a few rupees. Kartick can write well and so can Gouri. Motihari and Telukdar have more trouble.

Gouri is the most intelligent of the four but is inclined to be bad tempered. He is greying, with a small moustache. He wears a light-blue shirt and grey shorts.

Kartick has black hair; one eye shows signs of a cataract forming. He wears a white shirt, grey pullover and khaki shorts. He speaks quickly. Ask him to slow down and he cannot.

Motihari is the youngest. Black hair, tall and thin, his teeth protrude and he smiles most of the time. He is a very willing worker.

Telukdar is the oldest and not very bright. He is stocky and powerful, wears a light green and pink pullover above his white shirt and short dhoti. They are all from the land. Two local unskilled men help them. I pay these two in full and they sign with thumb prints, pressing their thumbs first on the ink pad, then wiping them on their black hair.

Kartick jabbers on about Bhagbat's death. He was in the basement on his own, quite fit; not tired, not drinking, nothing wrong. Suddenly fell over and died.

I go to the office but see that Mr James is busy.

"I'd like to speak to you when you're free."

"I'll see you later Mr Bennett."

I am anxious to speak to him about Jenny and I hope he won't object to her coming. I expect my letters will arrive in Calcutta in two or three days and the one to England, maybe a week. I won't write to Jenny until I know what is happening. I'll have to sound him out carefully.

How different India is from Thailand where it is usual to have female servants. I will explain to Mr James that she is a close friend, perhaps she will want to cook for me. I must make sure that I don't antagonise Kailash. I don't think there will be a problem; Jenny can get on with anyone.

I can't see Mr James - he's busy all day. I'm impatient, but he comes to the bungalow in the evening. I am glad he has come here where he can relax, less formal than in his office. He accepts a Scotch with pleasure.

"Indeed Mr Bennett it is a long time since I had any but Indian whisky. Yes, this is a treat indeed."

We discuss work. Then I change the subject.

."The money order is very late. Do you have trouble with the post?"

"Not usually. From my home in Kerala, letters take but a few days."

"Do you find life lonely here, Mr James? Have you been here long?"

"I have been here for one year. It is too long." He sounds a bit disgruntled. "My family is at home in Cochin."

"Why do they send you up here, almost the length of India?"

"I was brought to Delhi for attending a course. When completing course, they say, "We wish you to relieve man transferred from Shanagar". Yes, Mr. Bennett, "Just for a few weeks," they say, yes, just for a few weeks. It is now too long. What to do?" He throws his arms out wide. "Administration course."

"For promotion?"

"That I sincerely hope. But I prefer south. Marianna took children home. Not liking here. Schooling difficulties. Children have language problem. I'm not liking bachelor existence Mr Bennett."

I pour him another drink. He makes a play of objecting, but he is glad to accept.

"Have you been in India since long?"

"Eleven years."

"And you like this India away from your home? England, isn't it?"

"Yes, England. This is an interesting job, Mr James."

Visibly he is relaxed and contented.

"Mr James, I have something to ask of you. I have a friend in Calcutta. I would like to bring her here."

"Ah yes, Mr Bennett, and why not?"

"Well you might think it unusual to bring a lady on tour to such an isolated place."

"Mr Bennett, why should not an officer bring respectable companion?"

I pour more Scotch. He ponders, "There is just one thing to consider. Yes, er, you see, sometimes senior man visits here with assistants."

"They'll want this bungalow?"

"There is the possibility that they may come. Just temporarily, Mr Bennett, I then would ask you to move to the Dak Bungalow."

The Dak Bungalow, on the rising ground behind the village, is where the mail, the dak, was sorted years ago, carried by a man on horseback; and where the District officer would stay when on his rounds.

"Of course, Mr James. Certainly I'll move immediately."

I hope I won't have to move, for that place is not comfortable; charpoys to sleep on, hole-in-the-floor toilet, no hot water. Still, it would be only for a day or two.

"Then I will write to my friend Miss Sandakan and ask her to come. Thank you Mr James. She will cause no trouble. She'll get on with Kailash, she is no difficult memsahib."

"I find this place lonely," he says, "Captain of ship is isolated man. I am indeed so very pleased to have your company. Good people here, but I am stranger from the South. Very seldom do I partake of the alcohol. I am appreciating your hospitality."

"It's a pleasure. I know of course you can shop in Amritsar, Mr James, but is there anything not available that you'd like from Calcutta?"

"I will think. That is too kind."

I walk with him to the path, leading up steps to his bungalow, and he leaves, humming to himself.

Next morning I wake early and write a letter before breakfast.

"My dear Jenny, I hope all goes well with you. I arrived here on Sunday. I couldn't speak informally to the man in charge until last evening. Good news! He doesn't mind you coming. He is Mr Michael James from Cochin (his wife and children are there).

"Please study the instruction I wrote about the journey - plane to Delhi and Amritsar - then train to Dharikot, then bus. Please write to say the date you will leave Dum Dum. If all goes according to plan, you will reach Dharikot at 6.30 p.m.

"Please write immediately you have your ticket. Book four days ahead, I mean - post your letter to me four days before you fly. Letters may take three days. This will give me time to come down to the station to meet you. Stay in the "Ladies Only" waiting room in case I'm late. I expect to be on time, but if the car breaks down or something, then stay the night and wait. If you have to phone ask for the PWD bungalow."

She is not stupid, far from it, but I want to make certain that nothing goes wrong. Army training?

I'm about to seal the envelope when I see Mr James walking past. I call him and run to catch him up.

"I'm writing to Calcutta. Is there anything you'd like bringing from there?"

"It would be of the greatest help if you can ask your friend to bring me good quality travelling alarm clock working on battery."

"Certainly."

I can feel a slight change of atmosphere from last evening's bonhomie. He remembers he has the responsibility of being the senior man here.

"Mr James, our new supervisor Mewalal will be bringing materials. It would be difficult to bring them by bus. May I use the Estate car?"

"Certainly Mr Bennett."

He knows the materials are necessary so the job is finished quickly. I wonder when Mewalal will arrive. With a bit of luck he will be on the same train as Jenny.

10

Waiting for Jenny the days are dragging and I'm glad when Mr James asks, "Mr Bennett, would you like to come up the hill with me tomorrow? It is a routine inspection.'

"I certainly would, thank you."

"Then please, we will be meeting at the trolley at eight o'clock. Very prompt. Please, on time."

"I'll be there."

I am there as bidden. "You see, Mr Bennett, the trolley is pulled up rails by the cable, but you see, cannot go straight due to ground slopes. So goes in three stages."

Before starting I sign a form exonerating the electricity authority from responsibility should I be injured.

There is a lurch and we set off. The trolley is at a slope. At the end of the first stage, we clamber on to a level concrete platform and across to the next trolley.

I think of Brenda and Jenny; like these trolleys, crossing from one to the other. Call Jenny to England? Leave my firm? Leave my family? We move to the third trolley. Brenda to Jenny, Jenny to Brenda again.

We reach the top stage. There is a wonderful view. I hope I'll be allowed to bring Jenny to see it. Mr James says we are 2,000 feet above the power station. The top of the ridge ahead, covered by trees, is some 500 feet higher. Alongside the trolley rails are two huge pipes, bringing water from a lake on the other side of this hill, down to the power station turbines.

"Next week, Mr Bennett, I will take you to the valley and show you our lake."

He talks to the winch operator. Then we go down again, stage by stage. It is an enjoyable experience, but not for vertigo sufferers, for the trolleys run at an angle of forty degrees; you have to hold on.

I am not neglecting my duties, taking this time off. I have left the fitters with work to do. They prefer to be left alone and think I am a hindrance and a nuisance if I disturb their rhythm of work. I go to the station, am assured that all goes well. There's nothing for me to do there, so I walk back to the bungalow and read a book.

I go to bed early and fall into a deep sleep. Maybe it is something I've eaten, but my dreams are in turmoil. Out of the confusion comes fear. Part of my brain is awake. My heart thumps in my head and I know I am about to have a nightmare. I struggle in vain to become fully awake. I haven't felt like this since I was a child, when, what may have been a dream of death, drove me downstairs, screaming in panic to my mother's arms.

I battle but some dark force drags me into an evil dream. I am sitting on the trolley. The trolley becomes a car and I am in the driving seat. It is an old car with the hood down. Then I am looking at it from above. I can see it is an old Morris and my aunt is driving. Mother sits beside her. The road is very steep. Aunt is struggling with the gears, mother looks anxious. There is a cliff and a hairpin bend.

I look up the hill. There are rails and a cable that stretch a long, long way to the winch house. It seems they go off the ground, ever upwards into mist and exceedingly bright light, like Jacob's ladder. I can see myself in the car, yet I hover above. Then I am kneeling on the seat in the back of the car, looking down the hill. Below are Melanie and Jane, hand in hand, walking away down the track. Suddenly the car starts to move backwards towards the children, faster and faster. I try to shout to tell them to move out of the way, but I can't make a sound. The car comes near to them and then all goes black and I wake up with a loud cry. My heart is beating fast, I can feel it in my throat.

I put on the light. I'm shaken. It is half past three. I put on pullover and trousers over my pyjamas and go outside, walk in the driveway.

I had said to Jenny, "If it weren't for the children."

I can never leave them, even though I don't see much of them. Darling kids, I love them both equally, even though Melanie is not really mine. Melanie will never be told. Thank God they are happy together.

It is four o'clock, complete silence except for the distant rush of water in the tailrace. Whoever I desert will be hurt, and myself too. Perhaps it will all work out in the end.

In the morning, after that awful night, I am tired and I take my time. All is running smoothly with the fitters. In the afternoon I walk past the powerhouse to the village, and to the general store where beer and spirits are sold, all made in India.

I remember the owner, Mr Subharwal, to whom I presented some large pipes years ago, broken cast iron pipes, no use to us. They helped him irrigate his terraces on the hillside. I look round, hardware, utensils, second-hand paper backs, fruit, vegetables. I'm about to ask for Mr Subharwal when he comes in. In the ten years since we met, he has aged more than I have. His hair is white and he limps a bit. He stares at me for a moment, then remembers. His face lights up.

"Mr Bennett. What long time."

He takes me to see how he has used the pipes in the field. He has diverted water from a stream into channels among his crops. He grows wheat, vegetables and a few apple trees.

"A good place this, Mr Subharwal. Healthy."

"You like cooling hills, isn't it?"

"Better than Calcutta."

We walk back to the store and I buy bottles of Golden Eagle beer and a bottle of Black Knight whisky.

"Please send them to the bungalow Mr Subharwal."

"I have Lion beer next week, Mr Bennett. Much more better. I save you some."

"Thank you Mr Subharwal."

No doubt he hopes I will have some more pipes for him.

I walk back up the hill. Tomorrow I meet Jenny. Maybe Mewalal will be on the same train. I'm excited.

11

The driver is punctual. I throw in my bedding roll and we leave at two, arriving at Dharikot at six o'clock. Good timing; Jenny's train arrives forty minutes later. I see her looking out of the window and joy floods through me. I run towards the train and jump in as it is slowing. She is the only occupant of the first class "Ladies Only" compartment. She wears bush shirt and slacks and her hair is piled up in a green headscarf. I fling my arms around her and we kiss. Just then the train stops with a jolt and we overbalance on to the bench seat, laughing.

"What a long journey," she says.

"You're here!"

"Just about," she says breathlessly. I can hardly believe it. We sit and look at each other. She is a bit dishevelled and a wisp of hair hangs down over her forehead. I feel as though we have been apart for ages, yet it is only a few days. It is a glorious, relieved feeling. The gates of heaven have opened with this thrill of reunion. We met only two months ago, but I feel I've known her for years, as I hold her in my arms. There is noise on the platform, slamming of doors.

"We'd better get out." I pick up her bedding roll and suitcase and we walk the few yards to the waiting rooms.

"How was the journey?"

"No problems, but I had a fright this morning. I forgot to wind my alarm clock, caught the airway's bus just in time."

"I don't think anyone will object if you stay in the men's room instead of the ladies."

"I feel tired, but I don't mind. It's a relief to be here," she says, and collapses on the sofa.

"How are things at home?"

"Diana cried when I left her, but she's all right. Arthur is looking after my room. I warned him never to set foot outside, not even one step, without locking the door. I told him I would hire someone to murder him if anything was stolen."

"What would you like to eat?"

"Something light, an omelette, toast, tea."

"You go and order Jenny. I don't want to leave you in here on your own in the men's room. Oh and Jenny, beer, and a brandy for you - perk you up a bit." I smile, "Tell them it's for the sahib."

She returns, and after a few minutes the waiter brings the food and drinks. She will sleep on the charpoy. I'll make do with the sofa.

"I hope our supervisor will arrive tomorrow, about seven o'clock. He is bringing pipes, tools and things. Then we can go in the same truck."

We have our food. I drink beer and she sips brandy. I study the room. The furniture consists of an oblong table, bench, several chairs, a cane-bottomed armchair, the sofa, and charpoy. The place was built before the days of electricity, very high ceiling, with small windows which have cords for opening and closing. The walls are brown tiled up to the dado, then whitewashed and cobwebbed above.

Jenny sleeps, her hair spread all over the sheet. I lie down on the sofa, too short, so I have to bend my knees. I haven't wound down; sleep is difficult but eventually I drift off.

Noises on the platform waken me at six o'clock. Two old men come in but they take no notice of us, sit facing the door. Quietly I waken Jenny, whisper that we have company. I shield her from view while she slips into the bathroom. When she comes out the men have gone. I have a quick wash, don't shave. We pack up, then go into the refreshment room next door.

The waiter takes our order: "Andar rumbletumble, mukhan tost, marmlad, chae," he repeats my order for scrambled eggs, buttered toast, marmalade and tea. He fills the vacuum flask with fresh lime, sugar and ice-cold water. I go to find our driver. At seven thirty the train arrives, not bad, only about half an hour late after the long journey from Calcutta. I spot Mewalal in the crowd. He has gone to the guard's van and is supervising porters who carry the materials.

Like so many we employ, he is a farmer and one of the best, working for us to make extra much-needed cash. His garb is eccentric. He wears a brown smock-like garment and khaki shorts, grey stockings, black shoes and a dark-blue scarf.

Mewalal and the driver arrange the materials in the truck while I go back for Jenny and the luggage.

Jenny and I sit in the back seat and Mewalal sits next to the driver. It is annoying that I meet the driver's eyes in the driving mirror. We just hold hands out of his view.

"Jenny", I say quietly, "Mewalal is our supervisor. We call him a head erector."

"Oh yes. Is he a good worker?"

"Yes, he is a very good erector."

She muffles a giggle; Mewalal half turns round.

We reach Karampur and halt. Everyone gets out and we stretch our legs. Jenny has been to Bombay, Delhi and Cochin before, well travelled, but she has not been near the hills. She gazes at the snowtopped mountain across the terraced fields.

"Beautiful." she says.

There is a slight nip in the air.

"Later you will see the real Himalayas. Perhaps you won't want to go back to Calcutta. Shall we go jungle and stay here? Buy some land?" She smiles at the make-believe.

"Everything all right, Mewalal?"

"Yes, all things wanted I bring. Nothing missing."

Mewalal does not acknowledge Jenny. He is not rude, doesn't pointedly ignore her. He just takes her presence for granted.

We drive on round the twists and turns, ever upwards, arriving at Shanagar at midday. "There's the Post Office, Jenny, and that's the general store I use."

We pass the power station, water rushing under the concrete road bridge, and up the steep hill to the Rest House.

We pass the assistant engineers' bungalows on the way, by huge rhododendrons - trees rather than bushes. Kailash comes out as he hears the truck and helps with the luggage. I tell Mewalal to wait and I go inside with Jenny, dismiss Kailash and we are alone. "At last." We kiss, lie back on the bed and relax for a few minutes.

"I must take Mewalal down to the power house and see that he settles in comfortably. I won't be long. Have a look round. Ask Kailash for a cup of tea, he's a nice man."

"I can handle people."

"You're telling me!" I say, laughing.

At this, she punches me on the arm, purses her lips in mock anger. She reminds me of a cat when she does this.

"Don't be long."

"Put your cardigan on. It gets cool here."

Having seen that Mewalal is established as head of the gang, and introduced to Sharma, Assistant Engineer, I have a few words with Mr James. Then I trudge back to the rest house. Jenny comes out of the kitchen, followed by Kailash carrying a tray of tea things.

"I saw you coming," she says. "Thank you Kailash."

"So you've been getting to know him?"

"Yes. He told me about his family. We get on well."

I lift her up and swing her round, hug her tight.

"Put me down, I can't breathe."

"I can't believe it, Jenny, it's like a dream." She pours out the tea.

"It isn't for long, Bob."

We sit on the sofa, lean back and rest.

"I saw Mr James just now. Told him you were tired and that I wouldn't introduce you until tomorrow. So he won't be bothering us."

"I've brought two bottles of Black Label with me," she says.

"Wonderful, and Mr. James likes his Scotch."

"Let's celebrate our reunion in Scotch after supper, Bob."

"What's for supper?"

"Mutton chops, but first chicken broth. Kailash says he makes good bread and butter pudding."

We have one small Scotch each, then we eat. The food is good, but bedroom thoughts fill me.

"You want bed tea?"

"No thanks Kailash, just breakfast."

"What time breakfast wanting?"

"Aht baje, Kailash, eight o'clock."

"Bahut accha, very good Sahib." He tidies up.

When will he go? I can hardly wait.

"You can go now Kailash."

"Goodnight Sahib." Then, turning to Jenny, "Goodnight Memsahib", a compliment indeed, no sarcasm. He moves a chair, then at last he goes out.

We push the two beds together and rearrange the bedclothes. Then I check doors are locked, windows bolted.

"We are really alone for the first time, my darling."

She showers with me. I dry her and she dries me. I carry her to the bed. There is an animal urgency, passionate, violent and tender at the same time. No time for delicate love making, that can come later.

Afterwards I have a delightful slightly bruised feeling. I tingle.

She lies, eyes shut. For a minute she has a look of bliss, all hardness gone from her face; the determined mouth has relaxed. The lips are fuller, as a rosebud about to bloom. The slight frown of her eyebrows has gone. Even her nostrils, a touch flared, seem to have lost their defiance. My loved one is at peace, cares forgotten. I hadn't seen her look like this. We had always been worried about the time, about interruptions.

We sleep for a little while. Then she says. "I've never done that before."

"What do you mean, darling?"

"Gone to sleep like that. Bob, I've met so many men, never this."

No one will disturb us; no street noises; no blaring music; no rowdy people in the next room. I have work to do tomorrow, but it can wait. We just lie there in peace.

"Just talk Bob; I like to hear your voice."

"What shall I talk about?"

"Anything."

So I tell her about the power station, how it was built before the War; how the power is generated by the turbines, sent through the cables to the grid in the Punjab. She has her eyes shut. "Are you listening darling?"

"I'm listening."

"Let's have a drink."

I pour them out, top up with water.

She doesn't have a tuneful voice, but in her throaty way she sings.

"I like the way you walk, I like the way you talk."

"Can anything be better?"

"It has to come to an end."

"So does life." We have more Scotch. We are both becoming light-headed, but it doesn't matter; no early start tomorrow.

"The water comes down those pipes on the hill."

"What?"

"Those pipes on the hill. Water turns the turbines."

"Turbines? Oh yes, round and round. Let's twist again."

She flops with her head on my chest. We're sloshed.

"Don't leave me, Bob."

"How can I leave you? Don't be daft."

I haul her right up close to me. Not just tonight, but tomorrow night and the next. So it doesn't matter if we finish the bottle. I pour out big ones. Of all the millions in the world it is a miracle that I have met her. I can't believe it.

She lifts herself up, we touch glasses and drink.

"My head's going round, Bob."

"You don't feel ill?"

"No. I want to go to the bathroom, I'm dizzy."

She is only a little thing but she has kept up with me, drink for drink. I help her to the bathroom. She has a shower, and when she comes back her hair is wet. I lift her on to the bed and dry her hair. Then I pull the bedclothes from under and cover her. I go into the bathroom and when I return she is asleep. The bottle is threequarters empty. I half fill my glass and down it in one. I put out the light. With the two beds together, we luxuriate in the space. I feel I'm floating as I go to sleep.

I wake and she is stirring, we reach for each other. I think that in this world it is impossible to know joy to surpass this, my love for Jenny, my treasure. Whisky is supposed to reduce the performance, but I hadn't noticed it.

In the morning as dawn breaks, we make love again and then fall into a tranquil afterglow. A rattle, the kitchen door being opened and I hear Kailash putting plates on the table. Then Jenny wakes.

"I have to get up dear."

While I am shaving she comes into the bathroom. We shower together. I start to dry her long hair, then dry her body, kneel down to dry her legs. I hug her to me, kiss her navel. There is not a stretch-mark on that beautiful smooth bronze skin. I let my lips wander.

"Stop Bob, or you'll get me all worked up again." Gently she pushes me away.

12

At breakfast she is quiet.

Suddenly she says, "What are those big transformers for, out there in the yard?" So she had been listening.

"Transformers transform," I say wisely.

"Don't be silly Bob."

"They step up the current into a very high voltage. There is less leakage from the cables on the pylons that way. Then at the other end, transformers reduce the voltage again, OK?"

"Yes thanks."

"So now you know as much as I do." I kiss her.

"I've a mouthful of toast," she mumbles.

A little later, "If you told me you would take me away for ever, I would come."

"I wish to God I could."

After breakfast we go into the bedroom. She is wearing her housecoat, sandals and a white towel, turbanlike on her damp hair.

While I'm tying up my shoes, she says, "I want to cook, or I'll be bored here while you are working."

"Why not? Good idea."

"Will you be long?"

"No, I'll be back by one o'clock."

I walk away, then think of something and turn back.

"Jenny, I was thinking. Mr James will come here today, probably. You want to cook? Why don't you ask him to a meal?"

Later I see Mr James as he leaves his office and walk back up the hill with him.

"Everything all right, Mr Bennett? How is your friend liking?"

"Everything perfect, Mr James. What a lovely place this is; like a health spa. It'll do us both good."

We trudge up the hill, it's steep, past the rhododendrons.

" Mr James, have you time to call in, just for a minute or two? I'd like you to meet Miss Sandakan."

"Mr Bennett, I should like to do that. But just for a minute. Very busy today."

"I don't want to take her by surprise, Mr James." So Mr James kindly waits outside.

"I've brought Mr James to meet you, but he's in a hurry."

Jenny is reading, sandals off. She puts them on, runs into the bedroom, looks in the mirror, pats her hair.

"You've taken me by surprise."

"You look fine Jenny. I'll bring him in. I haven't mentioned a meal. You ask him."

I introduce them.

"Do you like our lonely place, Miss Sandakan?"

"Really lovely, oh yes."

"I have just called in to make your acquaintance."

"Very pleased to meet you, sir."

"I will call again; I cannot stay." He turns to leave.

"Mr James..." He looks round. "Mr James, I like cooking. Will you please come for a meal, a good Bengal curry?"

"That would be very nice Miss Sandakan."

"When would suit you?" I ask. "The day after tomorrow?"

"Yes, that would be convenient."

"Say about 6.30 on Saturday, Mr James."

He acknowledges with raised hand as he walks away.

"I suppose he eats everything. Kerala is full of vegetarians, but he is a Christian."

"Ask Kailash," says Jenny. "He's sure to know. I'll go shopping with him tomorrow."

"No Jenny, not Kailash; I'd like to come."

"Wouldn't Kailash know where to shop?"

"Not necessary, my friend Mr Subharwal will help, especially when he knows we are entertaining the big man himself."

Early next morning, when it is nippy and the sun has not yet peeped over the hill, we walk down towards the village. Jenny has her shopping list.

"What are you going to give us?"

"Chicken curry and rice, mutton pilau, dhal, dhai and chutneys. Maybe we can find some poppadoms. Kailash will make chapatis, and we'll have a vegetable dish."

"And if we have room after all that, what will you offer for dessert?"

"Wait-and-see pudding."

"Oh, I see."

My grandmother used to tell us it would be "waitandsee" pudding. These thoughts take me back to my family.

I have been so involved and happy that I have forgotten about home. We walk along, contented and silent. Melanie and Jane would love this place, but Brenda would be bored. My parents would be content with a walk now and again, sitting in the sun, reading, knitting.

Jenny strides along. I like the wiggle. She wears trousers and they suit her, but she can also wear a dress; she has hips enough. Thoughts of England disappear. Her walk differs from Calcutta step, freer and relaxed.

We cross the bridge. Water roars past below, like a freed beast, having done its work, turning the turbines, and now liberated. The sun has now risen above the hill and shines on an array of herbs, vegetables and fruit in roadside stalls; brown, green, golden, scarlet, yellow, orange. Mr Subhawal's store is the largest in the village. He is also a landowner, so is important in this small community. I introduce Jenny as Miss Sandakan.

"Mr Subharwal, we want your help. We have some shopping to do. We have invited Mr. James to a meal and Miss Sandakan is a good cook. It must be special so we have come to buy from you, Mr Subharwal."

He looks pleased, taking the compliment.

Jenny looks around and buys carrots, little potatoes and a spinach-like vegetable. She buys hot and medium mango chutneys and a lime pickle. He finds poppadoms for her. Then she goes to the trestle table outside and chooses cinnamon, cardamon pods, turmeric, coriander seeds, chillies, nutmeg, saffron and black mustard seeds.

"Kailash has some of these", she says, "but they may not be fresh."

She asks Mr S for almonds and honey. He goes into the store room for them.

"Where can we buy chickens and meat, Mr Subharwal?" She speaks in a mixture of Hindi and English: "murghi,"- chickens.

"Come," he says. He takes us down the street and we pass a stall with meat hanging up unprotected.

"The flies' dance floor, Jenny. I wonder if Kailash buys from here? What the eye doesn't see..."

Jenny asks Mr Subharwal if there is a better place.

"Chickens are all right," she says. "They are alive and clean."

Mr S takes us to a man selling them and we buy three. We need three for they are fully grown, but bantam size. Legs tied together, they are put into a wickerwork basket, squawking. Then we are taken to another shop, joints of meat protected by gauze. Jenny buys a leg of lamb for the pilau.

Mr Subharwal calls a boy to carry the things up the hill.

"Oh, I've forgotten onions, yes, and raisins," says Jenny. "Oh yes, and fruit."

We go back to the store. She buys oranges, apples and bananas.

"The trouble with writing a list is that you forget to put things on the list."

"I think that really is all we need," says Jenny.

The boy carries the hens in the basket on his head. Kailash will kill and prepare them tomorrow. Mr Subharwal sidles along with us.

"Thank you Mr Subharwal. Perhaps next week we shall have more pipes for you."

"Thank you very much, sir."

"Lion beer coming. Will send to you."

He leaves us and we walk to the rest house, our home.

13

Next morning Jenny says, "I'll be busy in the kitchen today, when will you be back?"

"Lunchtime. I won't go back to the station in the afternoon."

Jenny and Kailash are busy when I return. She has tied up her hair in a scarf. Thump, thump, Kailash is grinding some spices, while she tends pots on the stove.

"Make yourself a sandwich, Bob, but don't spoil your appetite. Please make one for me, too. I'll join you in a few minutes."

She comes and sits down.

"Everything going smoothly?" I ask.

"No problems."

"Do you want any help?"

"You can lay the table later, but I don't want you in the kitchen. You are too big."

Before going back to work, she lies on the bed with me. She pops in and out of the kitchen.

Time to stir myself. I get up to lay the table, find cups and plates and cutlery in the kitchen, including some I had never seen before.

Mr James arrives promptly at 6.30, dressed in a light-brown suit, white shirt, blue tie, very smart. I wear grey flannels, dark-blue pullover, artillery tie with its red zigzag pattern. She wears green trousers and an expensive-looking red high-neck pullover. I wonder who the hell bought it for her. It must have been imported. She has put up her hair, oriental style, with long black pins through it. Stunning! I'm proud of her.

There is a friendly atmosphere, helped by Jenny and me feeling at ease.

It is clear that Jenny captivates Mr James. He doesn't say anything for a few seconds, but just stands as if transfixed. Eventually he says, "Good evening, Miss Sandakan."

"Mr James, call me Jenny. I'm always called Jenny. I forget my name is Sandakan."

She brings a package from the bedroom.

"Here is the alarm clock."

"Thank you for taking so much trouble."

He asks the price and pays immediately.

"It is indeed very kind."

He sits in the armchair and we sit on the sofa.

"I hope you are comfortable here."

"Very comfortable, Mr James," she says. "It feels like home. I don't want to go back to Bengal."

"What would you like? We have Scotch, Carew's gin, Golden Eagle beer."

We all choose Scotch and water.

"I will propose a toast to you. May your stay here be a very happy one."

We clink glasses.

"I am much liking, but family not approving," he says, looking at his drink.

"How old are your children, Mr James?"

"Felicia is seven years old and Theresa is five."

He produces a photo of the two kids.

"Felicia, you see, wearing glasses, but doctor says it is only temporary corrective arrangement."

I am about to say that they are about the same age as mine, but Jenny says, "I have a niece four years old: Diana. She wanted to come with me." She gets up. "I must go into the kitchen."

While she is away I feel that Mr James wonders about me.

"My marriage has not worked out, Mr James. She is in England, doesn't like India."

He doesn't pursue my interpretation of the truth, just mumbles that he is sorry to hear it.

Jenny comes back from the kitchen. Mr. James is watching Jenny. I am watching him. He won't want her to return to Calcutta in a hurry. She goes out again. I can see him thinking. I imagine his thoughts, apart from a wish to go to bed with her, "Would my seniors reprimand me for allowing this European to stay in this bungalow with his girlfriend? Oh well, if necessary I can have them move to the old Dak bungalow by the village."

Jenny returns. "Nearly ready. I hope you have a good appetite."

"Indeed I have, Jenny, and I have eaten only little today, so that I may do justice to your repast."

"Just time for another before it arrives, Mr James."

I pour out more Scotch. He is relaxing and, I feel, really enjoying this little party, but I must make sure he doesn't have too much; he's not used to it.

"Jenny, you will please call me Michael. We are Christians, isn't it?"

"Thank you Michael," she says.

"Yes Michael," I say, "the officer commanding may be called by a more familiar name in the mess, but not when on the parade ground."

We laugh. It is so natural. We have made him feel at home. I raise my glass.

"I propose a toast. To the officer commanding!"

Michael waves us away. "Thank you very much, but oh! What a lot of rubbish you do talk."

"Ready to eat?" Jenny asks.

We sit at the table, he on my right; Jenny will sit on my left, nearer to the kitchen. Kailash brings in two large bowls, one with the chicken curry, one with rice, also the chapatis. Jenny carries a tray with a small dish and saucers on it. The dish contains a puree of potatoes, Aloo Bhurta, she calls it; and the saucers hold chopped banana, raisins, and grated coconut. Kailash then brings a bowl of mutton pilau. There is a jug of cold mountain water on the table.

"In Calcutta, servants borrow crockery from neighbours. It occurs to me, Michael, are any of these from your house?"

"I do seem to recognise them, Bob. This swapping of household goods is not uncommon."

After the curry and pilau, Jenny brings in a sweet dish. There are apples, oranges and bananas already on the table.

"She told me this is "wait-and-see pudding"."

Jenny says, "It's carrot halva."

"Oh yes", says Michael, "gaja karrah."

Jenny says, "Mother called it carrot pudding, made with milk, honey, cinnamon, cardamon, saffron and raisins."

We clear the things away and she brings in the coffee. I sit in the armchair; she sits with Mr James on the sofa.

"I hope you like Nescafe, Michael."

"Most certainly."

"You come from the south, land of good coffee."

"Yes it is good there, but Nescafe is good, too."

We feel contented and immobile.

"I congratulate you, Jenny. You are a very good cook. Surely you must be a professional?"

A professional of sorts, I think to myself. A sick joke.

"I have helped in a restaurant," says Jenny.

"But that is not your work?"

"Oh no, Michael, I was in the telephone exchange. I left the exchange; it was boring. Then I helped my mother, a widow, Michael. She was ill." She sounds so plaintive. "I have just lost her."

This is rather naughty of her, but I can't help smiling.

"My deepest sympathy, my dear."

"I thought this break would do her good." I add my little bitpart to the play. I'm quite enjoying it.

"I have plans to start a restaurant."

"What a good idea. I'm sure it will be a great success."

This is the first I'd heard of it.

All passes smoothly.

"Thank you for a very pleasant evening, a most memorable evening."

He stumbles a bit over the word "memorable". We see him out of the door, accompany him to the footpath.

"You made an impression. Sudden, this restaurant idea?"

"Yes, I thought of it last week."

We have yet another Scotch, then go to bed. We are in each other's arms.

"A restaurant, that's a bloody good idea."

No answer; just quiet breathing.

14

A few days later, Mr James says that he will be visiting the lake on the other side of the hill. "Would you like to come?"

"Very much, thank you."

"You bring food and hot drink."

"What time?"

"Eight o'clock."

"We'll be there."

We reach the trolley in good time. Mr James is there with two assistants. I have seen them often in the power station. Jenny and I sign the form excusing the authorities of blame in the event of an accident.

"Hold on Jenny!"

We start with a sudden jerk. As the view broadens rapidly below us, she looks at it wide-eyed, reaches for my hand, doesn't speak, just silent wonderment. She wears stout, sensible shoes, such as I had warned her to buy. At the halts where we change trolleys, I lift her over. At the top we sit on a rock and absorb the view. The ground to our front flattens towards the dusty horizon. To the left front is a range of hills and behind them, out of sight and many miles away, lies Simla.

"Now we have to walk." says Mr. James.

We follow the path by the side of the hill. The slope to our right is covered by trees. There is a mild uphill gradient. After half a mile we come to a tunnel; it is some fifty yards long, just cuts through the top of the ridge. We walk through this tunnel and the view on the other side takes Jenny and me by surprise. It is majestic. In front is a deep, narrow valley, the near side curves so steeply that we cannot see the end of the trolley lines. Beyond are the foothills, rising row on row, higher and higher, to the snow-capped peaks beyond.

"You've seen the hill people in the village, says Mr James. "They make this journey on foot, carrying heavy loads. They are very muscular. Once a year there is a big fair, a market, far up there in the hills."

We go down into the valley in two stages. It is not so far as on the other side, but very steep. At one point the trolley is on a sixty-degrees slope and we go down very slowly. The winch man has to be careful. We hold on tight. When we reach the foot, there is no sun and we put on our pullovers.

"Now one mile walk," says Mr. James. "No hurry. We go on ahead. We have work to do."

Shrubs cling to the steep valley sides, the bottom is about 200 yards across, flat and green. Down the centre a stream babbles over brown stones. We pass a water-wheel by a little stone hut. Inside a grindstone is turning, a miller feeding in the grist. We sit on the coarse grass by the stream. The sun reaches over the hill behind us and lightens the far wall of the valley, but we are still in the shade. I put my arm around Jenny.

Maybe this is the high point. Will all fall from here?

"Remember all this my love."

"I'll remember it all right!"

Three men and two women file past, carrying huge bundles on their backs. They have the loads secured to their waists and shoulders; the men's loads are also secured by bands around their foreheads.

"We had better move," I say.

We walk along slowly and we see Mr James in the distance. He is sitting on the grass by the lake.

"Good timing," he says. "Work just finished."

He points to a tunnel in the hillside.

"This is artificial lake, and that is the exit point."

On the other side the water flows through the two penstocks, 2,000 feet above the turbines. His two assistants are Hindus in their thirties. They wear grey flannels and pullovers - seems to be the standard garb here. One carries a theodolite and tripod.

We sit and have our sandwiches and hot coffee. Then we all walk back to the trolley and make the return journey. At the top we linger and take one last look at the glorious view, What a wonderful day it has been. At the bottom we part company with Mr James and the others.

"Thank you very, very much Mr James."

Jenny and I walk by the dry river bed to the rest house. We flop on the sofa for a few minutes. She gets up, walks to the kitchen door.

"I'll get some tea."

I follow her into the kitchen, wait until she puts the water on to boil, then give her a bear hug.

15

It is mid May. The weather is warm, very pleasant here, but in the plains of northern India it is torrid. Here more clouds sweep up from the south on monsoon winds. In Bombay rain usually starts to fall at the beginning of June, here a bit later. I am walking from the power station, where it has been agreed that Mewalal can finish the job. There is no need for me to stay. Our holiday is nearly over.

On completion, Mewalal will send surplus materials and tools back to our factory, close to the place where I met Jenny for the first time; the factory where I stored our belongings, Brenda's bric-a-brac, taken from the flat. I shall be with Brenda soon; parted from Jenny. I'll stop in Delhi on the way. I've something important to do there, a friend to see.
Jenny walks to meet me. The holiday, the exercise, away from Bengal, has made her glow with health, brightened her eyes. She has cut down on smoking.

"I don't think we'll be here much longer, Jenny."

"When are we likely to go?"

"In about a week."

We walk slowly up the hill.

"Then I'll be losing you."

"For a few months. I must go home, wish I could stay."

We arrive at the rest house. Mr Subharwal has sent twelve bottles of Lion beer; better than Golden Eagle. What quantities we drink in India! We open a bottle instead of having tea.

"Jenny, I must break my journey in Delhi. I've something very important to do. I have money there, a big amount. A friend, Ajoy, keeps it for me in his safe. I don't like to keep it in Calcutta."

"Why keep it in Delhi?"

"He's a rich man, used to large amounts. I don't want to keep it in a safe deposit vault. And Jenny----"

"Yes Bob?"

"I will be very busy so it's better if you go straight back to Calcutta. I'll only be one night there, possibly two at the most." I don't think she minds. "I always stay in Marsden's Hotel. It's expensive the firm pays. And I'll be very busy. I know Tony will ask me to call on customers."

I must have a heart-to-heart talk with Ajoy.

"You'll need money while I'm on leave, Jenny. And if you start a restaurant you'll need cash to get started. Tell me about your idea."

"Will you come to see Dr Rahman with me?"

"Dr Rahman. What's wrong?"

"Nothing. He owns the building. He has two rooms on the ground floor where I'm living. They're empty. Perhaps he'll rent them to me. If you're there it will help."

"Yes, as a guarantor I suppose. Course I'll come."

"If he agrees then I'll have to get permission from the Corporation. I think Dr Rahman will help, he knows lots of people."

"You'll need money. I suppose you'll need tables and chairs and cooking things."

"Lots of things, Bob. Cooker, sink and water heater. I wonder how I can manage."

"I'll pay, don't worry. And Jenny - very important. Move out of that place. Have a restaurant there, but please, please live somewhere else. What a bloody dump."

"I promise I will. First thing when I get back."

In the evening I phone Ajoy. The line is very bad, but I manage to convey to him that I'll see him in Delhi in a few days' time.

16

My friend Ajoy Bannerjay changed the spelling of his name from Bannerjee because he likes to be different.

"Too many Bannerjees," he said.

I met him in 1947 in Manchester, when I was training prior to my move overseas. He held an important post - I can say no more. It was a chance meeting in the Central Hotel. I'd been shopping nearby, so I though I'd look in. I had never been in the Central before. Sometimes Ajoy liked to drink in solitude, but he was interested that I was destined for India.

"We will meet there," he said.

A good-looking man, his friends at Cambridge had joked, "A thing of beauty is Ajoy for ever."

Some weeks after this first meeting, Ajoy was in a club where there was a police raid, as a result of a tip-off that drug dealers might be there. Ajoy was not involved in any way, but he was worried that if his name were linked with the club, his image, both at work and in society, would be damaged.

Next morning he phoned me, "Please meet me at lunchtime. It's urgent."

We met in a pub near my firm and Ajoy explained what had happened.

Mister Green's was a notorious club of the devious and deviant, certainly not a place Ajoy would have visited, but a party had dragged him in.

"Let me think, Ajoy." Silence. "I will give you an alibi. We'll have to work something out. Can you come to my place this evening?"

This gave me time to think.

On the evening of Ajoy's trouble, I had invited a girl to the cinema. We had quarrelled - just a petty tiff I had thought - but apparently she took it seriously and didn't turn up. I had bought tickets and waited for ten minutes after the show had started. I was annoyed and didn't bother to leave her ticket at the booth. Instead I had put it in my pocket together with my own ticket stub.

I returned home to find the ticket and stub in the pocket of the coat I had been wearing. Ajoy arrived in his Jag. I explained he was to say that he had been in the cinema with me. Then I tore the ticket in half, gave him to stub, threw the rest away. Rather a childish alibi, but it would have to do. It showed how worried Ajoy was that he agreed. Ajoy brightened considerably when he knew that, if necessary, I would perjure myself.

Over a whisky, he borrowed from Pooh-Bah, "Mere corroborative detail lending verisimilitude to an otherwise bald and unconvincing narrative."

"In other words", I said, "a terminological inexactitude."

After all this planning, like a plot in a poor detective story, thank heaven, nothing happened and we wondered why. But Ajoy didn't forget, neither in England, nor later in Delhi.

"I owe you a good turn, Bob old boy."

Later he helped me, and in so doing, helped Jenny.

Through his diplomatic connections, Ajoy discovered why nothing about this club raid was publicised. The police had found a member of intelligence in the ladies' loo, complete with dress, wig and falsies.

17

We leave tomorrow. I take Mewalal to see Mr Subharwal. Five large pipes have to be moved. They are damaged and of no use to us. Mr S is delighted. I give Mewalal one hundred rupees to share with his gang.

"Please move these pipes to Mr Subharwal's field."

They have done a good job and deserve it.

"Mr Subhawal," I say, "they have worked hard; now they are going to help you."

I wonder what his reaction will be. I wait.

"Er, yes, er, Mr Bennett", clearly a man not used to forking out unless he has to, "I know what, I will - I will give them a burrah khana, big meal."

"That's good of you, Mr Subharwal."

I tell Mewalal about this in front of Mr S so he can't change his mind then leave them discussing what they are going to do.

After lunch next day I take leave of Mr James and his staff, and then find Mewalal and say goodbye to him. Mr James has lent me the truck to drive us to Dharikot. Back at the Rest House Jenny has finished packing and we load our luggage. We have a few beers left, so we wrap up the bottles to stop them rattling. In the bedroom we look round to see if we have left anything behind. We pause.

"Goodbye forever," Jenny says to the place.

The moment grips me. The first day of the rest of our lives. No, rather, this is the last day of the dream. Have we reached the peak of our happiness? Can the path rise further or will it be downhill f.om now on? Where do we go from here?

I hug her. Being petite she cannot reach my shoulders, puts her arms around my body, lays her head on my chest. I kiss her hair again and again and breathe in the scent of it, lavender. Her long hair hangs down, secured by a clip, just like it was when first I saw her on the dance floor of scruffy Joshua's. She has changed. She is brighter and fitter, her eyes clear.

"Come darling, we must go."

She lifts her face and gently I kiss her lips.

"It's sad to leave", I say as we go to the truck, "but we must look forward now. No good moping."

We say goodbye to Kailash, give him a tip. The sweeper is there and I reward him. They are never absent at baksheesh time, can't blame them. We drive away.

At the foot of the hill, before the bridge, Mr James is waiting and the driver stops.

"I had no time to come to the rest house to say goodbye to you, Jenny. I wish you great success with the restaurant."

"Thank you Mr James, thank you for everything."

I get out and walk round to him. He meets me at the back of the truck. We shake hands. He looks serious.

"I hope all goes well for you, Mr Bennett."

"Who knows the future Mr James? I hope you have good news of your next posting. Good luck!"

I get back into my seat, wave goodbye and off we go.

"Take one last look, Jenny."

We look back at the power station as we pass through the village. Behind, on the hill, we can just see the rest house, surrounded and nearly hidden by trees. Then we look towards the two great pipes and the winch railway by the side of them; and the trees high up on the ridge where we walked to the tunnel and saw the valley below. We remembered the mighty snow-covered mountains beyond.

We look at each other, my arm around her. Nothing need be said. Memories. Now we must look forward.

It gets hotter as we descend. Jenny puts up her hair so as to feel cooler.

We reach the hotel in Dharikot and are shown to the old fashioned room on the first floor that had been reserved for us. There is a huge double bed, a dressing table with large mirror, a wardrobe, chest of drawers, two bedside tables and two armchairs, all maybe dating from before World War I. The place is clean, the bed sheets gleam white. There is a ceiling fan, but fans are useless when there is almost no humidity. Fortunately there is a khus-khus screen, tatty, rather like coconut matting, covering one window opening. Water is made to trickle down the screen, moved by a tiny pump set, and an electric fan drives air through the dampened screen. This cools the air delightfully. These arrangements have been replaced by air conditioning machines in most hotels.

There is a knock at the door. An immaculately bearded and turbaned young man introduces himself as Gulab Singh. He comes from the Electrical Authority offices.

"I have been asked by Shanagar Resident Engineer, Mr James, to see that everything is OK for you," he says, smiling, and snowing a set of gleaming teeth as spotless as his white turban.

"Please come to the station, where I have arranged for your rail tickets and berth reservations."

We go downstairs and see the driver. He has just finished drinking tea and throws the clay cup into the gutter. I tip him and he drives away back to Shanager. We walk the few hundred yards to the station. I collect the tickets, mine to Delhi only, Jenny's all the way to Calcutta. We have a two-berth non-air conditioned compartment. We thank Gulab Singh and he departs.

"It will be very hot on the train, Jenny. I think I can do something to make us more comfortable. Come."

"Where are we going?"

"To the ice factory."

We cross the passenger bridge and go out of the gate at the other side of the station.

"Is Gurbux Singh on duty?"

A man calls him.

"Ah, Mr Bennett. You come from Shanagar today?"

"We are staying the night, then take the express tomorrow morning."

"I am pleased to see you."

"Gurbux, may I please buy ice for the compartment?"

"No need pay. I send."

I tell Gurbux the number of our compartment.

"It is very hot weather. I have some Lion beer. You drink?" I had brought three bottles from Shanagar. "Please have these, Gurbux."

"That is indeed very kind, Mr Bennett, Bob. Tomorrow men bring special ice for you."

We are tired. The cooling khus-khus brings relief. After a shower we send for a cool bottle of beer. In the evening we ask for our meal to be sent to the room; tandoori chicken and naan bread, with to follow, that old standby in these little hotels, caramel custard. In these new surroundings, new bed, new room, and in the gentle cool of the khus-khus fan, we make love.

I adore her. There is no strain, no feeling of regret. We drift into sleep.

Next morning, after an early breakfast, a man takes our baggage to the train. Our two-berth compartment has a cubicle adjoining with just enough space for wash basin, toilet and shower. Sometimes the sun beats down on the roof tanks, giving only hot water. The windows have triple protection again heat, dust and prying eyes: three frames that can be raised and lowered. One frame has plain glass, one wire gauze and the third has wooden louvres. In addition there are metal bars to keep out intruders. The windows on the corridor side have blinds on them. Two adjustable fans hang from the ceiling. A table against the wall can be swung out.

Jenny wears grey cotton trousers, suitable for a journey, bush shirt and sandals. I wear a shirt and shorts, and sandals also. The fans beat stale air down on us. I watch two men cross the railway track carrying an object wrapped in sacking. I open the door as I see them looking for our compartment number. A huge lump of ice the size of a bolster is lifted in and slides across the floor. The workman grins and salaams as I slip him and his mate a generous reward. The fans play down on the ice, evaporation bringing coolness.

I close the windows tight to entrap the little remaining cool from the night. The fans keep up their good work. There remains a lingering smell of dust and disinfectant. I open my bedding roll on the top bunk while Jenny opens hers below. I don't think anyone else will try to come into the compartment when I leave Jenny at Delhi, for there is a reserved notice on the door. Slamming of doors, a whistle, the train moves.

We are a bit weary, so Jenny lies down and I climb on to the top bunk and we sleep. We are woken by the train stopping at a station. Each stop is for half an hour or more to enable hoi polloi to buy food and drink from vendors on the platform. The favoured ones like us can go to the dining car, or have their food brought to the compartment.

"Jenny, I'm going to the restaurant car to order lunch. The safest is curry, not European food. OK?"

"See if they have any cold bottles of soda."

I decide to walk along the platform instead of using the corridor. When I step out a blast of hot air hits me as from an oven. It is hard to believe one can exist in it. The tea vendor passes with his trolley. "Gurum Chaay!" What would India do without hot tea? It's darned hot in the station; the tea is even hotter, yet it cools you. I place my order in the restaurant car. It will be brought to the compartment when we reach the next major station.

The food arrives; chicken curry and a vegetable curry mixture of spinach and spuds. The attendant also brings four small bottles of soda water in an ice bucket. There is trifle and a pot of coffee, jug of warmed milk, container for sugar, all of bright metal. The curries are good. We don't use spoon and fork, but break off pieces of chapati, picking up the curry with them, using two hands on the bones. The trifle is made of strata of multi-coloured cake material, jam and moist rubbery custard. We leave most of it.

We keep the ice bucket, and push the tray with the remains of the meal into the corridor, bolt the door, pull down the blinds. Having given the food time to settle, we drink Indian whisky, glasses filled with the cool soda. Even with the ice on the floor, not yet evaporated away, it is very hot, so off with pants, bush shirts, panties and bra. We make love. It is a new experience. We can't help laughing, breathless laughter, as we sweat and bounce with the movement of the poorly sprung carriage.

Afterwards we both manage to cram into the little cubicle and have a shower. The water is warm from the sun. No need for towels, the fans dry us in a few minutes.

I am worried about the future, but as we lie there together I joke to hide my anxiety.

"Jenny, I read about a couple who make love on horseback; apparently not an uncommon occurrence among nomadic people in Asia. The horse has a bridle, otherwise it would be unbridled passion!"

"You're nuts!"

We put a few clothes on; the bare necessities.

"Darling, I'll have to leave you soon."

"Bob, it has been a lovely holiday."

"Just two nights in Delhi, then I'll be with you."

"Bob, why's your money in Delhi?"

"I bought some property years ago, sold it recently. I don't want the Income Tax people to find out." I change the subject. "You visited Delhi, you said?"

"Yes, my third brother became a Muslim. Changed his name to Ali and moved to Delhi. He asked me to visit him. He introduced me to his family, but I was bored because he was away working most of the time. Visited the Red Fort, the zoo, Qtub Minar, all the usual sights. I went to Chandni Chowk and looked at the jewellery and the men carving ivory. Not many women go there on their own. I was in European dress as usual. A man stopped in a big car. I was on the pavement right next to him. I hadn't been in a big air-conditioned car like that before. He was a Muslim, Nazir Ahmed, dressed in a European suit, wearing rings, a bit flashy. He took me home---------"

I jump up. The train has stopped. I look at my watch, open the shutters.

"Good God! We're nearly there!" Hurriedly we finish dressing and I pack up my belongings. Then, in sight of the station, the train stops again.

Jenny continues, "Yes, he took me to his home. Introduced me. Well educated women. My Urdu improved a lot. He bought me new clothes; no more skirts and short sleeves while I was there.

"I'm going to leave my bedding roll open on the top bunk, so that it looks as though the compartment is fully occupied."

"Yes, all right."

"I know there is a reserved notice, but this is an added safeguard. I'll be seeing you on Wednesday."

The train draws into Delhi Junction. I open the door next to the platform, the corridor being on the other side.

"D'you want anything, Jenny?"

"I'll go to the bookstall," she gets out. "I'm stiff', she says, "been sitting too long."

The station is like a small town, teeming with life and energy; even in the heat people are selling food, tea, old paperbacks, a man with a small suitcase surreptitiously selling "aids to enjoyment", beggars, some disfigured and one-legged, hopping with sticks, porters, pariah dogs slinking about. There are families with their baggage, waiting maybe for hours, with a resignation unknown in the West, for the train to take them on a branch line far from a town, to the station nearest to their village. Jenny returns with the morning's Hindustan Times and a magazine.

"Shall I order a meal for you?"

"Thanks."

"What would you like?"

"Any curry - mutton, chicken or vegetarian - anything. And some cold sodas, please."

I walk to the dining car, two coaches away. I persuade a waiter to come with me and I show him our compartment. He will bring food at the next stop, Aligarh. It will be kofta curry.

"Better hide the whisky, Jenny; don't be seen drinking it."

There is time to spare. Emotion hits me. I sit with head in hands and I can't stop the tears. She puts her arm on my shoulders and I turn towards her, put my arms around her. I get myself under control.

"Sorry to be so stupid, Jenny."

"Dear Bob, you will see me again on Wednesday."

I suppose her kind of life has toughened her.

The guard blows his whistle.

"Goodbye darling." We kiss. I get out and shut the door. "See you soon; keep the doors and windows bolted."

18

How lucky we have been. If Mr James had been difficult we would have been relegated to the Dak Bungalow. The gods and Mr James have smiled on us.

A porter picks up my suitcase and zip bag. I carry my briefcase and a roll of drawings. We cross the footbridge. I follow the porter who works his way through the crowd. Everyone seems to be walking in the opposite direction. We reach the booking hall, a palatial edifice built long ago by the British. I pick my way through, past groups squatting amid bags, tin trunks, tiffin carriers, cooking pots, bedding, children and flies. The flies are thick on the stone floor, flitting away from each footsteps; none is squashed. I have Jenny in my mind and I imagine I see her in the throng. A little woman turns round; but she has a tikka on her forehead and a jewel in her nose. I catch up with the porter as he reaches the taxi. The empty seat beside me cries out to be filled. But she is on the way to Calcutta; soon she will reach Aligarh and her food will be brought to her.

The Sikh driver moves off, dodging a ruminating cow. She knows she is safe. The driver dare not hurt her or he might be beaten up. It doesn't take much to rouse the populace, especially in scorching May. Queen cow! The driver honks his way past St James's, the Skinner church named after that dashing Anglo-Indian soldier, with its gilded metal cross above, riddled with bullet holes, a reminder of 1857.

We pass through the archway of Kashmir Gate in the old city wall, still showing battle damage, where Brigadier General Nicholson stormed through, and at Mori Gate nearby. Opposite Kashmir Gate, on a lawn surrounded by bushes, there used to be a fine bronze statue of Nicholson, that mighty man, sword drawn; but this reminder of British supremacy and stirring times was removed from its plinth and tossed aside as one in disgrace a year or two ago. History is being edited.

We drive along a tree-lined road, a complete contrast to the over-populated city within the wall. We come to Marsden's hotel, sitting in lovely grounds, fine houses and gardens nearby. All is neat and tidy, no shops, shacks and shanties. I pay off the taxi, go to the desk. I am known in the hotel and my firm has used it for many years. Behind the desk is a slim middle-aged woman, her long, blonde hair hanging down, too girl-like for her age.

"Hello Bob."

"Good to see you, Barbara."

"Only here for two nights? Don't you love me any more? Why don't you take me home with you?" She knows I'm married, so is she, to an Indian, but she misses Blighty.

"Something very important, Barbara. I must get on Tuesday evening's plane to Calcutta. Can you help?"

"Probably Bob. I know Indian Airways. I'll phone them now."

Barbara has allotted a nice room to me, ground floor, opening on to the verandah. In front is the rolling lawn with trees and shrubs, stretching down towards the swimming pool, and children's swings and seesaw. I walk with the bearer carrying my case and bag, past the white tables and chairs on the verandah. No one is about, on the verandah or by the pool; they are indoors awaiting the comparative cool of the evening. No modern architectural nightmare this hotel, only ground and first floors, no matchbox tower block. It was built when land was not so valuable, and it could sprawl. It has the gentle air of times gone by.

I send for the dhobi, then go into the bathroom, take off my grimy clothing, wrap myself in a large bath towel lungi-wise.

Dhobi knocks on door, "Salaam sahib."

I count out the pieces, write a list.

"Must have these tomorrow morning, early." He collects them in an old sheet.

I phone Ajoy.

"Hello Bob, I've just got in. Was about to phone Marsdens, wasn't sure when you were arriving."

"I have some calls to make tomorrow, Ajoy, but are you free in the evening?"

"Yes old boy. But why not stay here? Come round now if you like."

"I've already booked in, Ajoy, just about to have a shower."

"Then stay tomorrow night. When can you get here?"

"Say six o'clock."

"I'll come for you, Bob. I'll be there about five thirty."

Now I can relax. I ring for the servant. I don't feel like a whisky or a beer, so I order a large jug of fresh lime. I remove the grime under the hot shower; then turn the regulator to cold. I imagine I'm Shah Jehan, with the love of his life, not Mumtaz, but Jenny, jewel of the palace, in the garden of the Lal Qila, the Red Fort, musicians playing and the nautch girls swaying to the rhythm, and the cooling stream flowing by. But now, no Jenny, no nautch girls, no music, but only the rush of the air-conditioning machine. I doze off.

When I wake, I open the envelope collected from the desk. Tony wants me to enquire about an import licence application at the Ministry, call on a mill in Sabzi Mandi and a chemical plant on Faridgarh Estate. I phone the desk.

"Barbara, I've just been on the phone to a friend in New Delhi. He wants me to stay with him tomorrow night. He's a great friend so I must go. I'll be leaving tomorrow afternoon."

"Oh I'm sorry Bob. We've hardly had time to talk."

Barbara is always glad to meet expatriates, has a yearning for "home".

"When are you off duty, Barbara?"

"In an hour's time."

We'll meet on the verandah. Later I'll ring Brenda and tell her when I expect to fly home. Tomorrow I'll tell Ajoy about my entanglement.

It's cooling as the sun dips low. I feel fresher, sit on the verandah and read a newspaper, then stroll on the lawn. Two ayahs walk with little toddlers. Children are at the pool, watched by their mothers. Men are coming back from their offices in New Delhi. I look towards the pool, where a daddy does a belly flop into the pool to amuse the kids, who scream with laughter as the shock wave splashes them. Dozens of parakeets fly squawking among the trees to their night resting places. I see Barbara and join her on the verandah.

"Your flight is all fixed, Bob. Call at Air India tomorrow and pick up your ticket."

I have a beer and she has a Tom Collins. She shows me a photo of her son, I show her snaps of Melanie and Jane. We have an early dinner. Then I excuse myself, saying I have reports to write and that I must phone home.

19

Next morning the pool looks inviting so dive in for two leisurely lengths. After breakfast I read the Statesman on the verandah, but my mind wanders to Jenny. She'll be halfway to Calcutta by now.

I phone the Import Department and make an appointment for ten thirty tomorrow. Sometimes one has to wait a week. That arranged, I take a taxi through the old city to Sabzi Mandi (vegetable market). It sits astride the Grand Trunk Road. We crawl along passing stalls which encroach on the road. The market will be moved to a less congested area soon.

I visit a cotton mill for payments. I am told, "cheque is in post." Maybe it is. Then I continue to Faridgarh Estate to the chemical works. The manager calls the Chief Engineer and we discuss the job. There's always something else for the unlazy, and I visit another mill to see our fitter; then a flour mill "to show the flag". It is midafternoon so I go back to the hotel.

In 1949, when I first saw Faridgarh Estate, there was hardly a building on it. Land was very cheap. One of our supervisors, they called him "the Munshi" (teacher) comes from a village in Bihar. He has a head for business. He persuaded me to invest with him in a plot of land on the Estate. I had to do it through him and he added his own cash. One has to keep an eye on land or someone will build on it, so I arranged that most of Munshi's work for our firm would be in the Delhi area. This was a secret between us.

By 1959 the price of land had rocketed, for the torpor following the horror and disorganisation of 1947 had been overtaken by an energetic and confident move to expansion. We had a tempting offer from an owner of an adjacent property, a sum beyond our wildest dreams, and we cashed in. Munshi was delighted and could have gone back to live on his small holding in comfort, but he prefers to continue working for us. It gives him a chance to travel away from his claustrophobic village.

What a blessing that I have this money so I can help Jenny. It's a godsend. It is secure with Ajoy; he is used to stashing away lakhs of rupees. To me, my cash is a large sum; to him it is nothing much.

I pack up and take leave of Barbara. Ajoy arrives on time in his air-conditioned Merc. It is great to see him, first time for six months. He is good-looking, light-brown Bengali, medium height, round face, easy to smile and showing slight dimples when doing so. He considers English to be his natural language. Ajoy has been separated for years. His marriage had been arranged. He still likes the woman, but he is much too restless to live a normal married life, and his wealth enables him to be independent. He is a hard worker, very successful in PR.

"Bob, pity you can't stay longer. Next weekend I have a house party. I assure you that you would not be disappointed."

"Thanks Ajoy, but you know I wrote to you that I had a friend with me, Anglo-Indian. She's gone straight back to Calcutta. No, Ajoy. If you had asked me two months ago, I might have accepted gladly, but now I'm smitten."

I tell Ajoy about her, describe her and her background.

"Anglo-Indian, Bob? More Southeast Asian."

"I remember this coming up in Parliament some years ago. It was agreed that an Anglo-Indian was probably Christian, main language English, wearing European clothes, adhering in the main to Western culture more than Indian. Ethnic origin doesn't seem to matter. Could be half Hottentot and half Eskimo!"

"Ha! Interesting."

"Anyway, Jenny and family call themselves AIs."

"I'd like to meet her," says Ajoy.

Ajoy's house in South Delhi is in a quiet side road and surrounded by trees. It is convenient for the Diplomatic Enclave and government departments. Ajoy leads me into his lounge, pours whisky.

"Pani, soda or just ice?"

"Just ice."

"You say you're in love. It's a long time since I fell. Kept clear of it for years. A disease, easy to catch, difficult to cure."

"I think it's easier for you, Ajoy. you can afford to be separated."

"That's true. Easier to sin if you have cash. It distresses me when you are worried, old boy."

"It is good of you to listen to my woes, Ajoy. It's up to me to sort out my problems. I don't let them get me down. I work; I don't mope; I don't drink to excess."

"Why don't you stay with me for a few days on the way back to England? I assure you I would throw one hell of a party for you."

"It's no use, Ajoy. I'm in love."

Ajoy laughs in a kindly way.

"Self-inflicted torture."

"I suppose it is."

"Bob, so often it is the sensitive and creative who suffer; the easy-going often achieve nothing of importance."

"I suppose so Ajoy."

"Bob, I don't know what to say. I'm the last person to give advice."

"Ajoy, I am grateful to you for keeping my cash. I need some now."

"How much d'you want Bob?"

"It's difficult to estimate. My rescue of Jenny includes helping to start a little restaurant. Tables, chairs, kitchen equipment, new sink, cooker, cutlery, crockery. Mostly second-hand I expect. Maybe structural alterations. Say fifteen thousand."

Ajoy goes upstairs to his safe. He come back with wads of hundred rupee notes.

"How are you going to carry this, Bob? Not in your luggage and don't put it in your jacket pockets. I've a money belt."

We divide the notes into the compartments in the belt. I try it on under my shirt.

"Let's put it back in the safe until tomorrow."

I mustn't forget it. Ajoy is a little taken aback when I explain Jenny's poor circumstances. "You are besotted Bob."

"No Ajoy, not quite; I won't desert my family. The hell of it is that I want both lives and I won't give up either of them."

It is getting late.

As we move Ajoy says, "I can't think what I would do in your position. I could afford to keep two establishments, one in England and one in India - keep them apart. Perhaps it is easier to be a good man if you are needy."

I go to bed and it takes me some time to calm down my thoughts. I go to sleep dreaming a muddle of Jenny, trains and taxis.

Next morning at breakfast, Ajoy says, "Have you anything else to do apart from asking about your import licence?"

"I have to collect my air ticket, then look around Connaught Circus and the shops in Janpath if there's time. I must take presents for the kids."

"Bob, I have to visit a couple of embassies in Chanakyapuri. How about the Ashoka for lunch?"

"A good idea, Ajoy. What time?"

"Say twelve thirty in the main bar."

"I'll be there."

"Right. Twelve thirty."

The Import licence visit doesn't take long. The official smilingly says all is being processed. Why does it take so long? After all, we need spares to help keep Indian industry running smoothly. Then I go to India Airways.

I walk round Connaught Circus, then branch off and go down Janpath (People's Way), which used to be called Queensway. I wish Jenny could be with me. Women are better than men at choosing presents. I look in the row of little shops and see a wooden toy shaped like a table tennis bat with holes in it. Three wooden hens, painted red, sit on it. Attached to them are strings connected to a weight. When you swing it round, the hens peck in turn as if feeding. This should amuse the kids.

I go into the Cottage Industries Emporium, a distinct contrast from the little shops. All is cool; attractive, saried ladies sedately serving. I buy two puppets in very colourful Rajasthani dress. Can't think of anything else. I must get something better - I'll have to ask Jenny for suggestions. I would like to take something for my parents. Ah, that should please them: a teak elephant with baby elephant following. The big one pulls a log on a rope. They are fixed to a wooden stand. Yes, the "aged Ps" should like this.

Taxi to the Ashoka hotel, then wait for Ajoy in the air-conditioned bar. Looking out of the window, one can't believe how darned hot it is outside.

I mustn't forget the money belt, now secure in Ajoy's safe. I order a Campari and soda, slice of orange. Ajoy arrives with a partner. She is bronzed, dark-brown hair, the same height as Ajoy. He introduces us. "Gabriela, this is my old friend Bob."

She is in her twenties. she smiles and shows a perfect set of teeth. She wears a terracotta two-piece, short- suit, loop ear-rings, a gold band over the top of her head. She works in the small legation of a central American state, was Coffee Queen of the Americas, or runner up.

After lunch, Ajoy runs her back to the legation.

Ajoy says to me, "Now see what you are missing. Sure you don't want to change your mind, call here on your way to England?"

"Isn't it strange, Ajoy, I'm not interested. Anyway, I'm not paid well enough to keep up with her."

"Poor old Bob, I understand. Let me know if you think again."

Ajoy drives us back home.

"Bob, these affairs don't last for ever. Won't you tire of her?"

"Can't imagine it happening, Ajoy. I don't believe it."

"Supposing you lived with Jenny all the time, has she much conversation? Will you get bored? Perhaps she'd become restless."

"I can't imagine ever tiring of her."

"Will you bring Brenda back here?"

"Yes, I think so. Yes I will."

We have tea. I fit the money belt under by shirt. I wear a lightweight jacket to hide the bulge.

We drive to the airport. There is a queue as usual.

"Thanks Ajoy, many, many thanks. Don't wait; it's a weary business. See you soon."

20

"Fasten your seat belts."

It is bumpy. We land with a bounce in the crosswind. By taxi to Jenny's place and I dash upstairs with my luggage. It's very quiet.

Jenny's door is padlocked. My spirits plummet and I flop onto the sofa. From the next room comes big Bella, whom I met in the Sailors' Club.

"I remember you Bob. Jenny said she was waiting for you."

"Where is she?"

I'm frantic.

"She's taken Diana back home to her Mum."

Mum? Surely a slip of the tongue. I let it pass.

"When did she go?"

"About an hour ago. Like a drink Bob?"

She brings beer and glasses from her room. She hasn't daubed herself with war paint as she had when last I saw her and she looks better for it.

"Jenny tells me you've been in the hills. Where have you been?" she asks a bit cheekily.

"Near Kashmir, Bella. Very lonely power station. I'm glad to be back."

"She's been away, too, visiting cousins in Bombay."

"I know. She wrote to me. Tell me, Bella, how long have you lived in this building?"

"About two years. I came here about the same time as Jenny."

"You mean when Jenny moved from the Killarny block?"

"No, no. She was here, then she moved to live with a boyfriend. Now she's come back here again. They quarrelled."

Bella doesn't mean to tell tales, but she's a bit downright.

She doesn't notice my concern as she lights a cigarette.

"You've no idea... Jenny's changed. Bloody amazing! She's madly in love with you, man."

"Then why did she tell me she lived in Killarny block?"

"She was falling for you, didn't want to, thought she'd ditch you."

"Oh hell!"

"She loves you; she won't leave you. Are you going to take her away, Bob?"

"I'd like to Bella."

"I wish someone would take me away. I wouldn't muck around." she says quietly. "She's got a bad temper, Bob. You haven't seen it. She had a quarrel with her friend, made it real bad so she could leave him and come back here."

I see Jenny coming.

She shouts from the top of the stairs, "Sorry Bob, that bloody silly brother of mine."

Bella says, "I'll leave you."

"Thanks for the drink, Bella. Oh Jenny, what happened?"

"That fool brother, I told him I'd bring Diana but he took Sadie to the pictures so I had to wait."

We go into her room and sit on her sofa. She nestles up to me, leans her head against me. She reads my thoughts.

"Sorry dear. No love making. Wait a day or two."

Ah well, it's good for my self-discipline.

"What's that you've got under your shirt?"

"It's a present for you."

She chuckles, "You must be deformed; what's all these lumps?"

"Take my shirt off and have a look."

She sees the money belt.

"Well, take it off and open it."

She gasps as she sees the money.

"Oh Bob!"

"Fifteen thousand rupees; that's for the restaurant, and to keep you while I'm away. For heaven's sake don't tell anyone."

She jumps up and bolts the door.

"We'll put it in the bank, but first, tomorrow, I must go to Donald's flat. Be there about an hour."

"I've seen Dr Rahman. He will rent me the two rooms. I told him you worked for a British firm and that pleased him."

"Yes, guarantor for the rent."

"Can't see you till Thursday."

"I'll be there."

We go to bed early. I won't mention that Bella told me about the Killarny block and Jenny's quarrel there. I don't want a row in our last week together. But I must ask her about Diana. I can't get it out of my mind.

"Jenny darling. Bella said you were taking Diana back to her Mum. Surely...?"

"I was going to tell you. I tell all the sailors Diana's mine. That way they are more generous. Sorry Bob, I should have said right away. Yes, her Mum is Sadie and Lucy's her little sister."

With her beside me I can forgive her anything.

"She makes up for not having one of your own, darling."

We hear the girls returning with their newmade friends. A record player is turned on. There's chatter and laughter.

"I don't know how you can live in this place."

"I need money. I'm going to educate Diana."

Then a male voice, beery and maundering, sings loudly: "Oh her cheeks were pink, like a 'orses dink..." coming nearer, someone banging into the side of the passage, 'an 'er hair was a cow muck brown."

"Go away!" shouts Jenny.
"An 'er tits hung loose, like the balls on a goose."
"Bugger off!"
"An she came from a chicken shit town. Open the door, baby."
He leans against the door. Jenny is boiling over, jumps from the bed.
"Fuck off! Leave us alone," she bellows.
No more noise. We hear him stagger off. She comes back to bed.
"D'you know who that is?"
"No, I don't, but I'll damn well find out which silly bitch brought him. We don't have mother suckers like that here."
I hold her tight.
"You must leave this place, Jenny." I feel tears coming. "I beg of you, get out of here."
"I mean to leave Bob."
Firmly I say, "I want to see you out of here before I go on leave."
"Yes Bob, I promise. I'll look for a place tomorrow."

Next morning, I take my luggage by taxi to the flat, then back for Jenny and we go to the bank. She deposits most of the cash, but keeps some for immediate use. I drop her home, call at BOAC, then to the office.

In the afternoon I collect my car. While at the factory I explain to Gopi, the fitter, the work needed at the restaurant. He'll be pleased to make money on the side.

I drive back to Jenny.
"Good news, Bob. I've found a room."
"Marvellous! When are you moving?"
"It's a place in Nizamuddin Street, near Auntie Lulu. Rosie Stevens. I've known her a long time; she's a widow."
"Yes, but when are you moving?"
"She has two girl lodgers, office girls. One is leaving in three weeks' time to get married."
"It's a pity you can't go now."
"Rosie won't want you to stay there."
"We could go to a hotel."
"Why waste money? This room is OK."
"All right."
It is seven o'clock so I kiss her and leave.
It's early, but I must spend some time with my host.
Donald can't hide his disappointment when I tell him I'm flying home soon and will spend most of the remaining time with Jenny.

92

"Why do you bother with her? She'll have been to the clubs while you've been away."

"Oh no she hasn't. She went to stay with cousins in Bombay."

"Are you going to bring your family back, Bob? I hope you don't see Jenny when you return; word will get round. People will say, "Brenda ought to know". Why don't you stay here with me, leave Brenda in England?"

"Donald, Jenny is going to open a restaurant."

"Ha, ha. Don't be daft, Bob. She'll drift again."

"I'm damn sure she won't." I'm getting annoyed. "Donald, you don't like it but I'm going to see Jenny all the time I can, so it's better if I move from here. I'll hardly be here at all."

He is upset. "All right, Bob, go!" he says petulantly. "Go now; don't waste time."

"Donald, I'll go tomorrow morning."

"Let your family down! Stay with that dirty little woman."

I've had enough; I'm stung by what he says and I'm getting angry. I nearly blurt out that I feel unclean living in the same flat as a bloody queer. But I don't mean that. I like him and don't want to hurt him. I don't like to upset the fellow.

"I'm going down to see Micky," I say.

I'm glad I didn't lose my temper. I like this lonely man and I admire him. I'm beginning to have doubts about myself, mustn't get to like him too much; just as well I'm moving.

Micky greets me in his usual hearty way. I tell him of the restaurant idea.

"If she has any electrical work, can you help, Micky?"

"Certainly, Bob, certainly."

"I've had a row with Donald. I'm leaving in the morning."

"Had a quarrel? Has he tried to make love to you?" He laughs.

I'm not sure how serious he is when he says, "You should stay on with him, rich man, he might remember you in his will."

"I'll stay the nights with Jenny, but I must have an address somewhere else. Can you imagine someone asking, "Where are you living, Bob?" and I answering, "Bentala Street". I think they would be more than a little astonished."

"Then stay here with me, Bob."

"You mean I can use your flat as a base, a respectable address?"

"No, Bob, I mean move in."

"Seriously?"

"Of course, Bob, yes, and bring Jenny with you."

"You really mean it, don't you?" He smiles and nods. "I'm very grateful, Micky."

"I'll be glad of your company."

"Micky, I must phone home. Do you mind?"

"Carry on Bob."

"I've got myself in a tangle. I didn't mean to. By chance I've met Jenny. I feel guilty. I have a lovely family - two sweet kids - and yet I've fallen in love."

"Plenty of people are in the same mess, Bob. They just get divorced."

"I don't think I'll do that."

"Perhaps you'll cool off being away from her."

"I doubt it. Mind if I phone now?"

"Carry on. I'll leave you to it. Back in a few minutes." He goes into his bedroom.

I dial and there is a delay. I'm not used to lying, but I'm learning. Brenda flew home only a few months ago, yet in that time I've changed. I didn't know I'd meet Jenny when Donald took me to Joshua's Bar. I wasn't looking for a woman, or anything at all. At last I get through and Brenda answers. She is pleased I am coming home and I will have time to spare before we go to Scotland. First, I'll stay with my parents and then make the usual obligatory visit to Head Office.

"I'll meet you," she says.

She'll come with the kids in my father's car. When we meet at Heathrow we should fall into each other's arms joyfully. I can't see it happening; it's not her fault. She must feel as I do.

I tell her I've bought presents for the kids. I'll buy her perfume on the plane. I ring off.

"Micky, I'll move down tomorrow, before you leave for work."

When I go upstairs, I'm glad Donald is in his room and I needn't talk to him. I've only a little packing to do.. I tidy my dressing table and note that Donald has removed the photo of himself he'd given me. I'm sorry for him; he hides sensitivity in a mist of gin. His health is not good. I wish him well.

21

In the morning, before Arif has returned from the market, I flit.

"Make yourself comfortable," says Micky. He gives me the door key. "See you this evening, and Jenny too."

I drive to Jenny's place and she is surprised to see me so early and she is just dressing. She is delighted that we will be together at Micky's.

The last few precious hours will be in peace, no shouting, swearing, interruptions from unwelcome visitors. But when I think I'll soon be leaving her, my stomach turns over.

We go to see Dr Rahman, a wizened little brown man with horn-rimmed glasses. He wears a long-sleeved white shirt and dark-grey slacks. We agree the rent of the restaurant rooms. As he feels payment is secure, he relaxes. On the walls of what is both office and consulting room are framed photos of himself wearing flying helmet, of biplanes, and some sort of flying certificate. Fixed vertically to the wall is the wooden propeller of an old plane.

"I belonged to the Flying Club when I was young," he says proudly.

The gallant doctor has had an interesting life. Now he rents rooms to these ladies of charm. No doubt his specialist medical skills are at their disposal. He will put Jenny in touch with the right man in the Corporation for permission to start the restaurant.

In the evening I move Jenny to Micky's flat. Arthur will bed down in the restaurant, locking himself in.

Thanks to Micky, we are able to spend these last few sweet, sad days together in peace. I tell Tony I want time off and make it a long weekend, returning to work on Tuesday.

I have to buy presents for the children and Jenny suggests salvar qamiz, those loose garments worn by Punjabi women. But what sizes? I remember the 1959 diary where Brenda had entered their measurements when they had fancy dress outfits made. I find the diary in a trunk at the factory. Jenny chooses bright red and yellow material, the same for both kids and we tell the dirzi to make the clothing larger to allow for growth. Then we buy slippers to match.

We are sitting one evening on the verandah. Sheila is there. She has agreed to go to England with Micky when he retires.

"Are your brothers working, Jenny?" asks Micky.

"Dennis works in the Granada cinema. He's senior usher. He's cleaned up the place. People weren't coming because of the rats; they ran across people's feet. They were looking for scraps of food. It was Dennis's idea. They caught them with rod and line and a hook with bait, just like fishing. When they caught a rat they bashed it with a club."

She is talkative. We have all been drinking.

"There's a racket in the cinemas", she says, "run by the ushers and box office. They print their own block of tickets. When there's a full house, I don't know how, but they make a profit for themselves."

"What about the brother in Delhi?

"Ali, the Muslim, he's the youngest. I stayed with him, then left and stayed in that man, Nazir Ahmed's, zenana. Wanted me to convert to Islam but I wouldn't. So I came back to Calcutta. Went to see Harry. He was having a party. No one recognised me. I was all covered up and veiled. "Please give me work," I said; I was whining. "I beg you to give me work. Allah will bestow a thousand blessings if you help a poor woman." I went on and on until they were going to throw me out. Then I went up to Auntie Lulu and said "Hello Auntie". She did get a shock. Oh man, you should have seen their faces. They were so pleased to see me. I didn't know, but it was Dennis's wedding party, to Mary So I joined the party."

Sheila was relaxed, lying back on the sofa, puffing a fag.

"Don't go clubbing any more. Thanks Micky. Micky's done this for me. Getting me a passport. No more clubs for me. You know every evening all us girls go in taxis to Kidderpore. Heard of the Fishing Fleet have you? Micky says, before the War, memsahibs brought their daughters out in the winter by P & O. Tried to marry them off to bigwigs, ICS, you know, "The Heaven Born", Army officers or burrah sahibs like bank managers." She giggles, drinks and splutters, then more giggles. "Us girls are a downmarket fishing fleet. The sailors were the fish, but not for me now. When we finished with the sailors we threw them back in the sea." She giggles. She reaches out and clings to Micky. "I've caught Micky see! I don't throw him back in."

"Everyone frightened of being found out," says Micky. "Little women were smuggled up the back stairs of the snooty Bengal Club in laundry baskets."

Next morning Gopi comes to the restaurant rooms and we show him what has to be done, sink here, shelves there. Micky will come to deal with the lighting. We buy a gas stove and men take it from the shop on a hand cart.

Then I drive up the river road to Chandernager. We sit by the river as we'd done before, reliving precious moments, we stay the night in the Astoria hotel and again feed cigarettes to the little goat. On Sunday we drive back to Calcutta and on Monday collect the little outfits from the dirzi for Melanie and Jane. Then we buy chairs, tables and cooking equipment.

"What're you going to call the place, Jenny?"

"The Blue Room. I'll paint the walls light blue."

"You could have headed paper and bill forms printed."

"I'm going to start with tea, coffee, soft drinks and simple snacks, Bob. Then, later perhaps, I'll start cooking."

"I'll look forward to hearing of your progress."

On Monday evening I have to visit my flat to see how the Wrights are faring. All is well. we have drinks together. I go to the factory late in the evening, where I collect two suitcases and some clothing and things that Brenda wants.

Then I return to Micky's place. Jenny and I walk by the Hooghly. I can hardly bear thinking of Friday. We go back indoors and sit with Micky.

"See that she is all right, Micky, please."

"I will Bob, and I'll see the work is progressing."

On Tuesday I go back to work. It is a defensive operation, keeping clear of new jobs, tidying up what is on my desk.

In the evening I say, "Let's go to Joshua's, Jenny, for old time's sake, to Joshua's where we met."

I tell George that Jenny will be opening a restaurant.

"Yes George," says Jenny, "I'm opening in Benatala Street."

"That's good news. I hope it goes well."

"I'm going on home leave on Friday, George. I'm sorry I'll miss the opening."

"I'm calling it the Blue Room," says Jenny. "Please pass the word round."

"Get some cards printed," says George.

"Good idea," I say. "You could leave some on the bar here."

"When are you opening, Jenny?"

"Maybe at the beginning of July, just in a small way."

"Good luck to you."

We move to a table by the dance floor. A man with a guitar comes in. Looks cheerful, Jamaican I guess. I point to the empty chair at our table, invite him to sit down, buy him a rum and coke. He is talkative. Oh yes, he knows London, played and sang there. I introduce Jenny.

"Play for us Frank."

The band is resting; there is a lull, so he plays and sings, softly and melodiously.

And when she's weary,
women do get weary,
wearing that same shabby dress,
and when she's weary,
try a little tenderness.

He's good; it's moving. He says he used to play in Snake Hips Johnson's band in the Cafe de Paris, that dance hall restaurant in Coventry Street, just off Leicester Square. He was lucky to be absent when two bombs fell in 1941. The band and many dancers were killed. I remember that on the wall in the foyer is a brass plaque commemorating Snake Hips and all the other casualties. Frank says he will be sailing tomorrow, maybe he will never return to India. Such is the life of a seaman.

On Wednesday evening I take Jenny to Princes. She looks a picture. She wears a green dress slit at the side, Chinese style, and she had fixed up her hair with those long black pins, same as when we entertained Michael James in Shanagar. I wear black dinner jacket and white trousers, Calcutta style, and as we walk to our table we are stared at. The gossip will start, but I don't mind. I am with the one I love and I'm darned proud of her. This is an evening we shall always remember.
We eat and we drink and we watch the cabaret. We admire vivacious Dolores at the mike. We dance and we dance until midnight. We live for the present.

When we leave, we sit in the car, silent.

Next day, the last, I tidy my desk and speak to Tony.
"See you in December."
"What are you doing for transport?"
"Thanks, a friend is taking me to Dum Dum."

Then, without looking up from his desk, he says, "There's some talk of your being transferred, Bob, but I hope not. I've told them I need you here."

"Oh hell! Pakistan?"
"Yes. Contracts negotiated in Head Office."
"Thanks for warning me."

I hope I'm not moved. The family would hate it. And, oh God, I'd hardly ever see Jenny. I won't mention this to her. Maybe I won't go after all.

I had told Jenny I wanted to show her the Orphan's Home in South Calcutta. On the way we call at a shop and buy some goodies. The Home is very tidy. Stoutly built huts stand on welltended lawns. There is a serene atmosphere but silence is broken when we appear, and Jenny hands out sweets, nuts and pieces from chocolate bars. One curlyheaded boy with huge, wide eyes clings to Jenny's jeans and smiles up at her. She lifts him up.

"What is your name?"

Shyly he mutters "Bishu".

"Hello Bishu."

She kisses him and gives him another piece of chocolate. I introduce Jenny to the lady in charge. I contribute regularly to this place.

"Try to visit them Jenny. If you do well, perhaps you can bring them some food from the Blue Room."

Children love Jenny. Maybe it's because she is petite. What a pity she doesn't have a family of her own.

We leave the children, then drive alongside the river southwards into the country at Diamond Harbour, no diamonds, no harbour, but best of all no people, which is unusual for Bengal. There is just the open unfenced road and a green bank by the wide grey river.

We are starting to say goodbye, bit by bit.

"Take me away," she says.

We are in a situation where there is no chance of winning.

"I love you Jenny."

"Love you too Bob."

We drive back and Micky comes in a few minutes later with Sheila. We have drinks on the verandah.

"Ready to eat?" asks Micky.

It is like the condemned man's last meal. There is a tense atmosphere. Micky and Sheila sense it and we are silent.

22

Tomorrow is D for Departure Day 1960. I feel like I did in June 1944, when we invaded Normandy and surprised the Germans.

Half an hour before we landed, Gunner Barstow had muttered, "Dear Mother, it's a bugger, sell the pig and buy me out."

Tense excitement as we neared the shore and the self-propelled guns left the ramps of the landing craft, clawing their way to the beach.

"Kind of you, Micky, taking us to the airport."

"We'll miss you."

"Yes, we'll miss you," says Jenny to herself.

"We'll leave you alone. I'll take Sheila home now."

"I'll set the alarm for 5.30."

"No need," says Micky. "I always wake up early."

Sheila says goodbye.

"See you," says Micky.

Jenny helps me pack, folds the Punjabi outfits, the presents for Melanie and Jane, folds them with special care as if she feels they are part of us.

"Put me in a case and take me with you." She smiles broadly for once, revealing the gold tooth.

"Oh no! I won't do that. A Customs Officer might confiscate you." But we say little. We have a sweet, sad embrace, sleep soundly.

I stir at five o'clock, kiss Jenny and we make love, still not properly awake. I kiss her neck, bury my face in her long hair, breathe in. Micky knocks on the door which snaps us into cruel wakefulness. Simultaneously the alarm goes off.

"Breakfast at six."

"Thanks Micky."

We shower, dress, all is packed. I see the beautiful long, slightly wavy, hair hanging loose down her back. When will I see it again? Quickly she puts on a little makeup and red button earrings. We hug and kiss for the last time in private.

"Morning! Hope you slept well," says Micky, forever hearty.

We pick at our toast and papaya, drink the coffee, quiet, not a word. Cases in the car, Micky drives away, tilting the driving mirror away from us. Doesn't try to make conversation. He's a strange man, brusque and crude at times, but he can be gentle and kind. We reach Dum Dum.

Jenny has Ajoy's address, the flat in St John's Wood, North London.

"I'll write as soon as I arrive, but I'll be in Scotland, so won't be able to collect your letter for about three weeks."

"I'll tell you how the restaurant is going."

We don't feel like talking. My stomach is turning over.

"Look after her for me, Micky."

"I will Bob."

I turn to her.

"Jenny, work hard. It'll make time pass quickly."

I have to tear myself away. I see people who know me. They will wonder who that little lady is with Bob Bennett and the fat man in shorts.

"Oh, of course," they'll say, with a note of amused triumph, "of course, Brenda Bennett went home early. Ahha, yes!"

I hug her and kiss her, hold her close. She never has much natural body scent, but I breathe in the slight lavender perfume in her hair. The neat little woman in light blue jeans; the deep husky voice with a catch in it as she says goodbye; that vivid image I will carry on to the plane and beyond. It has to last a long time.

I shake Micky's hand. Jenny and I see each other full face. Her look is difficult to explain, anxious, eyebrows knit together. Then I am through the barrier, no looking back. I have made the break. When will I see her again? Will I be transferred from Calcutta?

Flying bores me, and Economy seats, designed for dwarfs, are uncomfortable. I try to think forward; my mind tends to look backward. I remember the words on my firm's calendar; "If your morals bore you they must be wrong." How can I equate this with my feelings? I can see no happy alternative to living two lives.

I don't want a divorce; neither does Brenda. I think it would be better for the children if we stayed together. It is all frustrating. If Brenda and I had to think of ourselves alone, then I suppose divorce would be the answer.

As the plane descends to Heathrow, I force my thoughts from India to England, immersed in the bustle of the present. At the barrier, Brenda points me out to Melanie and Jane. I manage to kiss and hug them while controlling the luggage trolley. I kiss Brenda on both cheeks.

"Have a good flight?"

"Fine thanks. How is everyone?"

"Everyone, everything is all right," she says. But after a pause - and I wonder if everything is all right - she says, "Oh Bob, I'm sorry to bother you straight away. Head Office phoned. They want to see you urgently. Here's a letter."

No peace, that's why it is better to escape by sea.

We walk to the car park. The kids have grown, especially Jane. They are both glowing with health, their fair hair shining in the sun.

Melanie wears a shirt with narrow vertical stripes, light and dark blue, red and yellow. Her skirt is light bluey- with elastic waist. Jane has a yellow tee shirt with a picture of a tiger on it, and blue cotton shorts. They wear the sandals that Brenda bought in the Calcutta market at Christmas. Their clothes are new, the old ones having faded in the Indian sun.

We go to the third level and Melanie remembers where the car is parked. Brenda drives away and I read the letter.

"No hiding place, Brenda. Big Brother is watching you. A man from Pakistan will be visiting HO on Monday. I must meet him."

Tony had warned me.

"I'll have to catch a train to Manchester on Monday morning."

"Here we go again," sighs Brenda.

"Oh well, Brenda, I have the weekend to get acclimatised and see my parents. I'll be back on Tuesday."

The children want to talk to me and I turn round to chat. The time here is the equivalent of eleven at night in Calcutta, but I haven't begun to feel tired.

"Nana has been teaching Jane," says Melanie. "Now sne can read."

"I know my times tables", says Jane, "up to ten times."

"Pampa and Nana took us to Morecambe," says Melanie.

"They took us to Morecambe," repeats Jane. There's lots to tell.

"Let Daddy rest. He's been flying for a long time."

At my parent's house on the outskirts of Wheatham village, I arrive to a happy reunion with my parents, plus barks and tail wags from the Lakeland Terriers. Flip remembers me, but Binkle was born while I was in India.

"Have you presents?" Melanie asks, and excitedly Jane yells,

"Presents, presents."

So I open a case and produce the puppets, and the wooden hens that peck when the weighted string is swung.

Quietly I say to Brenda, "I have Punjabi costumes for them."

Melanie is quick and senses I have something else.

"Want to see, Daddy. What have you got?"

They come crowding me.

"Oh dear", says Brenda, "they won't be satisfied until they try them on."

The clothing fits nice and loosely.

Granny says, "You are clever, Bob, to get the right sizes."

I think of Jenny.

After the children have shared the evening meal with us, they are quietened down and packed off to bed. I begin to feel tired, and at ten o'clock, the equivalent of early morning in Calcutta, I go to bed.

"It's too early for me, Bob," says Brenda.

We have single beds. I feel very sad that Brenda and I have lost interest in each other.

I find it difficult to sleep as thoughts chase around in my head and I feel as though I am still flying.

I rise late and breakfast alone. We go shopping. In the afternoon we sit in the garden while the children play.

Late next morning, Granny and Grandpa having gone to Church, I ask,

"Would you like a walk in the woods?"

"Yes, yes." They are enthusiastic.

"Ask Mummy if she wants to come."

Brenda speaks from the kitchen,

"I'm busy. Don't be late for lunch. Make them put their denims on. Take their wellies with them."

We cross the road into the lane.

"Janie", I ask, just to hear her answer, "which is Flip?"

"That's Flip," she says, pointing at the light-brown rough-haired little dog, slightly greying. "Flip mummy and Binkle her puppy."

The dogs unleashed, dash off into the wood.

"Did you make a snowman?"

"Gander make snowman," says Jane.

"We put coals for his eyes and a carrot for his nose", says Melanie, "and pebbles for his mouth."

"Gander put red scarf on snowman," says Jane.

"Let's go to the stream," says Melanie. They put on their wellies, walk along the water edge and show me the tiddlers in the pool.

"Come across the stream, Janie," says Melanie. She paddles through a shallow part and Jane follows. They cross without mishap, climb a mound on the other side and stand like conquerors. "You come too, Daddy."

So I take off my shoes and socks. I step on a flat stone but it turns so that I fall flat on my back with a splash. I'm soaked through. They think it's a great joke. The dogs splash and bark. The kids' laughter is a joyous sound, mingling with the babble of the stream. It is worth getting wet just to hear them.

"I think we'd better go home, so I can change my clothes. D'you think Mummy will be cross with me? Janie, I'm going to tell Mummy you pushed me in."

Janie understands the joke. She chortles, "Janie push Daddy in water."

Melanie clings to my arm, rests her head against me.

"Love you Daddy." I am happy; I'm getting to know them after the short separation. I must make the most of it, for I don't see much of them.

On Monday morning early, Dad drives me to Watford where I catch the Manchester train. "Thanks Dad. Pretty certain I'll be back tomorrow. I'll be driving down."

I board the train, settle for a few minutes, then make my way to the dining car. I can't resist BR's huge breakfast of bacon, eggs and mushrooms. My thoughts go back to that rattling old carriage in the Punjab. The upholstered seat in this coach is comfort supreme, but better I was bouncing on bedding roll with Jenny, in dust, heat and sweat.

I write to Jenny, describe this train, compare it with the one in the Punjab. I will take a photo of Melanie and Jane in their salvar qamiz for her. I'm surprised to see that I have filled the air letter. I send regards to Micky. I pray all is well. The letter is full of love.

23

After a warm greeting at Head Office, Pakistan comes into the conversation. I am introduced to the customer, one Ahmed Seth, who is glad to hear that I will be meeting him again in Karachi in November.
My director, Douglas, sees me afterwards and apologises that my leave will be curtailed by about a month.

"Of course", he says, "you can add it on to your next leave, or take short leave in India."

He says that I will remain based in Calcutta.

I sigh and say, "Thank God," in relief. Douglas lived in India for years and knows about family problems.

"Please fly to Karachi in the first week of November, Bob. You can return to Calcutta in December, then Brenda can join you for Christmas."

It is good of him to consider us.

"I'm sure that is the right decision business-wise, Douglas. We are busy in Calcutta."

Maybe Brenda will prefer to spend Christmas in England. Then I would have more time with Jenny. Instead of flying, perhaps Brenda would prefer to sail. The ship can be fun. I remember a burra memsahib, in that blasé high-pitched voice, proclaiming that, "There were such gorgeous men on the ship. Oh! I was enjoying myself so much, and then the children came and joined us and spoiled everything."

If she sails I'll have more time with Jenny.

The firm lend me a car and I pay running expenses. Next afternoon I motor back to Wheatham. I break the news to Brenda.

"Tony had warned me that I might be transferred to Pakistan."

"Oh Bob! Bloody hell!"

"It's all right, they've changed their ideas. I was very relieved when Douglas told me. I'll have to cut a month off my leave. I must go to Karachi early in November."

"How long for, Bob?"

"I'll be back in Calcutta for Christmas."

I put the three alternatives to her: sail or fly to India, or spend Christmas in England.

"I don't know; I'll have to think about it."

"You'll have to decide quickly; the ships get fully booked."

Just one night with my parents, then we pack the car boot and luggage rack, say goodbye. We stay two nights with Brenda's parents near Lancaster, then off again, north to the border.

I am enjoying the relaxation, the change, the rest from the harsh climate. Despite my love for my family, I can't get Jenny out of my mind. But this holiday in Scotland is a mere interlude and I will not dwell on it.

I drive all the way to Perth, stopping for breaks, but unrelieved by Brenda, who has enough to do keeping the children entertained. Fortunately they sleep for part of the way. We meet our friends, the Jamiesons, in Perth. We drive with them through the fishing villages of Fifeshire. I find time to write to Jenny. After a few days in Edinburgh we take the coast road to Eyemouth in Berwickshire. After three days there, we say goodbye to our friends who motor back to Edinburgh.

We return to Lancaster through the border country, staying two nights on the way at Keswick, exploring the Lake District. It is a happy time; Melanie and Jane enjoy themselves; that is the main thing. I leave Brenda and the kids with Nana and Papa, and motor south.

Mother is out and I am greeted by Dad.

"Bob, a fellow phoned from Delhi two days ago. I'm not sure of his name, think it was Banner Jay. Says he knows you well. Will be in London the day after tomorrow."

"Yes Dad, I know him well. Ajoy. I met him first in Manchester. He's an Indian, Cambridge man."

"I didn't detect any Indian accent."

"He has a flat in St John's Wood, Dad. I hope I can bring him here to meet you."

I can't wait two days to meet Ajoy, so I make an excuse to visit our London office and go straight to St John's Wood. Ajoy's cousin hands Jenny's letter to me.

"Yes, Ajoy is expecting tomorrow afternoon," he says.

"Please tell him I"ll phone him tomorrow evening, Sushil."

"Oh yes, OK, I will do," he says.

I go back to the car, open the air letter. Jenny writes:

"*Dearest Bob, Rec. your letter. I've looked at the map you gave me and I see where you have been. What a small place England is. It will fit in between Calcutta and Lucknow. I was very sad when you left and I am suffering now. Micky was good. He came to the restaurant and made some useful suggestions. We will have neon lights. I stayed the first night after you had flown, down there at his place so I could collect my things - I kept waking up thinking you were next to me but all I saw was a pillow then he brought me back home.*

I'm all right, Bob, but I miss you, words can't express it. I hope you are well. Rosie Stevens says I can move in on 30th June. You know Rosie's address I remember you put it in your diary. Anyway I'm keeping this Benatala room for an extra week, so I can move things without rushing.

Will close with all my love, yours for ever, Jenny.

It is a great relief to hear from her and I feel more at peace.

I phone Ajoy the next evening. He asks me to come to his place for lunch in two days' time. When I meet him he tells me he is selling the large house in Delhi, just keeping a small flat nearby. "I shall have to move the money I've kept for you, Bob."

I'm not sure what to do.

"Bob, I can get you sterling."

"How do you do that, Ajoy?"

"Leave it to me. Better you don't know too much. Via Nepal. But you will lose quite a hefty bit."

"Whatever you say, Ajoy. I'm very grateful."

"You see, Bob, the Government might change the configuration of the notes, then you would be stuck with the old useless ones. You would be in a panic to change them before the deadline."

"Yes, I see. How the hell would I change so many?" So that is arranged.

"Ajoy, I would like you to meet my family."

We arrange a day for Ajoy to visit Wheatham. It's a very successful meeting. Everyone, including the children, likes the man.

A week later we visit several boarding schools, looking for a suitable one for Melanie who will be nine years old next year. We choose one twenty miles from Wheatham. My parents will be thrilled to visit her.

"But not too often," says the headmistress. "It has an unsettling effect on some pupils."

Melanie is excited at the prospect of boarding school. Children play together in Calcutta and they see their friends leaving for schools in Britain. Most settle well, but some do not and mummy is then torn between child and husband, Britain or India. The children look forward to holidays in India, but not all parents can afford to bring them out more than once a year; it depends on the firm. The British High Commission and large firms can afford to be generous; others are not quite so lucky.

Brenda decides she will come by sea. The children will enjoy the voyage. So would I if I had the chance. The firm's Shipping department manage to reserve a suitable cabin on the Strathclyde. Early in November I shall fly to Karachi. Brenda and the kids will sail after I have left. Sometimes I wish planes hadn't been invented.

On arrival in Karachi I write to Jenny, saying I'll see her early in December. Jenny's reply is loving but short. She's relieved that I'm not going to be transferred to Karachi, but she knows we can't be together so often, because Brenda will be in Calcutta.

"I feel like I am an outsider now, Bob. In Shanagar I felt we were married."

24

I fly from Karachi early in December, sooner than expected. Brenda and the kids are due in Bombay in two weeks' time. After a night in Bombay they will make the thirty-eight hour train journey to Calcutta. Brenda will not enjoy the train journey. I don't envy her having the two kids in a small compartment for two nights and a day.

The Wrights had vacated our flat in midNovember, Our cook and sweeper are still there, so the Wrights must have been easy to work for. That first day I am so busy, going to the flat, in the office, then collecting my car, which won't start, that it isn't until evening that I can see Jenny.

I surprise her as I walk in. She is serving a customer and just stands there for a moment or two, dishes poised. Then she beckons me, walks into the kitchen and I follow. Work must come first. She washes her greasy hands, looks down at her apron to see if it is clean, then we hug and kiss. She is wearing a headscarf.

"Bob, I'm so busy. Rosie was going to relieve me but can't come, and Arthur has gone on an errand."

The dishes are piled by the sink.

"I'm going to do the washing up, Jenny."

"Oh Bob, don't bother, you don't do that sort of thing.

"Oh yes I do, I'm used to it; I'm an expert." I don an apron.

"I'll close at seven, Bob, earlier than usual, but I must get on now or the customers will grumble."

It takes me half an hour to catch up with the flow of dirty dishes through the hatch. It's nearly six o'clock when Jenny comes into the kitchen.

"I must dash down to the flat, Jenny. I expect to be back about seven."

I drive to the flat. I had told Bilbo to meet me there.

"Out tonight Bilbo. I will be back at eight o'clock tomorrow morning."

I have a shower, then dash away. Jenny lets out the last lingering customers by seven thirty. Arthur is left to clean and lock up the place.

"Where are we going to stay?"

"Arthur will sleep in the restaurant tonight. We'll use the upstairs room."

"Surely you don't stay here? I thought you'd left?"

"No Bob, I'm still at Rosie's place. I use this as a store, Arthur stays here."

We are back in the room where first we both knew we were in love. It is too cool to turn on the fan to keep mosquitoes away, and Jenny has a mesh screen across the window. She takes off her head scarf. She has cut off her lovely long hair. It is now collar length. I'm so sorry about this.

"I cut off my hair, Bob, because it was a nuisance when I was working.

"I'll miss it very much!"

From my bag I produce a pleated light-brown skirt and a light mauve cardigan. Delightedly she tries them on, parades for me.

"I've other clothes for you, too; I'll bring them later."

Then I bring out chocolates, two boxes and assorted bars. All these came from England and I kept them in a fridge in Karachi. Then I produce two huge tubes of Smarties.

"Have you seen these before, Jenny?"

I show her the multi-coloured button sweets that have chocolate centres. She tries one.

"They'll love them," she says. "Bob, you will be seeing me this weekend?"

"Of course I will."

"Then we will visit Sadie. You will find Diana and Lucy have grown. Diana has started school and Lucy will join soon."

On Saturday we visit Sadie and the kids. Harry arrived home a few days ago. His ship has docked and is loading. He has a family resemblance to Jenny, but is taller, wiry, not as dark as she is, and his thick, black hair is starting to grey. He looks a bit sly under his smile. Sadie is a little brown woman with a shiny, round face, hair pulled back in a bun. Diana is a bright little girl, thin, a small edition of Jenny, rather serious. Lucy is like her dumpy mother, more cheerful than Diana.

Jenny takes food out of a basket, sandwiches, an iced cake, and buns.

"This is uncle's treat for you."

Nice of her to say so; first I'd heard of it. Sadie busies herself laying the table.

Harry lies back in a chair and smokes a cheroot. Do I smell bhang? He thinks he has done work enough on the ship and is now home for complete rest. The kids stare at me, the stranger.

"I have something for you."

"Not too many now, Bob. It will spoil their meal."

I give them Smarties. They choose six each. As they pick them I make them name the colours. Jenny looks intently. I look up at her. She seems to be gazing right through me with a slight fond smile.

"What are you thinking about, Jenny?"

"It's nice to see you with the children, Bob; they like you."

"Cupboard love?"

"No, they like you."

She looks sad, turns away, gets up abruptly and goes to the table to help Sadie.

On Monday, I go to see Dr Rahman before work. I want to thank him for helping Jenny start the restaurant.

"Good morning Mr Bennett. It is indeed a long time since we met."

"Dr Rahman, I want to thank you for all you have done for Jenny." Thinking of the successful restaurant, I add, "I'm sorry I couldn't have been here to help."

"Always I look after the ladies, Mr Bennett, when they have enough sense to come to me."

"What d'you mean?"

"She was sensible and came to me early in the pregnancy." He sees that I'm shocked. "I'm sorry, Mr Bennett, I'm truly sorry. I thought you knew."

"No, doctor, no!"

"It was a boy, a little Bob Bennett." He smiles.

I can't say anything.

"Do not reproach yourself, Mr Bennett, do not reproach yourself. You are good to her. Some men don't care, they just disappear."

I feel really down. I just cannot go to the office yet. So I drive to the Swimming Club, sit in a corner, pretend to be reading notes. After half an hour I decide I'd better go to the office.

After work I go to her. She is busy cleaning up, so doesn't sense my tenseness. I help wash up. Upstairs she goes to the fridge to fetch a beer.

"I saw Dr Rahman early this morning. I had to thank him for helping you." She shuts the fridge door quietly. "Hadn't time to see you."

She puts the bottle and glasses on the table, says nothing. I take her hand.

"Sit down darling." She questions me with her eyes, brows knit together. She is about to speak, but I say, "Yes, I know darling. He told me. He thought I knew."

I put my arm round her. She nods, is silent. She rests her head on my shoulder.

"What else could I do?" she says.

"I don't know," I whisper. She draws away from me. I notice a tear; she looks away, pours out the beer.

"Oh Bob! What else could I do?"

"Dear Jenny." I have an overwhelming feeling of guilt.

"I had a dream. An old man with a beard called me and pointed to my baby playing in the gutter. I wouldn't want that to happen. If I can't have you then I don't want to be left with your child."

I feel quite dreadful, but she says, "I don't blame you."

"Perhaps not, Jenny, but I blame myself."

She comes back into my arms.

"I can't have children now. I made Dr Rahman see to that."

"Oh Jenny!"

"No, Bob, it's all right; I don't ever want another."

After a night of shared sorrow I have to leave her. The timing is quite dreadful, for Brenda and the kids will be here tomorrow.

25

Next morning I drive with Bilbo to Howrah. He guards the car while I go to the platform and collect three porters. As the train eases towards the buffers, we move along to where the air-conditioned coaches will draw up. I can see Jane jumping up and down and then wave. I was thinking of Jenny as I came to the station, but now in the hurly-burly, I switch thoughts to my family; emotional gymnastics. The hair of all three is bleached from the sea air and they have a clean, healthy look, complexion fresh and tanned, soon to be sallowed by the Bengal climate. I lift the kids up and kiss them. Brenda and I, the good friends, kiss cheeks as usual. There is a rush and a crush to get off the train.

We proceed to the car, porters with their head loads, children, memsahib sans solar topee, like a safari scene, great white hunter in the rear. We wend our way through the crowd. I drive away with the family and some luggage; Bilbo brings the rest in a taxi. We negotiate the mad scrum on Howrah bridge and North Strand Road, a traffic engineer's nightmare. I concentrate on driving until we reach the comparative peace of the road between Maidan and the river. Melanie and Jane chat excitedly.

"Daddy, look what we've got. She can walk and talk." I glance round quickly and they hold up a blonde doll.

"Daddy can't look while he is driving," says Brenda. "Wait until we get home."

"I'm looking forward to seeing your dollies," I say. "How was the journey, Brenda?"

"The voyage was superb, but I'm glad the train part is over. I've picked up a tummy bug since I left the ship, but they seem to be all right."

The cook and bearer welcome Brenda and the missie sahibs. We have a light lunch. At two o'clock our Nepali ayah arrives.

"Take them into the garden, Jetti," says Brenda. They go down in the lift. "I wonder how long they will last until the excitement wears off. I'm dead beat now Bob, I'm going to lie down."

"Then I'll leave you to snooze. I'll be back soon."

I go downstairs to the car. Jetti and two other ayahs are squatted down together gossiping. Melanie and Jane are busy with their friends who have broken up from school for the Christmas holiday.

I don't go to the office, but go straight to the restaurant. Jenny is sitting smoking a cigarette. "Hello," she is surprised. "Never expected to see you."

"You see, you can't get rid of me, but I've just popped in for a few minutes. I must go to the office." She gets me tea and we chat. Then two customers come in.

"I must go, darling. See you tomorrow, God willing," I say as I leave.

I drive to the office.

"Just reporting all present and correct, Tony."

He signals with his hand, "Good, see you later."

I look through the mail on my desk, open two or three that look important. I go into the main office and greet everyone after my six month's absence.

Tomorrow, office and family routine start, and with all that, the preparations for Christmas. I wish I could spend Christmas with Jenny. I'll see her on Christmas Day, I must.

On Christmas morning, Brenda is downstairs with friends, the kids are in the garden and I slip away. The Blue Room is closed for business, but open for Jenny's friends. Florrie greets me as I walk in. The radiogram plays Glenn Miller's String of Pearls. A smell of cooking comes from the kitchen.

"Jenny's upstairs, back in a minute," says Florrie.

Doreen I remember from the Sailors' Club; she is decorating a Christmas tree. A man sits nearby, tanned, smart in blue trousers and roll-necked pullover. Doreen goes and sits on his lap. "They've known each other a long time," says Florrie. "I think he's going to jump ship, settle in India with her."

"Has he found a job then?"

Florrie takes me aside and says quietly, "Plenty of cash, drug dealing."

She goes up to him and introduces us.

"Vince, this is Jenny's friend, Bob."

They stand up. He's over a foot taller than she is.

"Howdee Bob. Glad to know you. Have a drink."

"Vince is very good, Bob, he's brought things for the party," says Doreen.

Jenny comes in.

"Oh Bob, Bob! What a nice surprise." I can tell she has had a few; she is bright eyed. We kiss, she is very loving, doesn't care if people are there.

"We are having a party for the local children tomorrow."

What a pity Melanie and Jane can't come, but it just "wouldn't do". I have a box with me, which I had kept in the car boot, away from family questions.

"Here are presents for you, Jenny," I say quietly, and we go upstairs.

"Rosie is helping me, cooking at home. I'm cooking too."

"Happy Christmas," we both say. We kiss, she giggles, a bit tipsy, and I've had a few too. She flops on the bed. Naughty of me playing truant on Christmas morning. I can't stay long.

"Come now Bob, you have to go home. Don't get into trouble, and I must cook." She jumps up, "Something may be burning."

We go downstairs.

What a pity Melanie and Jane can't come to the poor kids' party.

26

It is 1962 and the pattern of the passing months has been much the same; home with the family; at the office; on tour; and with Jenny. Sometimes Jenny has taken time off, leaving Rosie in charge at the restaurant. I go on tour and we usually stay at the old fashioned hotel in Lucknow, with its beautiful garden, shading trees, and peace.

In August Brenda flies home with the kids. Melanie (9 years old) is taken to boarding school. It is unsettling for Jane to be taken from school in Calcutta. Mother teaches her and she loses no ground. The old fashioned teaching method pays off.

In December Brenda and the kids fly out. January Melanie flies home on her own. My parents take her to school. Brenda follows with Jane in May. December 1963 Brenda and the kids fly out. In January they fly home again.

June 1964 I fly home on leave. The firm tells me that my next contract will be shortened to two-and-a half years with four months leave.

In July Great Aunt Maggie dies, aged 96. She never married. I am a beneficiary and also an executor. She has left me her own house and also the one adjacent in the terrace. Brenda will be interested in busily modernising the houses.

27

In August, Jenny writes with very bad news. The police have closed the restaurant. There was a communal riot. Windows were smashed, and although no one was involved in the restaurant, the mob were outside and were about to enter. Fortunately the police arrived just in time.

The Police Commissioner decided that Benatala Street was not a fit place for a restaurant. In making his decision he did not overlook the activities of the ladies and their nocturnal visitors in the upstairs rooms. Perhaps if largesse had been substantial and prompt enough the closure might have been avoided. Jenny had asked Dr Rahman to intercede, but it was too late, or he didn't want to become involved. She tells me she is selling the contents of the restaurant, but then I don't hear from her again.

I have to call in Karachi and post a letter to her just before boarding the plane. I don't reach Calcutta until November and go by taxi direct to Benatala Street from the airport.

The windows of the restaurant are boarded up and the door padlocked. No one can say where Jenny is. I can't wait as I must go to the office where I am extremely busy. After work, Tony takes me to an important meeting. I just cannot get away. I have to attend a dinner with him.

Next day, I can't get away until lunch time. In the room outside her door, she is sitting on the sofa with a man, Filipino perhaps. She sees me coming, gets up quickly and goes into her room. I follow. She sits on the bed, face turned away.

"Jenny, what's happening?"

She shouts, "Leave me! He's my own flesh and blood."

I move towards her and I don't hear him come in behind me.

"Who the hell are you?" he says. "This is my woman."

I push past him and walk out. I feel beaten and my first reaction is fury.

"You bloody bitch!" I shout.

When I'm on the stairs he appears on the landing.

"No one calls my woman a bitch," he says.

I turn round and face him. He is of medium height and strongly built. He's a bit pale for a Filipino, but I don't know, they are such a mixed bunch.

I can do nothing. I can't start a fight. I feel in the wrong because I can offer her nothing. I go to the car; he doesn't follow me. I am horror-struck and feel as though I have been punched.

I drive away, but I'm too upset to go back home, so drive to Strand Road and park by the river. It is a terrible shock. Oh, why has this happened? She has lost the restaurant. Was she bored? Did she need money? How could she do this? I'm sure she loves me.

I want to be on my own, like a dying animal. I go to Joshua's where no one will care.

"Hello George. Give me a double whisky." I tell George my troubles. "Why George? Why has she done this?"

"I don't know, Bob. I hear the girls talking. One of them said Jenny is "real hooked" on you." He attends to a customer then comes back.

"Bob, this man can't be here long, he'll have to sail soon. Wait until he has gone, then go see her."

"Yes. May do."

"*The Adventurer* is in Kidderpore docks. He's probably on her," says George. "Thanks George." I go and sit on my own and mope.

George is right. I'll wait until the man has gone. If a revolver lay on the table in front of me, right now would I shoot myself? One second to pick it up, two seconds to pull the trigger. Or would I hesitate at that last moment? No, I wouldn't do it. Think of my family. It would be selfish. Oh damn the man. It's not jealousy; it's a feeling of powerlessness. I know that I could take her from him, but it would cause my mother grief, mystify the children, embitter Brenda, and the Major, my father, fine old soldier, would be ashamed of me.

Perhaps Jenny knew him long ago and he's come back. God knows! I must wait until the man has left, then go to see her. "Joy and woe are woven fine," comes to mind. Who the hell wrote it? Blake? Oh blast the whole set up.

"Another - George, please. George, can I leave the car here tonight?"

"Sure you can, Bob. Just tip the durwan."

Big Bella comes in.

"Bella, come and drink with me", and I add bitterly, "Jenny is busy."

"I know Bob."

"When is he leaving?"

"About another few days, I think, but can't be sure."

I get her a beer and I have another whisky. We shuffle around the floor to the music of a slow fox-trot. It helps me having someone to hold on to.

"Why is she with him, Bella?" I am a bit sloshed.

She slaps a great wet kiss on me.

"I wish I had you, Bob. I wouldn't mess around."

"Thanks Bella."

"I don't know what she's doing. They say he's a Filipino. Someone told him about her being Filipino too."

If Bella had wanted a customer this evening, then I have been wasting her time.

"Here's a present for you, Bella my dear."

I kiss her, embrace her, because I'm full of whisky. I roll up three ten-rupee notes and poke them down her cleavage. Then I stagger out to the main road and hail a taxi. The fresh air is making my head spin. And so home to the flat.

After five days of mixed feelings and misery, I walk down from the office. Arthur is standing by the car. Expressionless and deadpan, he says,

"She wants to see you."

"Get in. When did her friend go?"

"Yesterday morning."

"Has his ship sailed?"

"Yes, in the evening."

We are about to turn into Benatala Street when I stop. I hate the thought of going into that room where he has just been. I write a note:

"Dear Jenny, I don't want to come to your room; it reminds me of your "friend". I will be at Joshua's this evening at seven o'clock. I hope you will be there. I feel sick. Love Bob."

"Give it to her immediately." I give him two rupees.

I have to resist a desire to go to her. I sit in the car for a few minutes, then, with an effort of will, drive away.

I plough through the day's work, then drive to Joshua's.

"Evening George." I order a whisky.

George looks a bit grim.

"She came at five o'clock. She asked me to give you a note, but then she changed her mind."

"He's gone, George. He's sailed."

"I know Bob."

"How did she meet him?"

"He heard in the Sailors' Club there was a Filipino woman around, so he went to look for her."

"I can't believe it. She loves me."

"Sure she loves you."

"What the hell is she playing at?"

"Bob, I'm sorry. She says he'll take her to the States." He moves along the bar to serve a customer.

I go and sit alone. I feel numb. I go back to the bar.

"What the hell can I do?"

"Go and see her, Bob. Perhaps he'll change his mind. P'raps he won't come back."

"I'm going to see her now, George."

"Yeah, you do."

I drive away determined to go straight there, but I cool down, park on the racecourse road and think. If I stop her marrying, I can't afford to keep her. I wonder what he's like. How can I bear to stay in India if I lose her? If I go to see her now, God knows what I'll say. Better wait.

Next morning I go to her room. The door is pushed to, not closed. I feel like an interloper. There's no point in being angry.

"Come in." She is sitting on the sofa smoking. She doesn't look at me, makes no move. I sit beside her, but don't touch her.

"I got your message."

She doesn't answer. Silence. Then she turns to me.

I take her hand.

"He's asked you to marry him?" She nods, looks away. "Well?"

She pauses.

"Bob, what is there for me here?"

"Jenny, if I could take you away I would, you know that, don't you?" She nods.

I draw her closer, put my arm around her shoulders, kiss her gently on the cheek.

"I can't stand in your way, Jenny. What's he like?"

"He's a good man, not rough. Just a seaman."

"Not promoted?"

"Eyesight not good enough."

"You had my letters?"

"Yes." She hands me a note. "I was going to leave this for you."

I read: *"Dear Bob, The man you saw is Peter Brennan. He asked me to marry him. He will get a ship back from the States as soon as he can. We will go before the Registrar in Writers' Building. With love Jenny."*

I hold her in my arms.

"He wants me to find somewhere to live."

"You are at Rosie's still?"

"Yes, but he can't stay there."

"I'll help you find a place, if you want me to."

28

While I am on tour, Jenny finds a room in Burnside Road, and by the time I return she has moved in. It is on the ground floor; close by is a park. Burnside Road is in a residential area, no beggars or vendors with their pavement stalls are allowed here, and it is far enough away to deter any unwelcome scrounging visitors.

There are two rooms to the left of Jenny's, where an old couple live. Stairs on the right lead to two upper floors. Her room is about 12 feet square, she has bed, wardrobe and table, two chairs, one with wooden arms, and a stool. There is a smaller table covered with oil cloth where she cooks and a small stove by the side of it. To the left of her bed is the toilet room with a sink which serves also as a hand basin. The dressing table is against the outer wall between two windows which face a narrow passage. Behind the bed is a two-leaved door secured by a board screwed across it, separating her room from that of the old people. She has a radiogram and many records. Especially she likes Jim Reeves; poor Jim Reeves who was killed in an air crash.

The old girl next door, like her husband, is Anglo-Indian. She has, Jenny says, a "screw loose" but is harmless. She has a rough, greyish-white complexion, a big wart on her cheek with a hair growing from it. Her grey hair is tied in a bun on top. Outwardly surly, she is kind to Jenny, lets her use the fridge. Her husband is racked by a TB cough, and at each paroxysm she shouts in her gruff voice, "Die you bastard, die!"

Peter Brennan sailed back to Calcutta in January 1964. She met him at the docks and took him to their new place. He brought with him a lovely dress. He told Jenny it gave him a hell of a kick buying it. They were married while I was away on tour and I'm glad I was not in Calcutta. By the time I returned, he had sailed away again. A generous monthly allowance comes regularly to Jenny's bank account.

Peter sails to India every few months, at irregular intervals. When he leaves, she phones me.

29

Our firm must finish an important job by a given date. The penalty for late completion is severe, but there is a bonus for early completion. If we are late, Woodings, the factory manager and I, will be blamed.

"I think we are up shit creek," says Woody.

I'm sitting with Jenny.

"What's wrong, Bob?"

"Only work. I won't bore you."

"Tell me."

I tell her about the job at Gadavpur, near the Nepal border, about delays and thefts during transit by rail.

"You don't have the trucks escorted? Your firm must be crazy," she says. "I can arrange it for you."

I'm amazed; she really means it. I take her to see Woody. He has a girlfriend too, so he doesn't mind. He leaves home in the night to see her.

"Must see that the night shift is working," he says to Ilona, his wife. "They are lazy devils. I'll try not to wake you when I come back." Jenny has letter heads printed, "Bharat Escort Service".

"Escorts?" I say. "You could recruit the club girls. They would terrify the thieves and seduce the stationmaster."

There will be three trucks, so Jenny sends for Arthur and five of his friends. They have done escort work before. Two will sit in each truck, thus keeping off thieves. Financial incentives to the railway men will ensure that they don't leave the trucks immobile in a siding.

Woody sends Jenny to the office and she gets the order confirmed. She is not frightened of Tony, the burrah sahib.

"I've tamed more important ones than that," she tells me.

The materials arrive safely at site and Arthur sends Jenny a telegram. Next day, having travelled through the night, she arrives. Siddiqi, our supervisor, although a broadminded Muslim, is astonished to see this small woman who is clad in shirt and shorts. He is impressed when she recites from the Koran, speaks and writes Urdu.

Previous consignments have taken a month in transit; this lot has taken four and a half days. The job will be finished early. He and his men will be rewarded. Siddiqi orders a feast, a burrah khana.

Jenny organises one more job and that is enough for her.

"I did it only to help you, Bob, but the money's useful."

Woody decides to employ Arthur and friends direct. Jenny is a determined person. She says to her brothers when angry.

"You are useless. I am the one should have been born with the balls."

30

With no restaurant, and her visits to clubs limited, Jenny fights boredom and she welcomes my visits. She's married so I know I'm in the wrong, but I can't stop seeing her. When I go on tour she is alone for days, plays Rummy with friends. She's good at it and always beats me. At an Anglo-Indian club she plays Bingo. She visits the racecourse, where I hope she doesn't lose much.

When we make love, her bed creaks and the doubleleafed door is the only separation from the old folks' bedroom. We are sure they can hear us; they wouldn't care but it's embarrassing, so we put the mattress on the floor. Then in the afterglow of love we talk.

"Peter was born in Manila. His mother was Filipino. His grandfather came from Belfast."

"You said he lives in L A?"

"His grandfather married a Protestant Irish girl there. Peter's father brought his wife to L A from Manila."

"Is Peter in touch with his ex-wife?"

"I don't think so."

"Children?"

"Two sons, married. One in Houston, one in L A. The L A couple have a son and a daughter. His wife writes to me. Says she's looking forward to meeting me." She laughs, "Calls me "Mother"."

I wonder when I'll lose her. She sits up and lights a cigarette; smokes far too much. Time to stir. We shower, now in monsoon time with its heat and humidity we can't dry properly, remaining clammy under our cotton clothing.

While she makes tea, I think, can I ever really get to know her, coming and going as I do? Peter the sailor will never know her, except in the Biblical sense. His visits are brief and far between. What love is this?

"What d'you do when he's here?"

"Mostly stay in, play music, he drinks gin. Cinema, but not often. Oh yes, reminds me, has half share in a cinema in Manila."

"D'you ever go on his ship?"

"When we got married we were invited on board, but not many Masters allow us on."

"Doesn't he get fed up staying in one room all the time?"

"Hasn't yet. Has all he wants that he doesn't get on the ship. Doesn't dance. Drinks a lot, nice man, never violent, doesn't get drunk. He's funny, says he won't eat mutton because the shepherds get lonely. Made me laugh; argued the plural of "mouse" is "mouses". Hasn't much conversation or sense of humour, not our kind, anyway. If he stayed a long time, I'd be bored stiff."

Jenny gave him a book I lent her. She was surprised he read it, about heroic commanders of British ships in World War II. He referred to them as "Limeys".

"He asked me, "What happened to the Limey who came to see you?" I told him then that when I married him, you never came back."

When Peter gets notice that the ship will soon be sailing, he starts what he calls his "dryingout process". No more gin, only huge quantities of soft drinks and ice cream. He is always in good shape when it is time to sail. Then he and Jenny go to the dock gates by taxi and they say goodbye until the next time.

31

1966. Schools have broken up for the Christmas holiday and Melanie has flown out. Jenny is in Bombay with her husband. His ship won't becoming to Calcutta on this voyage.

Tony calls me into his office.

"HO have negotiated direct with the people in Delhi. Things have moved fast. They want us up there ready as quickly as possible."

"How long do you think I'll be there?"

"Sorry to spring it on you. It's not just a visit. They want you to open an office in Delhi."

The speed of development surprises me; I expected several long visits, but never thought I'd be told to open an office.

Tony continues, "I have to ask you if you are willing to move to Delhi permanently."

"I didn't expect this and..."

"Neither did I, Bob. Sorry about this; I'd rather have you here."

"Give me time to think. I'll tell you tomorrow."

In the evening I tell Brenda. "I'll have to move. I think you would like Delhi. Better climate. You don't feel so shut in there. Good social life, big diplomatic centre."

"I know I grumble about Calcutta, Bob, but I've got used to it. What if you say you won't go?"

"Probably, at the end of my contract, I'd be transferred back home and someone would take my place."

"Marvellous; back to London?"

"No, Brenda, it wouldn't be marvellous. A drop in seniority, less salary and the firm doesn't pay towards school fees."

"Oh!" She pauses to think.

"I'm supposed to dash up there immediately and find a place to live. Damn it, I'm going to delay it. I'm not going while Melanie is here with us. What a time to spring this on us, Christmas; and what's the point of bringing her out here if I won't see her?"

Ajoy isn't in Delhi at present so I can't ask him about accommodation.

I wake up at two o'clock and remember Barbara at Marsden's hotel. I'll ask her about the state of the property market.

Next morning I tell Tony I agree to the move.

"Find a place to live and work from home," he says. "Then find an office and expand your staff."

A letter arrives from Jenny:

"I hope you have a happy Christmas with the family. I miss you and wish we could spend it together. I won't be back as soon as I expected. Probably back in Cal. about second week of Jan. I'll let you know when I know. I'm writing this while he's out. All my love, Jenny."

I wonder if I'll be in Delhi when she comes home. I can leave a note for her.

I phone Barbara, "Barbara, this is Bob Bennett. I'm in Calcutta. I've been told to move to Delhi and open an office. It's urgent. Is it easy to find a flat there?"

"Bob, what a nice surprise hearing from you. Yes, there's always vacant property here." Then silence.

"Barbara?"

"Yes Bob. Just thought of something. Friends of ours are retiring in March, James and Mary Alderson. She's gone home in advance. I don't think he's got rid of the flat yet."

"Sounds interesting," I say, and it is arranged that I'll meet Alderson.

On 2nd January, I board the 6am plane, and during the flight, think of my future in Delhi. My territory will include Allahabad, Lucknow, Kanpur and Varanasi and I hope Jenny will meet me when I'm on business in those towns; and I'll make excuses to go to Calcutta.

She mustn't be bored, must find work; or she could take interest in the Orphans' Home. I hope that she doesn't go to the States. I'll have to be transferred back to England eventually. Better then if she joined her husband. But then I'd never again see her. I mustn't be selfish. She must do what's best for herself.

Maybe I'm more than a lover to Jenny. She said she was very sad when she lost her father. Soon afterwards her mother died. If only we could stay together. Her life is built on shifting sands; I could provide a solid foundation.

The hustle at Palam airport snaps me into the present and I switch to the job in hand. I am to meet Alderson at the Imperial hotel. As I arrive I see a man walk from his car who fits the description Barbara gave me, balding and with a Clark Gable moustache. Yes, it is Alderson and we make our introductions.

"Call me James. No point in going into the hotel."

He drives me to his ground floor flat, one of four in a block, two up, two down, with a small lawn in front.

James introduces the cook/bearer, Bocha Ram, a solemn bean-pole Hindu. One could imagine an evangelist with Bible under his arm.

"We call him just Ram," says James. "His wife helps him in the kitchen, and there's a part-time sweeper."

There is a large lounge, two large bedrooms with bathrooms attached, and a small one. I plan it out. Jane can use the small bedroom. One of the large ones will be my temporary office.

We agree terms, will sign up at the solicitor's office. Then we relax over a coffee. A little dog has been following us around, a smooth-haired miniature dachshund.

"Oh, this in Henry; do you like dogs?"

"Yes, we do. We have two in England."

"Then I'll bequeath him to you?"

"Yes, the children will be pleased."

As we walk to the car I say, "I'd like to give you a Letter of Intent."

"That would be excellent," he replies. So he too is keen to finalise.

We go to his office and I dictate a letter to his secretary and sign it.

"See you again very soon," he says.

In the evening I fly back to Calcutta.

I arrive home and the children come running from their bedroom. I am bombarded with questions.

"I'm sure you will like the flat, Brenda. Melanie", I say, "next time you come for the holidays, you will see Delhi." I am swamped with questions. "Jane, you will have a friend. He is called Henry."

"A cat?" asks Melanie.

"A dog?" asks Jane.

"It's a sausage dog, a little dachshund." They are thrilled. "He is six years old, very small, very friendly."

To Brenda, I say, "He's short-haired pedigree miniature, easy to keep clean."

To Melanie, "You will soon see Flip and Binkle, but we'll send you a photo of Henry."

Tony is surprised I've found a flat so quickly. I expect he wanted me to consult him first, then we'd have lost the opportunity while he dithered.

At lunchtime I go to Burnside Road. Nutty Auntie comes out, "Jenny gone away, Bobby."

"Happy New Year, Auntie."

"Yes happy," she wanders back inside. "Happy, happy."

Each day I go to see if she's arrived. A letter comes; she'll arrive by train. Next morning I meet her on the platform while Tulsi guards the car. She looks well and bright-eyed. I drive away. It doesn't seem an appropriate time to break the news while I'm driving through dense traffic.

"Have a good journey?" Yes, she did. "I hope you enjoyed Christmas." Yes, she did. She and Peter visited her cousins in Bombay. We're embarrassed with Tulsi sitting behind us. I drop him near the office, then drive down Strand Road.

"Where are you going, Bob?"

"I have to talk to you, darling." I park by the river. "I've bad news, Jenny." She says nothing. "I have to move to Delhi."

There's a pause. "Oh Bob, it had to happen sometime."

"I have to move in March." I look at her.

She smiles wistfully.

"So this is the end," she says.

"Oh no, Jenny, it isn't."

"You will come back here, Bob?"

"Could you doubt it? Also, I will be visiting Varanasi, Allahabad and other places nearer here. You'll meet me, won't you?"

"Yes Bob."

"Also I'll find reasons to come to Calcutta."

"You will come Bob?"

"Of course I will, Jenny."

"I'm used to saying goodbye, Bob. Many times. I say goodbye to Peter and I don't care if he goes, but with you it is different."

"It is not the end, Jenny."

We drive back to Burnside Road. The room is cool and she shudders.

"I feel cold, Bob, after Bombay." I switch on the electric fire. I put my arms around her. I should go to the office but to hell with it.

"You'll soon be warm." I take off my shoes, she kicks off hers. I lift her up and put her on the bed. I don't care if the springs make a noise and they hear us next door. We make love frantically. We lie there in each other's arms. Then I look at my watch.

"I'll come tomorrow, darling, but I must be with Melanie. She goes back to England in a few days' time."

The next few days flash by and it is time for Melanie to fly home.

This is an unnatural life. A family is meant to stay together as a unit, and yet the history of our islands has been one of dispersion all over the globe.

Will ye no come back again,
Better loved you canna be...

The heartbreak of the old days, for he would no be comin' back.

I feel deep emotion as we say goodbye and as I kiss dear Melanie, it hurts. My parents will meet her, take her home, then to school. Jane will join her in September. Then both will be away from me.

Brenda will be in England. Then I'm alone except for Jenny. The children gone, these dear ones, they are only lent to us, "a certain sorrow, an uncertain joy", so it is said. I hope we have done our best for them and that they will grow up not blaming us.

I take Brenda and Jane back to the flat. Then I take Jane to her school. Brenda stays at home. Then I go to Jenny.

"Jenny, we've just taken Melanie to the airport."

"When will you see her again, Bob?"

"She'll come to Delhi for the summer holidays."

"It's a strange life you people lead. You come to India and your home is England."

"My home is there, but my love is here."

A few days later, I fly to Delhi again. James Alderson and I visit a solicitor, sign over the flat. The official take-over date is 1st March. I fly back to Calcutta the same evening. Brenda has started to pack. Jane is excited; I doubt if she concentrates at school. I'm very busy at home and in the office. I go to see Jenny whenever I can.

32

I had seen Donald occasionally but not in the last few weeks. I hear that he is desperately ill in the Nursing Home and immediately I visit him. A fleck of blood runs from the corner of his mouth as he speaks.

"Doctor McCrae says he will fly home with me for treatment. I said to him, "Yes, I'll take the high road and you'll take the low road." Yes Bob, that's the way it is."

I don't think he'll make it to the UK.

Two days after seeing Donald, I have to visit Asansol, 140 miles along the Grand Trunk Road. In the early morning I drive there with Jenny. We stay for two nights.

Back in Calcutta I go to the Nursing Home, but Donald has died while I've been away. He had been cremated: no time is ever wasted in this climate. Too much gin, carelessness with his diet, had produced cirrhosis of the liver.

His death affects me more than I had thought possible. It was he who had introduced me to Jenny in Joshua's Bar. His intuition had prompted him to say to me, "This is the first time you have really fallen in love." He was fond of me. If he had been a woman, perhaps I would have responded; who knows! Poor Donald. He was too young to die. Sad business.

I wonder what would have happened to Jenny if Donald had not introduced us; would it have been better for us if we had never met? Perhaps without me she could have come to disaster; late nights, poor diet, drinking and smoking pot.

The time comes when I have to say goodbye to Jenny. Next day I leave for Delhi.

"Bob", she says, "I'm beginning to wonder if I should have married Peter."

"He'll give you security."

"He bores me. I don't know what it would be like in the States, just imagine, being with him all the time."

Tomorrow evening, Brenda, Jane and I fly to Delhi. I must leave Jenny, a bitter-sweet parting.

"Jenny, I will call tomorrow."

"No Bob, you could come only for a few minutes. No Bob, don't come." I take her in my arms.

"I'm going to tell Sadie to keep Diana out of school tomorrow. I'll take her to the zoo. I don't want to stay in."

"Darling, the morning after I reach Delhi, I'll write, and I'll see you again soon."

I go to the car. She stands in the porchway. She has a lopsided smile, a frown. I start the car. When I look up she has gone.

After lunch the next day, I drive to the office to collect a few papers and to say goodbye. On the way back I go to Burnside Road. I know she won't be there, but I leave a note:

"My darling, I hope you and Diana have had a happy day. This is just to let you know that you are always in my thoughts. I will write to you tomorrow my love. See you again soon."

33

The truck carrying our belongings is on its way to Delhi. We shall be anxious until everything is checked.

The plane takes off in darkness. Brenda leaves friends behind her, and a luxury flat she has become attached to. Jane is excited in going to a new place, and she wants to meet Henry. I leave Calcutta with a severe home-sickness for a little room in Burnside Road. There is challenge in Delhi; a new flat to break in; new office to find; new staff to train; new contacts to make; new clubs; much to be done. Life is not dull but Jenny haunts me; at home and at work I'm always thinking of her.

As we walk from the plane at Palam airport, the crisp, dry air strikes us. It is much cooler than the enervating humidity of Calcutta. We take a taxi to Marsden's hotel, where we shall stay for two or three nights. Brenda and Barbara get on well; she will show Brenda where to shop, put her wise to prices.

The truck arrives two days later and we move into the flat. Ram, the bearer, is introduced to Brenda, and to Jane, "the Missie Sahib". Ram introduces Henry, the dachshund, to Jane. The little dog soon makes himself a member of the family. Jane is thrilled when we take him for a walk and she holds the lead.

"What do you think, Brenda?"

"Nice. Not as luxurious as the Calcutta flat, but more private. Good being on the ground floor with a garden and with a separate entrance. Yes, it's all right."

"You think you can settle here?"

"Yes, when I can get to know people. Will you be touring?"

"I won't tour yet."

"I don't want to be left alone."

"I will have to tour, but I'll delay as long as I can."

"I don't know anyone but Barbara."

"You will, but, first priority, we must find a school for Jane."

We are arranging furniture in the lounge.

"Hello!" A voice at the open front door. "Anyone at home?" A smiling man comes in, neat, greying beard, good head of hair, green poloneck sweater, corduroys. Clearly not dressed for work; I'd forgotten it's Saturday.

"Charles Evans," he says, and I introduce Brenda. "Joyce is out. We knew the Aldersons; we'll miss 'em. We live opposite. Welcome to Delhi. D'you know the place?"

I explain that I've been coming here for years, but that Delhi is new to Brenda.

Brenda is delighted, for this will be a social break-through.

Charles works in the High Commission, not a very senior job, so there's no need to be reserved or aloof.

We had decided in Calcutta office to ask Murthy, a south Indian of great linguistic ability, if he would like to move to Delhi. He's glad to do so and I'm expecting him there. When he's found somewhere to live, he will bring his wife and two small boys from Calcutta. He's my first recruit. I shall have to find other suitable staff locally.

A week later, when I am organised, and when Brenda feels that she can cope, I fly back to Calcutta. I have to collect my car. Tony offers me accommodation and I'm taken by surprise. I make a hurried excuse. I tell him I'm going to a party that will go on until the early hours, and that I don't want to disturb him and Thora.

It is true that I'm going to a party; I shall be staying the night with her. I had sent a telegram to Jenny, so she's waiting for me. It's as if we'd been apart for months, not just a few days; it's a joyous homecoming.

"It gives me a kick, you coming back. When Peter comes off his ship, I don't feel anything like this."

"I can only stay two nights, dear. I'm driving the car back. I'll do the 850 miles in two days."

We go to an out-of-the-way place which serves good curries, east of Circular Road. We see two large fat men sitting there: Tweedle-dum and Tweedle-dee. One is an Englishman with a red chubby face and the other Australian, the same shape as his friend, but his face is tanned.

"Hullo mate, what're you doing here?" says the Englishman.

I tell him I'm lying low, so that I won't be asked to a party, but he thinks it is because I have Jenny with me.

"You should bring her in a burka," says Oz, and roars with laughter at his own joke.

We sit with them for a time.

Oz says, "I come from Queensland." He pronounces it something like "Quainslend" and has me practice saying it. "One and a half million people in an area two-thirds of Europe, and half of them live in Brisbane. Plenty of room for you and Jenny. Come and join us."

Oz and friend leave. Jenny and I eat. Then we dance to the radiogram. Dancing close makes us amorous, so we go home early.

Next evening, I have the promised drink with Tony and Thora, but she has arranged a light supper, so it isn't until nine o'clock that I manage to leave. Jenny is upset that I'm late.

"It's the thought that you're going that gets to me."

In the morning, I wake as she is kissing my cheek.

"Jenny, I'll be very busy settling in Delhi, but I'll come again as soon as I can."

"My life is made up of goodbyes, Bob."

"Au revoir, not goodbye. Try to get a job, won't you? Maybe part time."

"Tuition for little children, maybe." We kiss.

The same as last time, she comes to the porchway and, as I start the car, she waves, blows a kiss, disappears inside.

Tulsi is waiting for me by the office. It is eleven o'clock when I start for Varanasi, 430 miles away, half way to Delhi. As I leave the outskirts of Calcutta, my thoughts begin to wander back to Jenny.

A lorry comes towards me, hugging the centre of the road. Tulsi's gasp alerts me; he grabs towards the steering wheel and I come out of my daydream with a shock, swerving away.

In the evening I reach Varanasi and next day drive with hardly a stop to Delhi. I pay off Tulsi and give him a good reference. This chitti being more valuable to him than money. I give him his rail fare, bhata, his living allowance on the way, and a bit extra.

I've made the break from Calcutta, except for one tie that I will never be cutting.

34

Two weeks after my move to Delhi, Peter Brennan's ship docks. He tells Jenny he wants a bigger place. After he has sailed she finds a flat in Mohan Road, east Calcutta, not such a select neighbourhood as Burnside Road, but adequate. It is on the second floor, which to Peter is the third.

A month later business takes me to Calcutta and I see the place. Access is along a narrow passage with a wall opposite, private and secure.

There are two fair-sized rooms. One holds the double bed, armchairs, table and radiogram, the other a single bed, table, chair, storage shelves and cabinet for ornaments. In the bathroom there is a bathtub and shower above it, but bath water has to be heated on the stove. I may buy Jenny a geyser. The kitchen is well fitted, with sink, draining board, fridge and large shelves for cooking vessels. Diana is staying with Jenny and will soon be boarding at the Convent School.

It is May and very hot. I'm lying on the bed clad only in underpants. The fan beats down. Diana, her hand touching the wall to balance herself, walks up and down my back with bare feet, kneading with her heels, and her light weight drives the air out of my lungs. It is a delightful form of massage. After she has tired of this, Diana goes into the kitchen to help her auntie.

I can relax. Business goes well in Delhi. I have found a small office and taken on two Delhi men. We are busy but I see Jenny whenever I can.

The years go by and I miss seeing Melanie and Jane as they grow up. It is only when I'm on leave, that is twice in five years, and when they fly to India once or twice a year, that I'm with them. Of course they get to know mother better than father, but I am never a stranger to them. We get on well. In England, Brenda has comfort, the house, the children she can visit at the nearby school, the little car to make her mobile -and the man of many years friendship.

Jenny's cough worries me.
"Bob, I've smoked for years, never had a cough like this before. The bloody thing won't go away."
"What does the doctor say?"
"Says it's bronchitis. Gives me cough mixture and vitamin pills."

35

A month later I ask Jenny to meet me in Varanasi, which is about half-way between Delhi and Calcutta.

She writes: *"Dear Bob, I can't come to meet you. I'm too ill. Rosie says I should have an X-ray. The doctor only tells me to take cough mixture. I think he's an idiot. Perhaps one of your good doctors can help me. Arthur goes to the chemist for me. I feel so ill I can't make any effort. I hope you will come to see me. All my love Jenny.* Her writing is shaky. Obviously she's very ill.

I take the next morning's plane and I'm at Jenny's door at nine o'clock. Arthur comes to the door. Jenny is lying on the bed. I'm frightened by her appearance, her face has a shallow pallor, a deathly luminosity. Why on earth hasn't Rosie taken her to hospital or done something? It's bloody well beyond me.

"Darling, you're coming to my doctor straight away." I kiss her tenderly. She is wearing a low cut nightie which hangs from her. Her clavicle bones protrude rod-like. She is very thin. She coughs; it is a dreadful hound-like bark. I hold her to me.

"Oh Bob", she whispers hoarsely, "when I cough I feel I'm being torn apart."

We go to see Dr Mukherjee. I know he will be sympathetic. He helps those unable to afford standard fees.

"Jenny, my dear", he says, "you don't have a body, you have a structure."

Her shoulder blades stand out like wings, a walking skeleton. He tells her she has TB and that she must have her chest X-rayed.

"I can cure you, but a lot depends on you."

Then he writes a long prescription.

"Take this to Gooptu's Medical Stores. There are many pills that you must take at various intervals. You MUST NOT miss taking them, never, ever, not even one."

Turning to me, "Mr Bennett, you must help her fight and she will win."

Then to Jenny again, "You must have injections every three days. My assistant, the Compounder, will visit you."

He calls his receptionist. " Nurse, take Jenny with you and ring the X-ray department."

He writes a note and hands it to the lady. The nurse helps Jenny out.

"Mr Bennett, can you find someone to stay with her all the time? She must rest, no housework. Complete rest. These many injections will be painful as she is so thin. You must give her courage."

We take a taxi the few yards to the X-ray department of the Nursing Home.

"I'm very frightened, Bob. The nurse says that if I don't do what I am told, I will die."

"She says this to make sure that you obey the doctor's instructions. It is not as bad as all that, darling." There is no point in alarming her. I feel inspired to believe that I will help her to pull through.

After the X-rays have been taken, we go to Gooptu's Medical Stores, that reputable chemist near the big central market. Jenny is given the first instalment of 1,300 assorted pills, with instructions when to take the three different kinds.

Then we go to the analyst, Dr Dwivedi. Many are the stool tests and urine samples sent to him by the expatriates of Calcutta. I carry her up a flight of wooden stairs. She is so very light, poor Jenny. The doctor has to take blood. She cries, not with pain, but with exhaustion, and with the relief of being cared for.

"You'll be all right, my darling."

I take her home.

"You must not worry about anything. Rest and relax. Leave everything to me."

Sadie finds a poor Christian, Anjuli is her name, a widow who lives under a staircase. She will stay all the time with Jenny. Arthur will do the shopping, go to the chemist, while Anjuli remains with Jenny, never leaving her.

The doctor's assistant, the Compounder, comes every three days to give Jenny her injections. She dreads his visits, for the needle hurts. He suggests that he injects her in four places in rotation; first the left buttock, then the right, and then left and right arm. She finds she cannot lie down properly when injected in the buttocks, so he concentrates on her arms only.

By the grace of God I find business reasons to stay nine days and nights. I sleep in Jenny's bed. I had never been a religious person, but I feel strength flooding into me from an outside source. I am inspired by a holy confidence. Strength pours into me and I pass the power to my beloved. I am certain that she will recover.

At the end of the nine days I have to return to Delhi. I have to attend an important meeting, which cannot be dodged.

"I feel stronger Bob. I feel that I will get well." Her vacant eyes are looking; they are losing their blank dullness that had reminded me of a dying puppy, eyes wide open, nonseeing. Her hair that had lain matt, without lustre, is beginning to come to life, the lankness is going, the natural slight waviness returning. There is the semblance of a smile. Her body, called just a structure by the good doctor, is filling out again. The cough has eased. At last she can rest, for she has left the valley of the shadow.

I get up very early to catch the Delhi plane.

"I will come here again as soon as I can, Jenny. Rosie will visit you. I have told Arthur and Anjuli what to do. I haven't given him much cash. There's more in the box under your bedside table. Please write, just a short note, when you feel you can."

"Thank you dear. I have everything I need except you."

Weeks later, I take her to the old hotel in Lucknow, with its peaceful garden, for a complete rest. I manage to concentrate my work into the Lucknow and Kanpur areas, so that I can be with her.

Her illness has left her with chronic bronchitis, which keeps flaring up and she must take care to avoid a chill. She is never the same vivacious self for she has aged. No streaks of grey in her hair, but her face is thinner, her expression resigned, she seems to sag. She drinks very little alcohol, but against doctor's orders has started to smoke again; she won't stop.

36

1970: A year later, and I am transferred to London Office. I am fortunate not to be one of those who are made redundant, but the fear of unemployment is with me.

Jenny and I have parted with sorrow.

She writes, *"I cannot explain how I have suffered, just as if you were part of me taken away."* I think of her every hour. As I walk down the street I find myself looking for her. More than once I imagine I have seen her, go up to somebody, then realise my mistake. I find myself crying in bed, in self-pity.

1975: We write back and forth, trying to keep this hopeless love alive. While I continue to write regularly, her letters arrive at longer intervals, until she does not write again. We have been parted for five years. I have found it impossible to visit her for I am too busy. Time in England doesn't seem to be the same as in India; there is none to spare; nor is money so plentiful. Timing a visit is another problem. Would her husband be there? Perhaps he's found out about us. Perhaps she wants to forget me. Many years are to pass before the truth is revealed to me.

1978: Three years pass by and the hope dims, leading me to believe that Jenny, my love, has gone for ever. Then, when I had consigned her to fond memory, a letter arrives. It is addressed in handwriting unknown to me.

"Dear Uncle, I hope you are in good health. You remember me as a school girl. Now I am working. I have bad news, Uncle. Aunty Jenny's husband has deserted her. She wrote many times but he hasn't replied. She is in bad state as he has stopped the allowance to her bank.
Uncle, I am working for one of the best firms here in Calcutta, but what with helping my sister and all sorts of expenses, I can't do much for Aunty. She lives in a nice flat, but she has rent arrears and she is desperate. I wonder if you can help her? I am sorry to bother you. I am grateful to you and always will be, for helping with my good education, or else where would I be now?
Hoping to hear from you, with love, Diana."

I was settling down in England but now all is stirred up again. Much of the money that Ajoy had wangled out of India for me is appreciating, invested here in England. I write to ask for Jenny's account details, then remit a generous amount.

Jenny writes: *"Words cannot express my gratitude to you, I thought I would find myself in the House for Destitutes."* And she continues, *"That hobo sailor has let me down, yet only a short time ago he said he was arranging to move me to the States. His daughter-in-law wrote to me saying that I would be welcome. After a long gap he wrote to say that his ship would be coming soon and that he would cable me, but he didn't. He never wrote again. Then he stopped my money. I am doing tuition work for little children, but it doesn't pay much.*

"So, Bob, you have helped me again. You saved my life. My friends were amazed that an Englishman would stay with me when I had TB."

I write to tell Jenny how to use the money I sent and write in capitals, "YOU MUST NOT SPEND THE CAPITAL. YOU MUST INVEST IT AND LIVE ON THE INTEREST."

Jenny asked Diana, who took advice from her manager, and Jenny writes to say that she has invested the money in bonds which pay ten or twelve per cent. I sent cash enough for her to pay her living expenses until the six-monthly interest would start to come through.

Diana is now a young lady of twentyone years. I wonder what she is like. And Jenny has reached her halfcentury. How is she carrying her years?

37

Now I will piece together my story from Jenny's letters: I live on her letters: Jenny's brother, Harry, died. He had been a ship's cook, mostly on Indian coastal voyages, but occasionally he had visited the Gulf. Sadie came to Jenny with the news. He had been taken to hospital at Kandla Port, north of Bombay, with terrible pains in his head. He died before Sadie could see him. Jenny thinks he drank himself to death. He had been her favourite brother. She shared Sadie's grief. The only consolation is that she receives a pension.

Jenny writes that she has sorted out her most pressing financial worries except for the rent. She struggles to pay it. We work out that she will have to leave her beloved flat and move to a cheaper place. She had two working girls staying with her, but then they wanted their boyfriends to stay with them at weekends, so Jenny got rid of them.

After that Mr Perry's widow, who is one quarter English, and her two grown daughters, came to stay. Mrs Perry shared the rent with Jenny. Mr Perry had been one of the few British to marry locally and to stay on after retirement.

Then Jenny heard from relatives in Orissa State. She should visit them, for there is a chance of work in a school. She decides to go and see.

Rampul, in Orissa State, is twelve hours from Calcutta by train and bus. How can I see her now? There is no hotel worthy of the name in Rampul; there would be no privacy.

My life is changing. The centre of my emotions is shifting to a point nearer to England than to India. I will always have a deep affection for Jenny, based on happy memories. She has been everything to me and I will never desert her. She is still my love, however distant. There can be no one but Jenny; I never look for anyone else.

So Jenny travels to Rampul. The governors of the school have difficulty in finding teachers. They become bored in this uninteresting backward town, with only one cinema which never shows foreign films. She writes: *"I had an interview and I am going to teach the Kindergarten class. I have no qualifications and no references, but they need teachers badly. They don't pay much but I hope to get private tuition. They've given me a furnished room which is comfortable. I will be sending my share of the rent of the flat to Mrs Perry every month."*

What a transformation has come over Jenny, the bar girl, since we met! Now she is a teacher and I am proud of her. But I hope she won't become bored. She has a radio but no television and the town is just an overgrown village.

Jenny writes: *"I visit Calcutta when I have time off, to see that the flat is being looked after properly. The school periods are from 8am to 1pm. It is darned hot in the afternoon, so I have to do my shopping and cleaning in the early morning. I get up at 5am and do all my housework and cook. After school I have lunch, rest until 3pm and have a cup of tea. At 3.45 I go to give private tuition for an hour or more.*

When I took over, the Kindergarten class had no teacher of its own, so five teachers were coming from other classes. Not surprisingly the children were in bad shape, but after I worked hard on them, they improved. I prepared them for the final exams and I am glad to say that 22 out of 23 passed. Teaching is hard work, but you get good results with discipline."

In another of her many letters, Jenny writes: *"The school has an Oriya teacher with "BA Pass" qualification. She sits with me and learns how I work. So much for a degree! She helps to write out homework for the kids."*

Jenny cannot get on with the headmistress who lives next door to her, and on the other side lives the headmistress's married daughter. Jenny says "They breathe down my neck".

She stays for two terms but then can stand it no longer.

"They put pressure on me to run errands for them and enjoyed bullying me. One thing will show you what it was like, this is just one thing among many. I asked their servant not to chain their dog near my window, which opened on to the verandah. He made urine and the stink went through my window. I have handed in my resignation. The governors want me to stay but I've had enough."

Unfortunately Jenny's temper was her weakness, for tact and patience might have straightened things out.

The next letter was written in Calcutta: *"The bus journey from Rampul to the main railway line takes three or four hours. Then I got a place on the Puri Express, with a bribe of course. I left Cuttack at 8.30pm and reached Howrah at 5.30 next morning. Diana sent Arthur to help me. I had two suitcases, a bedding roll, two big travelling bags, utensils, stove, bucket and table fan. So my time in Orissa has come to an end."*

I am upset that Jenny has left the teaching post. I wonder what will happen now.

38

I have lost my job. The firm calls it "slimming down" when their employees are made redundant. I have found another job by not aiming too high, but the pension I take with me is most disappointing.

I can't expect much at my age, but the small firm I join welcomes my experience. By chance a visit to Dacca is necessary and I'm chosen to go.

Jenny had arrived from Orissa three days earlier, very fortunate or I'd have missed her. She asked Mrs Perry and her daughters to move out of the flat to give us privacy. Alas, I could steal only Friday of the firm's time and add on the weekend, flying back to Dacca on the Monday.

The love was still there, but not the passion. She had aged more quickly than I, but her hair had not greyed. One front tooth was missing.

She was wearing a cheap unbleached cotton sari, the sort that the poor wear. "It's more economical, Bob".

It upsets me to see her like this. She has let her hair grow long again, combed but unstyled. She senses how I feel, when I suggest we go out somewhere. She tells me she will dress up.

In the evening she changed into a plain pink frock, put up her hair, and we went to a restaurant and danced. There was warmth and happiness, and much to discuss. She is looking for tuition work with very young children.

I'm sorry I missed Diana who was staying with friends outside Calcutta, with her little girl, Munisha. Diana is often left on her own by her husband who has to travel away from Calcutta in his railway security job.

When I leave Jenny it is heart rending. Perhaps it would have been better if I hadn't come. She comes to the airport with me and I wave goodbye to my love as I board the Fokker Friendship and fly back to Dacca.

A few days later and I am on the way to England. I think of Jenny in her flat, and wonder for how long she will be able to stay there. If she moved to cheaper accommodation, she would be able to live simply, but comfortably. What more can I do for her? I drift in and out of sleep, aware of the airline's music in my headphones.

I have no reason to grumble about my life in England, but it is with Jenny that I have spent the most rapturous days. Now, as we age, it is a great affection that unites us. We shall be adoring friends until the end of our days.

Back in England, emotion swings from India, and a shock comes a week later. My father, walking in the garden, suddenly falls: mother finds him on the lawn minutes later. He was eightyeight years old.

At the funeral I try to hold back tears but they flood uncontrollably. I have a strange mixture of emotions, for at the same time I think of Jenny; tears are for her, too.

Mother is dry-eyed during the service, sitting erect and dignified. It is only afterwards, when the parson asked her if she would like to go into the Garden of Remembrance, that she shook her bowed head, tears falling, silent with my arm around her.

Melanie came from Edinburgh for the funeral. She had moved to Scotland with her AngloScot husband. They have a boy and a girl. Jane, single, works in a fashion house. She has a flat in Islington.

Mother, in her eighties, is happy that I am back in England after the many years I've spent away from home. She is moving into the house adjacent to ours and we are making a communicating door. This is the house Great Aunt Maggie left to me along with her own. The family house in Wheatham is being sold.

So I'm split in twain, but I realise with dismay that my love affair with Jenny is becoming a side issue. My family is the main theme of the symphony of my life, interspersed by the recurring refrain of Jenny and India, a haunting melody that will never go away.

Jenny and I write every month or five weeks. And so it goes on through the years, as Jenny's life unfolds to me.

39

It is August, and the monsoon will be in full swing. I remember the damp humidity, miserable, pouring with rain. It is hot water bottle time. More of them are sold now than in the cold dry season.

I haven't heard from Jenny for several weeks, but at last her letter arrives.

"I have been very ill. I could hardly stand as I had malaria. I was shivering and vomiting and had high fever. I can't understand how I came to get it. A week later I started to eat solids, and a week after that I began to feel better but I'm still groggy."

All her worries came flooding back. Her favourite brother had died; her husband gone; no more did she see me. Her marriage allowance came no more to the bank and her financial situation frightened her. I kept telling her she must find somewhere cheaper, and wondered why she didn't move.

Then she has a bit of luck. She writes, *"I have found a tenant, a boy of 24 from the Sudan who is here studying computers. He is a good boy, tidy, and he pays me well for a room. This is why I haven't moved."*

This is just delaying the move. I know that eventually she will have to leave her beloved flat. Who will look after her when she is really old? She is on her own, losing her charm as she ages. I pray for her well-being.

As a ghost I could be with her, could gesticulate, but she wouldn't see; could speak, but she wouldn't hear. At least I can communicate, even though parted by thousands of miles.

Has my meeting her all those years ago helped or hindered? I like to think that I have helped. Lord knows what would otherwise have happened to her.

40

Jenny teaches a girl of three years in the next building. It is October. I can remember Calcutta after the monsoon: the rains have gone; the beggar plays his bamboo pipe, the plaintive sound ringing out clearly in the drier air. The humidity's down; its less oppressive.

"*My tuition in the next building now includes a little boy. He has to be coached for his finals in November. He is weak in English Language, Social Studies and General Science. I have been ill again, and also I have sad news. Auntie Lulu died, aged 86. That is a good age, in this climate. I was too ill to attend the funeral.*"

I had met Auntie Lulu, who had lived in what was once a watchman's gatehouse, solidly built of stone. It measured only ten feet by eight but Auntie had lived here contentedly for many years. Once she had been moved to an old people's home, but discharged herself, wishing to be independent.

When I visited her in her little room she had said to me, "I am glad you are looking after Jenny. She has grieved me very much." Scornfully she added, "Earning her living lying on her back!"

Jenny is ill yet again. She writes: "*I was real bad and I believed that Auntie Lulu was calling for me. When I was fit enough I went to the hospital. I had a stomach X-ray, also chest examination, and blood and stool tests. There is a mistake on my hospital card. It shows that I am forty-nine, but I am fifty-three years old.*"

This is news to me. The year is 1978. I suppose, when she first met me, that she thought I would be more attracted if she took a few years off.

Letters flow between us. Jenny's friend Edna had married the seaman, Joseph, an old man, Filipino, who spoke broken English. He came and he went. Then there was an unexplained absence. Edna was not educated and didn't write to Joseph. His shipmates said he was dead. No cash had been arranged for her. Jenny helped Edna who was quite hopeless. After many visits to the US Consulate, and waiting a long time, she was granted a generous allowance. It was all thanks to Jenny.

Jenny writes; *"Edna got a bigger allowance because she had two daughters who were born while she was married to Joseph. Joseph was too old to have kids and both girls are from Danny Chater. Joseph kept him to look after Edna when he was at sea. When news of the allowance came through, Edna threw her arms around me. She cried with relief and thanked me again and again. She told me I would be welcome to go to live with her in Chandernagar, where she would be buying a house. Also she promised to give me Rs100 a month in gratitude .But Edna changed her mind. She had no more use for me. When I became ill again I asked for Edna's help. She sent Rs50 and a bottle of Horlicks. Then she sent a message to say that she would not be able to offer accommodation, telling me not to give up my flat. So after helping Edna and other people this is the ungrateful way I am treated."*

How lucky Edna had been, and how unfortunate Jenny was to be treated so badly and to be deserted penniless.

In her next letter Jenny writes that *"No sooner than I feel well, I am ill again. I have an internal pain. The doctor sent me to the Cancer Hospital in Bhowanipore. After a very painful examination I was told the result was negative and not to worry. I was given an assortment of medicines and pills. On my Outpatients' card the doctor wrote, "To attend Outpatients' Dept. in any State Hospital for further treatment."*

"I arrived at 8am at the hospital and finished at noon. Anything free means a long wait. Even though I had been told my first report proved negative, I was told to refer again to the Cancer Hospital. I was sick with worry and I couldn't sleep, but my worries turned to joy after this second examination. There was nothing to worry about as I had only a small cyst..

I was so grateful I prayed to the Holy Mother saying I will send Rs5 to her shrine in Bandel and go there several days in May as the whole month is dedicated to Her thanksgiving.

You must be wondering why I have not moved from the flat yet, after promising to do so. I hate to tell you this. A woman about twenty five years old has a man friend. Both are from the same firm, but he is married. They come here on Saturdays at about 2pm and leave at 4pm; then on Sunday, the same time. I receive them, and come back after they have gone.

I leave them alone, and since I have a Yale locking arrangement they just pull the door to and it's locked. She leaves Rs50 each visit under the clock. He is a big shot in the firm and does not want to stay in any of the hotels. Look what I have come to! The money covers my rent and electricity.

Talk about electricity! We are having power rationing. On Monday it was off for nearly seven hours - every day there is load-shedding two or three times. We never know when. They should have a fixed programme. It is now 10.45 and I am later than usual going to bed. We have had a power cut so I am writing with a lamp.

"More power cuts! This morning at 9am it went off until 2pm. At 8.20pm it was off again. It came on for a few minutes at 9.30pm then went off again.

"I have started and stopped this letter, but now I finish and post it tomorrow."

41

Jenny has received a letter from her landlord's lawyer saying that she had sub-let part of her flat to several people, and latterly to a Sudanese man. To sub-let contravenes the terms of the lease.

"I have no stomach for a legal fight", she wrote to me, *"so I have decided to leave the place. I have started to look around. As you know there are some awful bustees, shanty towns at their worst, out there are also some quite clean ones. In bustees often you pay for "Black" electricity, taken off any nearby line without the Electric Authority's permission."*

Two weeks later she wrote, *"I've found a place in Sealdah area. I've paid a lump sum of Rs3,000 for it. I borrowed the money from Rosie. After all the worry of hanging on to the flat, I feel a heavy load will be lifted off my back."*

Another letter followed. *"I moved yesterday at 4pm. I did it over a period of 3 days. The landlord was very helpful because he was so glad I was moving. Now he can put up the rent for the next tenant. He lent me his three-wheel Tempo truck and driver. I took the almirah, showcase and dressing table and the next day a bed and boxes. Everything else in the way of furniture, except two chairs, I sold. Finally I brought the tin trunks and the chairs. I brought the kitchen things by rickshaw. The landlord has let me off the last two weeks' rent."*

Two weeks later she wrote again: *"It will be comfortable here when I can get electricity. You know how hot it is at the end of April and the heat is driving me mad under this thin roof with no fan. I get some relief because some nights I spend at Rosie's place .I am not missing the old place except for the heat. The general toilets are clean and there is plenty of water. Best of all you are never lonely. Four of my old landlord's men lifted the furniture and placed it in the exact positions I wanted.*

I have pleaded with the factory owner nearby and I have taken a line for Rs90 per month. That is, for one fan, one light and a small night light. I had to buy 85 metres of wire, total with fitting charges was Rs127. I owe myself a lot of sleep and I am now making up for it."

Five months passed, and Jenny was without electricity again as someone was caught stealing from the line without paying the factory manager. He disconnected several people. She wrote : *"Thank heaven it is cool now, I don't need a fan. For light I have a kerosene lamp, also I cook on K. oil. I'm careful to keep kerosene in stock."*

This electricity problem went on and on. It was only because Diana knew the District Engineer that Jenny got a permanent supply, but she had waited a total of seventeen months.

42

Mother died. I was out shopping. Brenda heard a crash. She found Mother sprawled at the foot of the stairs with her head at an unnatural angle. The little telephone stool had fallen across one of her arms and the phone table was knocked over, the directories strewn on the floor.

Brenda explained it all vividly. It was assumed that Mother became giddy on the stairs, hit the corner of the stool with her temple as she fell. Brenda called 999 and the ambulance crew arrived promptly. I saw the ambulance as I came home and sensed the worst, for Mother was in her ninetieth year. She had been experiencing blackouts.

Melanie flew from Edinburgh. She and Jane stayed with us. The same as at Dad's death - I could not keep back the tears at the cremation service - but worse. Next day Melanie and Jane took me to the cinema. Their presence was a great comfort to me, but I don't remember the film at all.

I thought of Mother's tears at Dad's funeral, her great dignity. And now it was my turn, and I was head of the house, if that means anything these days. I remember her grief when William, my brother, was killed in the RAF; her sadness when I said I was going to India.

"You've hardly been with us, Bob. Boarding school, Army, now this. William gone. Now you leave us."

Then her apology for the outburst. Those wonderful picnics on the Downs. Building sandcastles with her, was it at St. Ives? Walks in the

woods at Wheatham and she scolding me for getting wet in the stream, where years later I took Melanie and Jane, and fell in the stream again.
All these memories flooded back. I had been blessed with good parents. The German quotation came to mind, "The death is nothing; the dying is the insidious invention." Thank God they had both died peaceably.
I went to my doctor unable to sleep.

"I am so sorry", he said, "it is grief reaction." He gave me a few sleeping pills. I was able to sleep soundly a week later.

I felt a little ashamed that I had recovered so quickly, but there was no lessening in the love and sense of loss. For years later when something interesting happened, I would say to myself, "Oh I must tell Mother!" Then I realised how much she meant to me.

Mother died in October. For a time my loss masked thoughts of Jenny. A yawning gap was left which could not be filled. If there had been no children with us, we might have felt differently at Christmas, but it is a festival for children; they were happy and cheered us up. Melanie, her husband and their two kids, Jane, Brenda and I, made it a happy party.

As I was dismembering the turkey, I was day-dreaming of India. Someone spoke to me; I didn't answer, Jenny was in my mind.

"Don't disturb him," said Melanie, "he's concentrating, hacking the poor thing to pieces."

Jenny sent me a Christmas card, a secret not shared.

"Letter follows," she wrote in it. The letter arrived rather late, on 10th January.

"I spent Christmas with Diana and Norman and the Sandakans," she wrote. *"We had pea pilau, chicken curry and salad for lunch. Duck roast and stuffing for dinner. I went to Mass first. After returning from Diana's place I exchanged greetings with my Christian neighbours.*
For New Year, Diana, Norman, Munisha, Lucy and her girl Anna, Diana's and Lucy's two brothers, John and Roger and three friends, all came to see me. It was nice to see them but they ate up all the fruit cake you sent in the parcel."

43

March: *"The third of this month is the Holy Festival for Hindus. It is Lent and we Catholics attend on Fridays. The Way of the Cross, Good Friday, is the last."*

May: *"It is our Holy Mother's month. I go every evening for devotions. Our Holy Mother has granted me a lot of favours - I got this place to live in - I prayed that a friend who had been childless for years would have a baby of her own, and this was answered. Through Our Lady my medical report was good and the Cancer Hospital found only a kind of cyst. The Hospital told me it was nothing and gave me tablets to dissolve it. So many favours I have received. One thing only I cannot have and that is you."*

August: *"I am going to Bandel church on 15th. Will spend the day in church, hear Mass, as it is the feast of the Assumption of Our Lady. I will take food, as there the meals in hotels are not good, for one thing the rice is very thick."*

September: *"I spoke to the priest of my parish and told him I got married by Registrar, but now I am living alone. He said I can come back and take part in the church in full. So I made my confession and since then I attend Mass and receive Communion. I thank God I have had my petitions answered. Rain has fallen for five days with hardly a break. My roof is leaking in five places and I've put down vessels and bowls to collect the water. It is a blessing that in this part of the town the floods go down fast and there is no waterlogging."*

The landlord did not help Jenny, so she put a new roof on at her own expense. *In this compound are two Anglo-Indian families, four Hindu families and the rest are Bengali Christians. One Hindu family opposite me have great sorrow; their girl of seventeen ran away. Two weeks later she wrote to her parents giving no forwarding address, saying she was married and very happy and they must drop charges against the boy, as if he were arrested she would commit suicide.*

We watch videos every Saturday. Each house gives Rs5. Two Hindi films to every one English. The balance of the video hire is given by Upen, liquor shop owner.

All are friendly here and the children love me. One Anglo-Indian girl, 12 years, always comes to me for help with her maths and English homework. The children are very helpful and do my shopping.

At 8pm every night I fill my water vessel for the next day. Morning and early evening filling times are difficult and there are small quarrels in the queue, so night filling is best.

If, as time goes by, I become weak with age or bad health, and unable to maintain this room, I will go into a home rather than be a burden on my relatives.

I have started giving tuition from 6pm to 8, in Canal Street, two boys in classes 1 & 2. The parents are good to me and give me tea, parathas and vegetables, with a sweet or curd, and that's enough for me, with my sparrow appetite. Then they give me a lift home in their car.

What I have earned I have spent on a pair of black shoes and materials for new dresses, the old ones fade and droop in the sun and damp. No good getting inferior cloth or leather as they don't last. Prices are high. Tailoring has gone up a lot. To stitch a pant costs Rs50-60. Gents' shoes are Rs120-300. Good material is from Rs25-30 a metre. Dhobis take Rs100 for 100 pieces large or small - sheets or handkerchiefs. I do all my own washing and I press with a coal iron.
How time rushes by! We are now getting ready for Christmas. It took me three days to mop, dust, wash the crockery, put clean covers on shelves, clean the oil stove, plus daily cooking and washing clothes. There are so many coal fires round here that everything gets dirty. I have painted the fan brown, as white is not good here because there is so much smoke from the coal fires. I was so tired I just rested yesterday.

I don't see many Europeans, you asked me if I did. I believe there are only a few, not like when you were here. Even for local people it is dangerous to be out late at night. It never used to be like this.

The Fancy Market (Black) store has been raided, so now no foreign things. I suppose it will be back when the authorities slacken off again. After all, they want black market goods themselves."

What a change for Jenny! Squalid surroundings; no piped water in her room; mud, smoke, electricity cuts, squabbles, shortages. Rationed rice has to be picked meticulously for little stones and gravel. All this, but once she had a chance to leave India. I wonder if she regrets staying on.

44 1985

I haven't seen Jenny for ages. I'll go to Calcutta in February, that is, in six weeks' time.

She writes: *"I can't wait to see you again. There is something I must tell you. I didn't want to tell you, but I must now. I'm sorry to tell you that Diana is not being kind to me. I don't know why she doesn't help me when I have been so good to her. She rarely sees me, even when she knows I have been ill. Still, we must visit her when you are here.*

I am excited that you will be here soon The weather will be nice then; it starts warming up in March after the Holi festival.

You will be surprised to see how much I have aged. I have lost most of my teeth, they fell out two or three at a time. I cannot walk fast or far without getting out of breath. When I look in the mirror I am sad, I am an old lady now."

So I fly to India. I have reserved a room in a Boarding House, south of Shakespeare Sarani (the old Theatre Road), where tourists often stay. I remember the place from years back, when young European bachelors from business firms stayed there, but since then it has been extended and modernised, with air-conditioning in all bedrooms.

The plane lands in the morning and Jenny is waiting at the airport. She had warned me that she had aged, but even so I am shocked and upset by her appearance. I am not prepared for what I see. It is not that she is wearing soiled clothing - of course not - she is as clean as always but she has neglected herself. Her hair hangs down without any styling. All its shine has gone; it is long as it was when first I met her, but still it has not greyed. She wears a plain sari and a dark blue cardigan. I put down my hand luggage and wrap my arms around her, while she, little lady, hugs me round my waist. She looks up and beams a smile at me. Her cheeks are sunken and I remember she said she had trouble with her teeth. I kiss her on the forehead. Then I hold her away from me.

We look at each other fondly. "Hello," I say rather inanely.

"Hello." she answers in a hoarse voice. I hug her again. We take a taxi to the Boarding House.

The Indian at the desk is hesitant.

"Yes, Mr Bennett, your room. Yes." Rudely he looks Jenny up and down. "Just one moment please," and he goes into the office behind. I hear talking.

Out comes a skinny, pale, bejewelled lady in a pale blue sari. I take an immediate dislike to her. She puts on a sickly smile.

"Good morning, Mr Bennett," she says, looking all the while at Jenny. "There has been some mistake. Rajan, silly man, has overbooked. He is off duty; I will reprimand him. Mr Bennett as a result we can offer you only a single room. I am sincerely sorry."

I am very angry.

"I wrote in plenty of time, madam." She reminds me of a vulture.

"I am truly very sorry, Mr Bennett, but that is the situation. I cannot remove guests from their rooms."

I decide to accept the room for now. Clearly the woman doesn't like the look of Jenny. I am most distressed to find that I can understand this, for Jenny looks unkempt. When I come down the proprietress has returned to the office.

We go to Jenny's place, along Circular Road, passing one of Mother Teresa's Homes, then cross the tram lines that run along the centre of the double-carriage way. We say little. I'm very upset at what has just happened at the Boarding House. I have my arm around her shoulders and we hold hands. The driver keeps looking at us through his mirror.

We enter a road half blocked by a small rubbish dump, dogs nosing through the junk for food and a little boy and an old, bent man searching for anything useful, be it rags, paper or tin cans.

Very little is wasted. We pass shops, stalls, thin light-brown pariah dogs with their washboard ribs. They wake from their naps and move away from the car wheels; half asleep. One yelps as its tail is touched. There are handcarts and people everywhere, goods for display in the narrow lanes, children scampering about.

The Sikh driver says, "This Muslim area, sir. Every family has a hundred children."

It is a warren, with street stalls narrowing the through way and we arrive eventually at railway lines. The rails are above the level of the road so that there is no level crossing. Vehicles cannot pass, but a mud road continues on the other side. Pedestrians cross at their peril.

To the left is a narrow passage, buildings on one side of it and a high wall, the railway boundary, on the right. The bustee area starts here. As bustees go, this is of a good standard. From the railway boundary wall to the roofs of the rooms, bamboos are fitted horizontally. These are used for drying clothes; or in hot weather, awnings can be fixed to provide shade.

We walk along this passage. Four side doors lead off the main passage into side areas open to the sky. On either side of each area are seven or eight rooms. The dark brown wooden door leading to Jenny's area has a wooden cross nailed to it.

"Most of us are Christian here," says Jenny.

Her room is third on the right. There is a blank wall at the end of this space marking the limit of the bustee landlord's property.

We come to Jenny's door. Two old Hindu ladies are talking close by, squatting in front of their room. They stare, for I am out of place here. Jenny opens the padlock and we go into her little room.

"I wonder what your neighbours will think of me?"

Jenny smiles, "I'll tell them you are from my church."

Jenny's door is on the left of the shorter wall of the room. To the right of it is a green wooden shutter.

"Look at my window," she says. It is rectangular hole in the wall, three feet by two, no glass. "I've fitted a tin shade outside to stop the rain splashing in. If the shutter is open, rain, wind and smoke come in. If I close it, I have to switch the light on, and it's stuffy."

To the right of the entrance is the cooking and washing area, a low brick wall separating it from the living area. One takes a step up to the main part of the room. In front of me is a table against the wall, and two chairs.

Jenny closes the door and comes to me. We are alone at last and we sink into each other's arms, no need to speak. There is a deep love, it will never die, but the spark has gone. I kiss her tenderly. Jenny half closes the shutter so no one can see in and switches on the light.

"Sit down, Bob, and I'll make tea. Are you hungry?" I had eaten on the plane. "I've made a cake."

I accept it. I don't want to disappoint her.

"That would be lovely." It is a plain cake, sliced across with jam inside.

I study the room while she lights the kerosene stove, fills the kettle from a bucket of water, using an enamel mug. There is no sink, no tap, only a stone slab and a drain hole in the floor. She takes a teapot from a shelf in a wooden framework against the far wall. Above is a larger shelf on brackets screwed to the wall where she keeps her large cooking pots and vessels. She takes her good cups, saucers and plates out of her glass-fronted showcase. The showcase is next to the low wall and contains her *bric-a-brac*.

I remember the brass ornaments and the Toby jug. There is an empty vase on the showcase, two candle sticks, a writing pad, an air letter form and a pen. She puts the cups on the table, gives me a kiss on the cheek then goes back to the boiling kettle.

In front of me against the wall is an almirah, with drawers under it. It is tall and reaches almost to the ceiling, with just enough room for a suitcase on top of it. The ceiling is underdrawn with boards.

Jenny fills the teapot and brings it to the table with half a loaf, jam and butter.

"Have some bread, Bob."

"I ate on the plane, dear, but I couldn't resist your cake."

She has bread and butter for she hasn't eaten this morning. She pours the tea. She sits to my left and behind her is her bed against the wall. Each leg is raised on two bricks to make room to store her tin trunks. On the wall above her bed is her little altar with a picture of a haloed Jesus and the Sacred Heart, and on the shelf below are models of Christ and the Blessed Virgin. To the right is a garish Indian calendar showing a Hindu goddess, and to the left is a framed photograph of me, Melanie and Jane, taken years ago. On the wall behind me is another framed photo of Jenny and her errant husband.

"This place is clean, Bob."

"I can see that, Jenny.

"I mean the whole area, Bob. My neighbours are clean. We all keep our rooms and the yard well scrubbed. There are no rats and no bugs, and only a few cockroaches fly in."

The place is neat and tidy but I wish she could have found somewhere better. I'm surprised that she seems to be contented, perhaps resigned to her lot is a better description.

Two cages are hung from the ceiling. There are two Red Muneer birds in each cage. They are about the size of wrens.

"These are my friends, Bob! When I was cleaning a cage last week, one of them flew away and never came back. I cried, Bob. Those two are called Buddha Boy and Lalu."

She says "Lalu" with that break in her voice that attracts me.

"In the other cage are Kali and the new one I've called Junior."

I get up and look at the little birds. Jenny fills their water bowls and gives them seeds.

"At night my other friend comes out, a tiny mouse. I call him Tom Thumb and he lives on the ledge there next to the ceiling. He comes down and looks for crumbs on the floor. He is my lodger. I feed him and the only charge on him is to keep me company."

"We are not going to stay at that place, Jenny. I'll see if we can get into the Boarding House in Ashutosh Road."

"No, I don't think they liked me at that place, Bob."

"They got the wrong impression. You were wearing a simple sari, Jenny, dear. They couldn't place you." She looks thoughtful and pats her hair. "Put your European clothes on, Jenny. I'm going to cheer you up."

"What do you mean, Bob?"

"A pleasant surprise."

As she changes she hides her body from me, unlike the old days.

She wears a plain brown skirt, a white blouse and a light blue cardigan.

We send a boy for a taxi.

"Where are we going, Bob?"

"I'm not sure."

"Why don't you tell me?" She smiles.

"Be patient," I say to her.

"Park Street," I say to the taxi man.

Then to Jenny, "Where is the best hairdresser, or beauty parlour, whatever you call it.? I'm going to beautify you."

"A magician couldn't do that, Bob."

"Wait and see. Where shall we go?"

"It's not the most fashionable, but there's a good place in Free School Street. Chinese girls."

"Have a super shampoo and set, perm, manicure, whatever you want."

We are lucky. There is a cancellation, no waiting. I make a fuss of Jenny. It is clear who is paying so the staff sense generosity and get cracking. They must wonder why this large European is so attentive to the ageing little old lady.

While Jenny is having a perm, I take a taxi to Armstrong's Boarding House. These Indianmaintained establishments often keep the old names.

The manager, Mr Duty, says, "We are too pleased to welcome you."

"I worked here years ago, Mr Duty."

"Things are not what they used to be, Mr Bennett, isn't it?"

"Very true, Mr Duty. I would like to move in tonight."

"That is quite all right, sir."

I go back to the other Boarding House.

"I will not be staying here."

"But sir, you have booked room."

"I booked a double room, not a single room, and you acknowledged in writing. I will pay for one night."

I take my luggage to Armstrong's, then return to the beauty parlour. I have quite a long wait.

150

Jenny emerges, glowing and happier. Being fussed over is something she hasn't experienced for years, a real morale booster. I approve of all I see with just one small criticism. Her hair is cut to neck length but the perm has hardened the attractive natural wave. She wears nail varnish to match her cardigan.

"I haven't used nail varnish for years, Bob. The girl, Gamin, persuaded me to."

"You look terrific, Jenny. Now let's go and buy you a fashionable pair of shoes."

We go by rickshaw, past the Fire Brigade HQ and to the main market. It brings back moving memories to see the chemist's shop nearby, for it is where I bought hundreds of pills when Jenny had TB over twenty years ago, we go into the huge covered market and Jenny buys a pair of peep-toe shoes.

As she tries them on, I say, "You should have had your toe nails varnished to match. Shall we go back and have it done?"

"Don't be silly, Bob."

As we walk back from the market to the Golden Dragon restaurant, I tell her that I've moved to another boarding house.

"I like the people. We will be comfortable there, Jenny."

We walk very slowly. She stops twice on the way to get her breath back, once when she pretends to window shop and once when she makes no pretence. How I wish she would move into a Home and be looked after. We reach the small restaurant and sit at a corner table.

We order sweet sour prawns, chicken with cashew nuts, special chow mien rice. Jenny says she is hungry but I eat twice as much. She uses her chopsticks effortlessly, while I have to concentrate on mine.

"This is my favourite restaurant, Bob. Do you have many Chinese restaurants in England?"

"Hundreds of them Jenny."

I refill her cup with green tea from the huge pot.

"How are your investments going, Jenny?"

"All right," she says, with her mouth full, swallows, then says, "I can't show you the certificates. My friend Rani is visiting her parents in Madras and the documents are locked in her safe."

I can't help feeling that she should have kept them for me to see. Still, I don't want to argue; I'm not here long enough.

We take a taxi to Jenny's place. She packs her things in her old suitcase. I must buy her a new one.

"Just a moment, Bob," she says and walks along the row. "I've left the duplicate key with Helen; she'll look after my birds."

Helen pokes her head out of her doorway. I suppose she wants to see what I look like.

That night we snuggle close, happy; but the fire now only smoulders.

45

Next morning I say, "I'm worried about the future, Jenny. Why don't you move into a Home? It'll become too much for you here. Besides, the smoky air is bad for your chest."

"I know I'll have to go, Bob, but I don't want to lose my freedom."

"When will you move? You wrote to say you would move."

"Not this year. Next year, I think."

"Which Home?"

"The Catholic one in Kidderpore."

"Is there a waiting list?" She is silent. "Jenny, you must do something about it. I'm terribly worried. I don't want to leave you here and go back to England until I know you will be looked after."

"We'll go tomorrow."

"That's good, darling."

I'm still worried; perhaps I can persuade her to go this year.

It is sad, we seem to be drifting apart, but we've been separated for such a long time. I remember how Jenny had said, "We may be parted, but it will take more than that to kill the fire between us." Now I know what that is: age. We have reached our December.

I wonder what she does while I'm away. She doesn't tell me much. I must see her settled before I leave Calcutta.

We go everywhere by taxi. I wish I had a car; I could hire one, but I think it is risky. I might have an accident. Bengalis in a mob can terrify you when they lose their tempers. We go through the gates and walk up the drive to the Roman Catholic Old People's Home. A nun directs her into a room. After a very short time she returns and I am surprised she has been so quick.

"What happened?"

"They say I can have a place."

"When?"

She hesitates.

"Next year."

"Next year? Couldn't you go this year?"

"Early next year, probably."

I'm not happy about this as she seems so vague.

"Don't you have to get a proposer or something?"

"The priest will speak for me. I filled in a form."

"Can't you get a doctor's certificate to give you priority?"

"I'll ask him Bob." She doesn't seem enthusiastic. What more can I do?

Conversation dries up. I'm worried, for I'm beginning to doubt her. First she doesn't give me information about her money, then I can't understand what has happened at the Home.

Next day we cross the Hooghly bridge and take the road past Howrah station, to the Botanical Gardens. There is the banyan tree, reputedly the largest in the world. It is not tall, but its branches reroot themselves, forming a huge shade that covers a large area. We sit on the grass. Her life is empty, we have drifted apart. There isn't much to talk about. My home is in England. Is my heart still in India? I am sorry for her. "I wish I could stay here with you, Jenny, to make sure you are well looked after."

"You could never settle here, Bob. Look at poor Mr Stevens. In his last days he never went out. He had stomach trouble all the time and lived mostly on dhal and bread. You wouldn't be like that, of course, because I'd feed you, but you would go mad here. Calcutta is hell. I will die before you, Bob, then you would be left on your own."

A few days later we go to see Diana and her two kids. Norman is away on security duty. I have never met him. The taxi drops us on the main road, not far from Jenny's home, we walk down a side street, then turn into a passage, too narrow even for a rickshaw. There are huts on one side and a high wooden fence on the other. We dodge people squatting down, cooking and cleaning pots. After a right and left turn we come to a wider path and, to the left, a hut.

Jenny leads me in, passing a lean-to shed where Sadie is squatting down in front of an open fire, cooking. She beams as she sees me.

"Hello Bob. It's a long, long time."

The little round chubby-faced woman's hair has greyed. Then Jenny takes me into the hut. Diana and her sister Lucy are there. They are dressed very smartly because they expected me. Diana wears a red dress with a white flower pattern. She is a good-looking woman. Diana still bears a scar on her left cheek. I remember she grazed it deeply when she fell years ago, the little girl who had walked up and down my bare back as I lay on Jenny's bed.

Lucy wears a red sari. She has a tikka mark, although she is a Christian. I remember her as a cheeky little girl with an upturned nose, but now she is a beautiful woman.

153

Diana holds her baby in her arms. The child is dressed in pale pink, her black hair tied in ribbons and sticking out at the sides. Munisha, aged eight, has her shoulder-length hair tied loosely in two tresses. She wears a dress of red, white and yellow patterns, and a thin, light-blue knitted cardigan. She has a serious expression. Lucy's daughter, Anna, is all smiles. She wears a blue Punjabi outfit and an unbuttoned pink cardigan.

The room is sparsely furnished. On the wall behind one of the two beds is a framed picture of Christ. I would have loved to have stayed, but Jenny wants to move. I can't understand why, for all seem to be so happy here. I know she told me she had quarrelled with Diana, but Diana is friendly.

She says, "Uncle, I'm here temporarily, while my flat in the block on the other side of the main road is being decorated."

I have little time to talk as I am taken away by Jenny. I am most disturbed about this.

"She isn't nice to me," Jenny says as we walk away. "She has a good job but she doesn't help me."

I can't understand why Jenny needs help. I have calculated that her income from investments should suffice.

"I think she has her hands full already, Jenny. I am very sorry that you don't get on. Why oh why do you Anglo-Indian people have to quarrel so much?" She doesn't answer.

I think about Diana. People where she works will see this smart business woman. They will not imagine the poor surroundings she lives in. How easy it is in this huge city to drop down into poverty. If it hadn't been for Jenny educating Diana, what would have become of her? And now I am worried about Jenny. I'm not in Calcutta long enough to sort all this out. I don't want to argue with her, but I pray she will go into a Home.

"I wish you would live with them or with Diana, Jenny. Why must you quarrel?"

She is silent.

46

It is Sunday; we are driving northward to Bandel church. The original church had been built at the end of the sixteenth century by the Portuguese.

"I feel at home here with you, Jenny."

"I hope I die before you, Bob. When you're away I feel lonely."

"Come now darling, move into a Home; you'll feel better, no stress, no chores."

I remember when I drove her to Bandel many years ago. Since then a bypass road has been built and the taxi driver turns on to it. This avoids the narrow road, passing through the string of villages including Chandernagar. No doubt in a few years time cluttering villages will spring up along this route among all the palm trees.

We reach Bandel in mid-morning. It is a beautiful February day, sunny, with few clouds.

"Mother used to bring us here."

"Peaceful place, Jenny. It has a holy feel."

We go into the church where the congregation fills almost every pew. Little girls in smart grey skirts and white blouses, from a nearby school, form the choir. She leads me to a pew at the back.

"Please stay here, Bob," she whispers, and goes to sit at the front.

She takes Communion. After the service she comes back to me.

"Why did you want me to stay here?" I am upset and show it.

"Bob, only Communicants sit at the front."

"Well, I would have taken it with you. Have your forgotten? We both took Communion in the Protestant church in Lucknow."

We walk out of the church and down steps. In front is a large, grassy expanse, leading to the bank of the Hooghly. We sit on a stone bench. To our left are two trees, their wide-spread branches giving shade to vendors of soft drinks and sweetmeats.

"Jenny, you do remember going to church in Lucknow, don't you?"

"Yes Bob. I'm sorry about just now."

"I don't think it matters which church you belong to.

Was she worried to be seen with me? By the priest, maybe?

She leads me back through the church and up a narrow, spiral stone staircase to a platform above the church. We have a view of the river to our left. Here in a shrine stands a figure of the Blessed Virgin holding the Christ child. Both Virgin and Child wear golden crowns. It is the Shrine of our Lady of Happy Voyage. Seafarers came to be blessed.

"Mother came here when my father was at sea."

This holy place draws us together, but I have a foreboding about the future.

"Jenny darling, remember this peaceful place, and when i write in my letters, "Yours for ever", I mean it."

"Me too, Bob."

"There's something peculiar about this place. It makes me want to tell you something. Have you ever thought how we met?"

"Perhaps we were destined to meet."

"The reason we met is that Brenda flew home. If she hadn't gone back to England, I wouldn't have met Donald and he wouldn't have taken me to Joshua's Bar. I really believe that meeting you has kept me out of trouble."

"Perhaps we'd have met anyway. It was Fate."

"All I know is that I love you deeply. I want to tell you something, Jenny. No one else knows except Brenda."

"What do you mean, Bob?"

"Melanie is not my daughter."

"Oh Bob, how can you say that!"

"Because I know; there is no doubt."

"But you are very fair, so is Melanie, and you say Brenda is too."

"It makes no difference. I found out by chance. When she was a baby, Melanie had some trouble and the doctor took a blood sample. She cannot be my child."

"Are you sure Bob?"

"Yes, it's certain. Jenny, I can guess who the father is. Brenda still meets him. But I love Melanie as if she were my own, just as much as I love Jane. Brenda doesn't know that I know about Melanie, and I'll never tell her; and of course Melanie must never be told. So you see how I trust you my darling, telling you this."

"Bob, this will all die with me."

We go down the spiral stairs, through the church and sit in the shade of a tree, where a man is crushing sugar cane through a mangle-like machine. We eat our picnic and I throw a banana skin to a goat that devours it. It is time to move, so we look for our driver. We find him outside a restaurant in a row of huts. Above the entrance, painted white on a green board, in Bengali and English, are the words "Baba-Cabin. Special meal supply." Outside, a tiny but fullygrown cow is grubbing through green coconut husks.

This time we take the narrow (formerly Grand Trunk) road that wends its way through riverside villages. We pass signs of previous settlers. There is a Danish church, falling into ruin, a Dutch burial ground, signs of a brief German presence. We British came last, Portuguese and Dutch pushed out. Then in 1951, the French were removed from Chandernagar.

In just two days' time I have to leave her. She is so frail. I ought not to be leaving her. Maybe I won't see her again. I feel sick at the thought that I am deserting her.

"Darling, please, please move from that bustee. You must look after yourself. If you can't get into the Kidderpore place, try Tollygunj."

"I will try, Bob."

47

As first light appears, the alarm goes off. I wonder how the condemned man feels on the morning of his execution. We lie in each other's arms.

"Oh Bob, will I see you again?"

"Yes, you will. Now, look after yourself."

A servant brings our breakfast. Will there ever be another one, the tea, papaya, toast and marmalade? I have a feeling of foreboding.

I phone the desk, "Please call a taxi." A man takes the luggage down. We drop Jenny's case at her place. People in the bustees are stirring, for they rise early.

We go into her room. Again I have that dreadful feeling that it is for the last time. Jenny removes the covers from the birds' cages and they chirp. We cannot wait. I look around the room. The altar, the photos on the walls, Jenny's bed, the glass show case. I hug her.

Helen arrives at the door. We had agreed I would give her something and I hand her Rs100. She is a plump Bengali Christian, wearing a light green sari, untidily draped, for she has dressed hurriedly.

As we walk to the taxi, I say, "I want you to keep a separate account in your bank, Jenny. You must save, you may have to go to hospital. I'll remit something extra to your bank when I get home."

"All right Bob."

There is silence. I have my arm around her.

"I hope to come back for Christmas, Jenny. Otherwise it will be the same time again, February."

It is cool in the early morning. She wears a dark-blue woolly pullover and denim trousers. Her hands are cold. We have been through all this before, this goodbye, this tearing apart.

"Goodbye darling."

"Don't say goodbye, Bob. Say "cheerio", or something." She hides her face.

We hug and kiss, and then I go through the barrier. I told her not to wait. It is a miserable business waiting. I want to spare her this forlorn sadness. I take my seat in the plane next to a window.

I look towards the verandah. There is a little woman standing in the crowd by the rail. She is wearing a dark-blue pullover.

48 1986

Back in England at the beginning of March, the overcast sky and drizzle match my mood. The day after I arrive, I go to the bank. We had spent too much on the house for comfort and my account is low, but I send Jenny the promised cash.

"I have sent you Rs8,000. Please keep it separate for an emergency. Also I hope you will buy a fridge. I hope you are keeping well and I'm waiting anxiously to hear that you have a definite place in a Home."

In reply she wrote:

"I felt very low when you left me and your letter helps. Many thanks for the cash. I'll keep it for an emergency. I've bought a small fridge. Word got round that I'd got one and now people ask me to cool their bottles of water, which I do if I have space in it. I've not been to the Old People's Home again. I haven't had time. I mean the one in Kidderpore. If not there then I will try the one in Tollygunj. It is further away but I can go on the Underground."

I had taken Jenny on the Calcutta Underground railway, her first trip. We just went for two stations along the side of Chowringhee. Surprisingly all was spotless, no graffiti, and well policed, no beggars allowed near the entrances.

In April, Jenny wrote about another visit to hospital:

"My X-ray report says, "Old calcified lesions with bilateral emphy... (I can't read it) changes shown. Cardiac contour normal." I was given cough syrup and capsules to take and Benzoin tincture inhaler.

"Sadie is very ill with kidney trouble. Given oxygen. I get so tired. Last week I bought five corrugated sheets to repair my roof. Helen's brother-in-law did the work. He also repaired the back wall behind my bed because dampness was coming through. While this was being done, I spent some time in Helen's room as I was dead beat. I will have to get the walls distempered and colour washed. All the smoke from coal fires makes the place look grubby."

In May she writes, *"Things are not too good. There are many long power cuts, processions of party against party, price increases for almost everything, shortage of kerosene oil. Some Christians have been attacked. In a district of the U. P. two nuns of St Mary's School were molested and raped. A former Government Minister suggested to Christians that they should leave India and go to the USA or Europe. How can any of them go? They can't get entry permits."*

June: *"We have a priest from South India. He gives good sermons. Sometimes he mixes in stories, some facts, some fiction. One evening he said a priest had a habit of tapping the mike to see if it was working. One day he tapped it and no sound came. It was turned off but he did not know, so he said "What's wrong with the mike?" Not hearing him clearly, the people thought he said, "The Lord be with you," so they answered, "And also with you!""*

July: *"I was very ill again"*, Jenny wrote, *"and while I was confined to bed, poor Sadie died. I was too ill to go to the funeral, so Rosie went for me. I have got better. Rosie was here a long time, so now she has gone home for a few days to look after her house, and will come back soon. I am getting to the stage when I can't do without her help."*

August: *"I went to the Home in Kidderpore and they say it will be at least a year until I can go. I can't do much until I feel well, but soon I will go to Tollygunj and ask them there."*

She wrote again a week later.

"I have been to Tolly. I took the priest's letter and they say I can be admitted in the spring. I saw them enter my name in the book. I suppose they have to wait for someone to die."

September: *"When I went into hospital, tests showed that I had malaria, liver disorder and urine infection. As you can see from my writing, my hands are trembling. Now I am back home and Rosie has been with me all through - a Godsend. She cooked me mutton and potatoes one time, another time goat leg soup, cheese sandwich. The money you sent last month paid for my stay in hospital. God bless you for everything."*

October: *"One of the Anglo-Indian boys in the compound has been murdered. He was 26 years old. He was standing near the railway lines at the entrance of the lane when two men, his enemies, threw two bombs at him. This was around 8.20 or 8.30pm when I heard the bombs explode. He was rushed to hospital where he died. The mother, sisters and brothers were so grieved that although I didn't like them - they are always squabbling - I went to console them. After the post mortem next day 3.30pm the body was brought to his home next to mine and was there all night. I stayed there till 2.30am saying the Rosary and prayers, then I went home and slept.*

The boy nearby is absconding as he was the informer as to Robert's timing of movements. It was all arranged that night there was no light in the street. Later they noticed that the neon tube in the light had been broken deliberately. I don't know the reason for this murder. Everyone liked Robert here in the compound, he was good natured and helped everyone. Many times he got me 1kg of sugar from the ration shop. I miss him."

November: *"I have a letter from my cousin Fred in Australia. The family are coming here and want me to find accommodation. I feel so tired and wish I didn't have to do this. They are coming in Dec. I must go round about and find somewhere cheap and decent."*
It seems unfair that Jenny has to do this. Perhaps it is that she is the only one reliable and educated, and only she can help. Diana could help but she is very busy. He doesn't know how unwell Jenny is. He will be shocked when he sees her.

18th November 1986: *"I have had a very exhausting time running around with Rosie's help and finding a place for Fred and family to stay, and sending price lists. I've told him to cable which one to book in, as the post is too slow. He has already sent me cash in case an advance is needed.*

Dear Bob I am feeling so weak and I am sinking. I get worse week by week. My hand is trembling. I will be happier in the Old People's Home. Now I know that I should have gone this year, but I didn't want to lose my independence.
So will close and God bless, Yours for ever, Jenny XXXXXX"

Her letter arrives on 24th November.

Two days later I reply, "I hope Fred looks after you and buys all that you need. I have written to Armstrong's Boarding House. We will stay there, as we were happy there last time."

On 11th December I send a Christmas card and write again, saying I hope she is enjoying Fred's visit and is keeping well. Then I wait expectantly for her next letter and her Christmas card. She had written every year without fail in time for Christmas, and sent a card. But this year nothing comes. I don't feel too bad, because there can be a delay in the mail. But after Christmas nothing comes, so I become worried. Perhaps she has gone into hospital again. I wake suddenly very early one morning with the disturbing feeling that something has happened to her.

49

On 2nd January I write to Diana asking for news. Then, a week later, as I have still had no letter from Jenny, I get really worried and I phone Diana at her office.

"I haven't heard from Jenny since November, Diana."

"Uncle, you will be sorry to hear Aunty died two days ago."

The phone makes Diana sound unfeeling; this, along with the awful news, stuns me, as if I'm sandbagged.

"Hello Uncle, are you there?"

"Yes."

"We buried her yesterday."

Still I can't speak.

"Uncle, did you hear?"

"Yes, dear, yes. Please write to me."

"Yes Uncle."

"You will write, won't you Diana? Write today."

"Of course Uncle, yes I will."

"I don't feel like talking, dear. So you will write?"

"Yes, Uncle, of course I will."

"Goodbye dear. Please write today." I hang up.

I must get out of the house, so I just walk, anywhere. Then I take a bus, any bus. I've reached the woods, so I get out and walk. I sit on the wall of the children's sandpit, deserted as it is in winter. The wind blows and it suits my mood, cold outside and in, alone, desolate. I must cancel my air ticket. I won't see her again, hard to believe. A man comes past, throws a stick for his spaniel to fetch. He looks at me, ill-clad, an oddball sitting in the cold, that's what he must think.

Jenny dead! She knew I loved her. I don't think I could have done more for her.

Suddenly the cold gets to me; I'm freezing. I walk the few yards to a pub on the main road, take a double Scotch and sit in a corner near the fire. I had half expected something to happen, as she was so frail, but I find it hard to believe.

I take a bus, then a tube into Town. I was going to my club, but went past to Victoria. I'll go to Westminster Abbey. Then I see the cathedral, Holy Roman, Jenny's. So I go in, kneel, rest my head on my arms. It is very quiet, few people in the nave.

"Dear God, look after her. Father forgive. She had so many good points. Give her the great love that the two of us glimpsed." I try to empty my head of everything except thoughts of her. I pray for her peace. No one in the world loves Jenny more than I.

50

Diana writes: "*We took Aunty to hospital by taxi just before Christmas. Rosie stayed with her but she couldn't talk. I was so busy with Christmas arrangements and with the kids. I meant to see Aunty soon after, but I became ill. I felt dreadful, 'flu I think.*

I managed to go to the hospital on New Year's Day and Aunty seemed much the same, I didn't think she was in real danger. She died very early in the morning.

Jenny's son, Tommy, was with her most days, when Rosie didn't go. I wanted to see Aunty, but Tommy hated me. Two days before she died he saw me coming into the ward and he told me to get out. I think it is because you helped me. Of course, you didn't know about Tommy. I couldn't face a quarrel in the ward so I left, but my brother visited Aunty every day and told me how she was. It surprised us at the end that she went from us so quickly or I would have gone to see her, even if Tommy had been there. Even before she was ill he hated me to go to her house or to have anything to do with her."

Jenny's son? I read Diana's letter again. No, there could be no other meaning. I had never pressed Jenny for information about her past. Surely he can't be my son. Surely she would have told me, or would she? It doesn't make sense.

Then Diana writes and I begin to understand. She tells me Jenny had been married before to one John Wilden. Of course, Wilden. Doreen in the Sailors' Club had told me, but I thought, "Wild"un" was a nickname, and I had joked about it. Diana writes that Jenny married Peter Brennan while John Wilden was still alive, so she committed bigamy.

"*Wilden had since died. Uncle, I apologise for not telling you this, but Aunty was a funny person and she would have been angry with me if I had told you. And Uncle, Aunty was not telling you the truth about her age. She is 61 years old. Tommy is 42, and she has a daughter Sylvia who is 44 years old.*"

So Tommy can't be my son for he would be thirteen when I first met Jenny. I wonder how she could have kept him in the background so that I never met him. All those years she had kept her secret. I suppose she was frightened to tell me in case I would be so unhappy or angry that I would leave her.

She loved me, I know she did; of that I am certain. She didn't want to lose me, so she didn't tell me. Apart from the secret I knew her so well. We were good friends, the best, and the loving, how we loved. That little body, I knew it as my own and I never saw any stretch marks, no signs of childbirth. I suppose that was because she was so young and supple when she had Tommy and Sylvia.

Diana writes: *"When she was sick sometime in September and admitted to hospital, I went to see her twice. The day she was discharged I went to see her at her house, but Tommy was angry and told me to go away. So I used to refrain from visiting her after that because I knew it would only cause unhappiness for her, and Tommy would fight with her. She seemed afraid of him because he would drink and act nasty with her.*

So Uncle, you see why I didn't often see Aunty. Tommy never once came to inform me when she was sick. He hated the sight of me."

A few days later, Dennis, Jenny's eldest brother, writes: *"Dear Bob, This is to inform you that Jenny died on 7th of Jan. Sorry to say she has not nominated any one name. She has got her son Tommy which you don't know. The house only is in his name and nothing else. To the last Tommy has looked after his mother and Rosie was with her in the Hospital.*
"Now Tommy has nothing to look forward to. So please do something for him. Dennis and Mary and Patrick send their regards to you. Thanking you and God bless, signed, Dennis Sandakan."

It looks to me as though someone else has written it for him.

I didn't want to get involved, so I didn't reply. If I started to send money to Dennis for Tommy, would it ever stop or would it be a kind of running sore? I had already stretched my resources to help Jenny and Diana. I just can't imagine what would have happened if I had known about Jenny's past, and Tommy and Sylvia.

Poor Jenny, I suppose I might have been her means of escape. She wished I would take her away from her tangle of problems, but it was impossible.

Diana and I swap letters. She writes: *"You know Aunty had a scarred lip. Well, Uncle Dennis tells me Aunty's husband hit her and that's why she left him. They had violent quarrels because she stayed out all night. He said he wondered if Tommy was his child. When Aunty deserted them she was only nineteen years old. Sylvia was three and Tommy just one year. Her sister-in-law had to look after them.*

I made all the arrangements for Aunty's burial. Then I went to her house, and then Sylvia and her three children came in. They and other relatives and Tommy were there. They made me feel unwelcome, so I went home. Neighbours told me Sylvia and the rest squabbled over Aunty's belongings. Tell me, Uncle, who would want to be involved with unscrupulous people like these?

Tommy is gambling Rs30 or 40 every month of Aunty's cash she had in the house. He sold her earrings and wedding ring, also gold bangles. This I hear from the neighbours.

You know Aunty's relatives came from Australia? Well, she made all the arrangements for their stay and was overtired. She exhausted herself visiting them in the evenings and coming home late with a chill. This caused her death.

You will remember that I asked you long ago to help Aunty - you see Norman, my husband, was unemployed. I had Mum, my brothers, sister and her daughter also to help. I would help Aunty, in fact whenever she needed money or anything, I was always there. Tommy is not educated, and worked as a security guard on a low salary, but Aunty used to make him leave his job and stay home to help her in the housework and errands. Whenever she had a problem with him, she came to stay with me.

I appreciate all that you and Aunty have done for me as a child (your initial step in admitting me into a good school). Today I hold a good job. I first thank God and second Aunty Jenny and yourself for your kindness towards me.

I am sorry to say that Aunty did not invest much of the money, but put it in her bank, where it dwindled. She used to smoke 3 packets of cigs a day, which was bad for her health. She also loved to play cards which she did regularly. Losing Rs 100 or 200 would mean nothing to her."

All this made me very depressed. Then I thought about Tommy, the son I had never known about, and Sylvia. Jenny had quarrelled with their father, made a clean break and took no interest in them. Instead she helped Diana and put her through school. This would be enough to make

Tommy very bitter. It would be worse for him than for Sylvia. Sylvia had a man to support her.

Another letter from Diana: *"Aunty told you and others that I was unkind to her. This isn't fair and it isn't true. My door was always open to her. There was never a day that I got rude to her. My regret today is that I should have gone to the hospital, irrespective of her son acting funny with me. I loved her and I know she loved me. I remember her every single day in my prayers.*

Tommy started to live with Aunty when she was in the flat. She had to take the teaching job in Orissa because she needed the money. It was on a very small salary. Tommy stayed in the Calcutta flat while she was away.

I paid many of her bills. Her daughter Sylvia, together with Sylvia's daughters and their husbands, started visiting her. In fact they were the cause of her having to leave the flat as they were very notorious and had anti-social connections. She was told to vacate the flat, if not, she would be taken to court.

She enquired from you if I had written to you because she thought I would write and let you know that she had two children and that Tommy was bullying her.

Uncle Peter, Aunty's husband, did not know about Aunty having two children. This he gathered from her daughter Sylvia, who was living an immoral life, once when she went on a ship and met him by chance. That was the reason he broke off all contact. Uncle Peter was a nice man and he must have been very badly hurt.

Tommy told me sometime ago that he had sold the fridge to get money to order a cross for his mother's grave, but he didn't buy one. It is all very very sad."

I asked Diana to buy a simple stone or cross for the grave and to tell me the cost. As for Tommy, I feel very sorry for him. Jenny deserted him, then, too late, tried to make amends. I will not support him; I fear that any money I sent would be squandered. I can't afford it anyway. From time to time I have qualms of conscience about this; but I'm determined not to weaken.

Months later Diana wrote to say that her uncle Dennis and his wife Mary, had allowed Tommy to stay with them. At first, after Jenny's death, they would have nothing to do with him, but they have relented. It seems that he had changed his ways. Dennis, now in charge of the cinema staff, has brought Tommy in as an usher. I'm relieved about this and wish Jenny could know. It has been a sad business. Pray that Tommy will keep the job and be good.

51

My thoughts went back to the time, over many years, when Jenny and I first fell in love. I was with her whenever possible. If a business call took me near Benatala Street, I would spend a few minutes with her.

Once I returned from tour much earlier than expected and I saw a different Jenny. I suppose that, chameleon-like, she adapted to her environment; with the girls she was one colour, with me, another. In the room at the end of the passage stood Florrie and Bella. As I walked towards them, they appeared not to notice me. Then I saw Jenny; she was unkempt as I had never seen her. She wore an old crumpled floral dress with hem stitches coming loose. Her hair was all over the place, as an unmade bed. Her down-turned face was tear-stained and grim. She wiped away the mucus that emerged from one nostril.

As Jenny walked barefoot into her room, Florrie called after her, "It's no use crying over spilt milk."

I didn't know then why she said this, but now I understand. Florrie was referring to Jenny's past.

As she lay in hospital, Jenny was too ill to speak. In her silence, still I know that she had loved me; certainly no one loved her more than I did. What course, I wonder, would our lives have taken, had we met when we were young and uncomplicated!

EPILOGUE

A year later I was sitting in the Old People's Club with Ronnie, brilliant pianist in his time, now in his arthritic eighties. We were discussing the music hall show. Rehearsals would start soon.

A member came in and nodded in recognition, He had with him his middle-aged guest. She was a dark good-looker, a big woman, Jamaican at a guess. She was singing to herself as she passed.

"You've got a good voice," piped Ronnie.

She stopped, beamed, "Thank you very much," and moved on.

"Wait." Ronnie half stood up, raised his hand towards her. "I know a good voice. Will you sing in our show?"

They sat with us and she agreed that she would sing. Ronnie would accompany her.

The way she sang, full of emotion, grabbed me:

Don't know why, there's no sun up in the sky,
Stormy weather.
Since my gal and I ain't together,
It's raining all the time.

Still the song haunts me, day after day; can't get it out of my mind.